Cover Design and Interior Format

HIGHLAND RESILIENCE

6 THE BAND OF COUSINS

KEIRA MONTCLAIR

THE GRANTS AND RAMSAYS

FAMILY TREE (1280s)

GRANTS

LAIRD ALEXANDER GRANT and wife, MADDIE
John (Jake) and wife, Aline
James (Jamie) and wife, Gracie
Kyla and husband, Finlay
Connor
Elizabeth
Maeve

BRENNA GRANT and husband, QUADE RAMSAY
Torrian (Quade's son from his first marriage) and wife,
Heather—daughter, Nellie (Heather's daughter from a
previous relationship) and son, Lachlan
Lily (Quade's daughter from his first marriage) and hus-
band, Kyle—twin daughters, Lise and Liliana
Bethia and husband, Donnan—son, Drystan
Gregor
Jennet
Geva (adopted)
Emma (adopted)

ROBBIE GRANT and wife, CARALYN
Ashlyn (Caralyn's daughter from a previous relationship)
and husband, Magnus—daughter, X
Gracie (Caralyn's daughter from a previous relationship)
and husband, Jamie
Rodric (Roddy) and wife, Rose
Padraig

BRODIE GRANT and wife, CELESTINA
Loki (adopted) and wife, Arabella—sons, Kenzie (adopt-
ed) and Lucas, daughter, Ami (adopted)
Braden and wife, Cairstine—son, Steenie (Cairstine's son
from previous relationship)
Catriona
Alison

JENNIE GRANT and husband, AEDAN CAMERON
Riley
Tara
Brin

RAMSAYS

QUADE RAMSAY and wife, BRENNA GRANT
Torrian (Quade's son from his first marriage) and wife,
Heather—Nellie (Heather's daughter from a previous rela-
tionship) and son, Lachlan
Lily (Quade's daughter from his first marriage) and hus-
band, Kyle—twin daughters, Lise and Liliana
Bethia and husband, Donnan
Gregor
Jennet

LOGAN RAMSAY and wife, GWYNETH
Molly (adopted) and husband, Tormod
Maggie (adopted)
Sorcha and husband, Cailean
Gavin
Brigid

MICHEIL RAMSAY and wife, DIANA
David
Daniel

AVELINA RAMSAY and DREW MENZIE
Elyse
Tad
Tomag
Maitland

TO THE READER:

This book will be closely tied to the last two books in the series: Gavin's story and Connor's story. As such, each hero and heroine will get their happily ever after, but a string or two is left unsettled. The three are best read together. Thanks for reading!

Keira Montclair

CHAPTER ONE

MEREWEN BAIRD AWAKENED WITH A scream in her throat. Normally, she would have quelled the need to let it out, but not today. Not when her sister's side of the bed was empty. Not when she knew in her heart something was wrong. She wailed like a banshee—a high, keening sound likely to be heard over most of Ramsay land.

After screaming loudly enough to rouse half the clan, she bolted out of bed, grabbed a gown, and threw it over her head.

She rushed out of her chamber into the small central chamber of their hut, her gaze catching her mother's wide-eyed stare. "Lass, why are you carrying on so?"

"Linet. She's gone. Something awful has happened. I can feel it in my blood, in my bones, in the hairs now rising on my arms. Where is she?" She raced to the door, yanking it open to yell her sister's name into the Highland winds. "Linet! Linet! Where are you?"

Grabbing her mantle, she dashed outside, ignoring her mother's pleas.

"Merewen, wait for your sire! He'll find her."

"Nay, Mama. I must find her now. You know once Papa is working, he'll not leave. 'Twill be too late by the time he returns." She adored her only sister, so she would not ignore her hunch. Something had happened, of this she was certain.

Her heart pounded as she hurried along, looking about for any signs of her sister. As she searched, she tried to remember everything she could from the last time she'd seen Linet. The more she remembered, the more her gut clenched. Her sister had returned from a visit to the chapel, her hands crossed in front of her belly. It had been late, much later than Linet had ever been out before.

The look on her face should have prompted Merewen to question her, but she'd been too self-involved to do so, even though Linet had clearly been out of sorts. Merewen's courses had just returned, and the painful, relentless cramps had demanded her focus.

While she still felt the cramps, they were nothing compared to the ache deep in her belly for letting her sister down.

Linet had whispered to her in the middle of the night, and rather than answer her, Merewen had groaned and rolled over, giving her sister her back.

But she could still hear her sister's last words.

"Merewen, please? I must tell you something."

And now she was gone.

———◆———

Gavin Ramsay brushed his long hair back from his face as he made his way to the stables. He needed to ride, needed to move to ease the restlessness in his blood. These past few days, he'd been tempted to ride off alone to the northeastern part of the Highlands, where they'd last heard whispers of the Channel of Dubh, the underground network responsible for the kidnapping and sale of lasses and lads across the water. His sire, of course, had forbidden him to do any such thing, but that wasn't the reason he'd restrained himself. His cousin Gregor had persuaded him there was wisdom in waiting for his sister Maggie and her husband to return.

Maggie and Will oversaw the group he and Gregor had

fought and spied with for the last year. They called themselves the Band of Cousins, because all the members *were* cousins, aside from the siblings, and they'd dedicated themselves to stopping the Channel of Dubh for good. None of them would rest until they prevailed.

Patience and a calm sense of reason were two qualities Gavin lacked completely. Like his sire, he had an intense craving for adventure and a deep-seated desire to roam the beautiful lands of Scotland. But Gavin's impatience sprung from something much deeper. The only son of Logan and Gwyneth Ramsay, he had reached an age where the onslaught of pressure never left him.

Pressure to measure up.

His parents worked for the Scottish Crown, secretly at one time but now openly. His mother had the reputation of being the best archer in all the land, and his sire?

His nickname was the Beast.

Although Gavin was proud of his work with the cousins, he'd never taken on a leadership role. He felt the need to make his own reputation.

But how?

He had just mounted his horse when an intense cry, unlike anything he'd ever heard before, reached his ears from the small village of huts outside the castle walls. He turned his horse in that direction, his gaze raking the area for anything unusual.

Then he saw her. Merewen Baird stood outside the village in the meadow, her expression as stricken as if someone had taken a whip to her. Her long tawny locks whipped about in the early winter breeze.

As he got closer, he realized she was shouting her sister's name as she ran. She paid him no mind, so he dismounted and approached her on foot.

"Merewen," he shouted as he drew closer. "Merewen, what is it?" The Bairds had lived on Ramsay land for as long as he could remember. The lass's sire was a gifted blacksmith. He was a hardworking clan member, although he was known for being a strict father.

"Merewen, what is it?" he asked again, an appreciation for her beauty suddenly enveloping him. She had always caught his eye, but this morn she looked like a wild faerie queen, her hair loose and long, her brown eyes sparkling with gold flecks. He forced himself to rein in his carnal thoughts as he took another step toward her. "Merewen?"

She spun around to face him, freezing in position, her breathing as fast as if she'd just run to the keep and back. The look in her eyes reminded him of a cornered animal, wild and frantic.

She swallowed and whispered, "Linet. She's gone. I can't find her anywhere. She came back from the chapel late last eve, and then she left before I awoke this morn."

"I'll help you look for her. Have you checked the chapel yet? Is your sire aware she's missing?"

She shook her head twice, as if to answer both questions, making a face at his suggestion. "My sire is at his smithy hut. He won't wish to be bothered."

"When his daughter is missing?" Had he heard her correctly? Was the man truly so cold?

"He does not like to be bothered when he's doing his duties. Please, can we not search for her before we go to him?" She rubbed her hands together in the cool morning.

There was no point in delaying their search any longer. "Come. I'll give you a ride to the bailey. We should inform your sire, but we'll check the chapel first." He held his hand out to her, hoping she would trust him.

She'd always been a bit of a mystery to him—beautiful and intriguing yet wrapped up in her own world—except for that one time they'd shared a kiss. About a year ago, he'd found her at work in the butts, trying to shoot with a broken bow. By the time Gavin had come upon her, she'd started crying out of frustration, for as much as she'd tried to repair the weapon, it would not function.

She'd told him the whole story then. Her sire had been furious when he'd caught her trying to use a bow and arrow. His response had been to snap her bow in two, declaring that bows were for lads only. No lass of his would shoot.

Gavin had quickly gone to retrieve a new one for her. His family had so many that it had been an easy task for him, but Merewen, her brown eyes rimmed with grateful tears, had hugged him with excitement and quickly kissed him on the lips.

Gavin hadn't let it stop at a simple brush of the lips, instead deepening the tantalizing kiss. Her taste had enchanted him, but he was the one who'd pulled away—he'd known all too well his loins would get him in trouble if he did aught else.

Ever since then, he'd had an eye for Merewen, but the Band of Cousins had come along and kept him busy and away from home. Away from *her*. Still, he'd thought of her from time to time while traveling on various missions. In fact, he had to admit she was the only lass on Ramsay land whom he had ever held more than a passing interest for him. Had he made a mistake walking away from her?

"Nay, she's not there," she replied, her big brown eyes darting back and forth. "And Papa doesn't know anything, either."

"How do you know this?"

She brought her hand up to her heart. "Something's wrong. I can feel it here. I cannot explain how I know, but she's far away from Ramsay land. Linet and I...we are so close that we know what the other is thinking. I cannot explain it, but I just know."

The two had been inseparable, of that much he was certain. Was it possible to be so close? He often knew what his cousin Gregor was thinking, but not to the point where he knew where he was at all times.

The certainty in her eyes swayed him. He wasn't sure he

believed her, but his sister Molly knew things no person should. He knew it was possible.

"Let's talk with my uncle and your sire before we look elsewhere. We'll decide what to do then." His uncle was the clan priest, and there wasn't a warmer or more helpful soul in Clan Ramsay.

After a long pause, during which he felt quite certain she would reject him, she finally nodded and followed him back to his horse. He gripped her waist and lifted her onto the saddle, then mounted behind her. At least he had her to a point where she was under control and not running blindly, something the Merewen he knew would never do. Yet he could tell she was gravely unsettled by how she sat as though she were flat against an arrow and didn't dare move.

He urged his horse forward and she fell back against him, something he didn't mind at all. All soft curves, she smelled of the wildflowers that grew in the valley.

He hadn't gone far when two horses flew toward him. He knew the riders well—his cousin Gregor, half-brother to Torrian, their laird, and Kyle, Torrian's second-in-command.

Kyle's shout carried to him first. "We heard the screaming. She is hale, Gavin? Was she attacked? Reivers?"

Gavin shook his head out of her line of sight. He was considering what to say—how to describe a hunch that was more than a hunch?—when, to his surprise, Merewen spoke.

"My sister Linet has disappeared. She was upset last night, though I know not why, and this morning her side of the bed was empty. Mama has no idea where she is. Papa is in the bailey."

"I'm sure we'll find her soon. She couldn't have gone far. I take it your brothers haven't seen her?" Kyle asked.

"Struan and Mal always leave at dawn for the lists. I know not where she is, but she's gone from Ramsay land.

I can *feel* it. Who would steal her away? Who?"

Gavin shared a glance with Gregor, and neither of them needed to say a word.

The Channel of Dubh. Could the heartless smugglers they'd been hunting with the Band of Cousins have finally reached Ramsay land? Their adversaries had never been so daring, preferring to do their evil out of sight.

Kyle turned his horse around and rode abreast of them. "Even so, I'll go to the lists to check with your brothers. Gregor, ask around and then see what her sire knows. Where were you headed, lass?"

Gavin said, "Linet often visits Father Rab, so we'll visit him at the chapel to see if he knows aught."

"Then we meet in the hall in half an hour," Kyle said. "I'll speak with our laird."

Merewen leaned forward, frantic again. "And if she truly is gone, what will we do? Will our laird send a patrol out for her? I wish to go along. I'm good on a horse. I can..." She spun her head around, but then bit off her sentence and sat back, her face turning the shade of a fresh autumn apple.

Gavin couldn't help but wonder what she had been about to say.

Apparently Merewen Baird knew something they didn't.

CHAPTER TWO

M EREWEN HAD NEARLY CONFESSED HER secret in her worries over her dear sister. She couldn't tell anyone what she could do, and it would be especially dangerous to tell Logan Ramsay's son. Gavin Ramsay was a handsome lad. He always wore his hair long and free, and he had the green Ramsay eyes that reflected the color of the forest. He was the jester of the clan, always quick to make others laugh.

She recalled the time that she and Linet had gone up against him and Gregor in the three-legged race at one of the Ramsay festivals a few years ago. She and Linet had made it to the finals against Gavin and Gregor.

Gavin had spent the entire race trying to unsettle them or upset them. He'd kept up a never-ending stream of comments meant to distract them.

"Look out! There's a mouse by your foot!"

"I see a snake headed right for you, Linet."

"Your legs are untied. No fair!"

She'd giggled but ignored him, while Linet had chided her for her giggling. She'd been unable to stop herself. Gavin's sense of humor had always amused her.

They'd beaten the lads because at the very end, Linet had shouted out, "Watch out!" and Gavin had fallen over.

After the event at the festival, she'd teased Linet, suggesting the two of them could marry cousins: Gavin and Gregor. But her sister had bellowed a quick refusal. Linet didn't understand. She thought Gavin a brute. And she wouldn't budge from their pledge to each other.

They'd promised each other never to marry unless they could marry brothers. Their bond was so close that they could not bear to live apart. They had to marry brothers.

No brothers—no weddings.

And yet there was no denying Merewen felt a soft spot for Gavin Ramsay, especially after he'd kissed her so thoroughly that her toes had curled. She didn't mind at all being this close to him on his horse.

He wasn't as tall as his cousin Torrian, but his shoulders were broad and he fought like a demon. Linet had caught her watching him spar with his sister's husband, Cailean MacAdam. The two were known for stripping to the waist and fighting for their own entertainment, their colorful taunts heard across the lists.

Hopefully, she would be more successful at keeping her other secret to herself, lest she suffer from her sire's wrath.

Kyle Maule took off toward the lists, and Gavin steered his horse toward the curtain wall, his knees managing the huge beast with just the slightest of movements. She had to get him to promise to help her. If anyone could save Linet, surely he could.

"Gavin, will you not help me?"

"Of course. 'Tis still possible she's at the chapel and has lost track of time." When they reached the bailey, he dismounted and helped her down, handing the reins of his horse to one of the stable lads. They had begun to walk toward the chapel, but Merewen couldn't wait to speak with him privately. She needed his word.

"Nay, you do not understand," she said, tugging him out of sight. "You must promise to help me find her. I meant what I said earlier. She's not here. I'm as certain of that fact as I am of my given name. Someone has taken her, and we must go after her. Will you help me?"

Gavin stared at her for a moment as if finally understanding the severity of the situation. "You truly think she's been stolen from Ramsay land? No one has dared to come this far on our land to commit such a crime. We have daily patrols to warn reivers and…others away."

"I'm certain of it. She's gone. Promise me? Please?" Holding his gaze, she said, "This Channel everyone speaks about…the smugglers…could they have taken her? If so, then you must help me before 'tis too late."

Gavin gave a slow nod. "I'll help you, lass. I'll do whatever it takes to find your sister. Could it be possible she's run away with someone else? Decided to marry someone your father did not approve of?"

"Nay!" Her voice had risen again, without her realizing it, and her shout had brought them much attention from passersby. She dropped her voice. "Nay, we vowed to marry brothers or not at all."

She noticed a slight curve in the corner of his mouth begging to bloom into a large grin. That grin normally pleased her, but not today. Not when Linet was gone.

Furious, she grabbed his wrist and squeezed. "We are serious. Do not take this lightly. She would not have gone anywhere without me."

His mouth stopped quivering, and he became serious again. "Come, let's find Father Rab. Even if he hasn't seen her, he might know something. We'll decide what to do after we've spoken with him." His hand fell to the small of her back, a soft warm pressure that gave her strength, and they moved forward toward the chapel in silence. Gavin reached for the door of the chapel, holding it open for her to enter. Father Rab stood at the end of the chapel in front of the cross, silently praying if she were to guess.

"Uncle Rab…I mean, Father Rab," Gavin said, his hand at the small of her back again, a wee bit of intimacy that she liked.

"Gavin, how good to see you," Father Rab said, his eyes crinkling at the corners with his big smile. "And you've brought Linet's sister with you today. Is there aught I should know?" His uncle darted a look at the hand Gavin still held at her back, waggling his brow, but Gavin just stared at him.

"Aye, something is amiss. Linet disappeared this morning."

"Aye?" Father Rab asked, pausing to consider the events of the night. "She was here last eve."

"I know," Merewen said, her panic bubbling back to the surface. "She was out of sorts when she came home. I was nearly asleep, so I didn't speak to her, but when I awakened, she was gone." She paused, then added, "Father Rab, was she upset when you saw her?"

Father sighed. "Aye, she was a bit upset, but she often is. 'Twas not unusual for her."

Merewen eyed the priest carefully. She had a special place in her heart for the priest because he would often find books for Linet to read, something she loved to do. "Father, she was upset last eve, but I disagree. I do not often see her in such a state."

Father Rab scratched his chin and said, "Seems I've made a mistake, lass. Have you checked everywhere?"

"We're getting to it," Gavin said. "Kyle has gone to the lists to fetch her brothers. We'll meet Gregor at the blacksmith's hut to visit her sire."

"Godspeed to you," Father Rab said. "I hope you find her hale. I'll advise you of anything I learn."

As soon as they stepped out into the cold wind, Merewen rushed toward her sire's hut. While she knew her sire would not be happy about her bothering him, at this point, she didn't really care. It was possible he may have seen something.

Gregor stepped out of the hut and headed straight for them. The younger Ramsay cousin was much more serious than jesting Gavin, but although he was quiet, he was known for being a quick thinker and deadly with his bow.

He and Gavin had been inseparable for as far back as she could recall.

"Did you learn anything, Gregor?" Gavin yelled.

Gregor shook his head. Merewen strode past him and headed straight for her sire's hut. She stuck her head inside and asked, "Papa, have you not seen her at all? Where can Linet be?"

Wallace Baird simply shook his head. "I know not. You should ask your mother. I'm too busy to monitor you lasses."

Gregor and Gavin had followed her inside, but no one said anything for a long moment. The door opened then, and Kyle came inside with her two brothers, Struan and Mal.

"Lads, have you seen your sister?" Wallace asked, Merewen stepping away from him to face her brothers.

"Nay, we've not seen her," Mal replied. "We stopped off in the great hall. Our mistress has not seen her either."

Gavin and Gregor passed a sick look between the two of them. A *knowing* look.

Her sire said, "I must return to my work. Notify me when you find her. I'm sure she's scattered to the wind somewhere."

Merewen stared at her sire in shock. Her sister was never scattered to the wind. She was always focused and purposeful. Her hand went to her head as a sudden dizziness overtook her.

Her father had no idea, her mother didn't either. Neither of her brothers had seen her, and nothing unusual had happened at the keep.

That could only mean one thing.

Most everyone knew about the wicked men who stole girls and sold them. This meant that Linet hadn't left. Someone had taken her.

The Channel of Dubh.

Gavin and Gregor ushered the two brothers, Merewen, and her sire, despite his complaints, into the great hall. There was no sign of Torrian, but their laird's sire, Uncle Quade, sat near the fire with Aunt Brenna. Gavin led the family over to the hearth, intent on fulfilling his promise to Merewen. He would help. He would find her sister.

As he reached the fire, his sire, Logan, and his mother, Gwyneth, came down the stairs.

"What has transpired?" Logan asked, immediately picking up on the tension.

"Linet is missing," Wallace Baird said. "She disappeared from bed this morn. Could she have been kidnapped by this Channel everyone speaks of?"

Merewen stood behind the chairs arranged around the hearth. Her face looked pale, her brown eyes huge. Gavin wished to comfort her but didn't know how. "Can we not stop talking and just go after her?" Merewen cried out. "Where is this Channel? I'll go along."

Both her brothers snorted. Mal asked, "And how will you help?"

"I can help. I can ride a horse. I'll be able to see her at a distance. You know I can see farther than either of you."

Gavin could see her brothers didn't take her seriously. It seemed they didn't get on with their sisters, or at least not with Merewen. Her sire paid none of them any mind.

"All this panic is likely for naught," Struan said. "She probably just wandered off somewhere. She'll be back. No reason to panic."

Mal nodded. "I'm going back to the lists."

"Not if I tell you to stay," Uncle Quade said. The words had been spoken in a whisper, but his tone brooked no argument.

Struan quickly adjusted his attitude. "I'll do whatever you like, Chief." Most clan members still referred to Quade as chieftain, even though that title had been passed to his eldest son.

Torrian entered the hall at that very moment, his steps quick, his expression intent and serious. "I've heard Linet is missing?"

"Aye," Uncle Quade answered him. "And no one knows where she is."

"I'll send a patrol out immediately. Struan, Mal, get to the stables and await Kyle's orders. Get twenty men gathered, Kyle. I'll be right there. If these fools think we'll allow them to steal lasses from Ramsay land with no consequences, they're about to find out how wrong they are." The group got up to leave, Wallace Baird taking his time as if he had something to say, a definite attitude change. Like many others in the clan, his respect for the old chieftain and his son drove his actions. Uncle Quade had made sure that Clan Ramsay had prospered.

"How do you know where to look for her?" Merewen asked, kneading her hands until her knuckles turned white.

"I don't. But she could still be on Ramsay land. The verra first thing we'll do is send out a patrol. Kyle will be in charge of that mission, and the rest of us will decide what comes next."

"I agree," Gavin's sire said. "'Tis the best way to start. We'll discuss the next steps here." He made a motion for the Baird family to take their leave.

Merewen didn't move.

Gavin edged closer to her. "I promise to let you know if anything turns up."

Merewen smiled sweetly at him. "Would you mind escorting me home? My brothers are heading to the stables, and my sire will surely return to his duties." She dropped her gaze to the floor. "I'm afraid I'll be stolen away, too."

Gavin shrugged his shoulders and glanced at his sire, who gave him a brief nod indicating he should do as she asked. He motioned his arm toward the door and followed

Merewen out.

As soon as they were out of the others' hearing, she whispered, "I need you to keep your word. You must help me find my sister."

"Lass," Gavin said, "the whole clan will be looking for your sister. You heard our chief. We're patrolling the land, and if she doesn't return by the end of the day, we'll have another plan in place."

"I already do." She crossed her arms and lifted her chin a notch, her lips in a straight line.

"What are you saying?"

"I'm saying I'm going after her myself. I'm leaving around the evening meal. No one will notice me then. I'd appreciate your help."

"Do you think your parents will truly allow you to leave after your sister disappeared?"

"I don't need their permission. If I must, I'll save her myself." The clench of her jaw told him she wouldn't be swayed.

"Mayhap you should reconsider, lass. But you have time to think on it."

"I won't change my mind."

He decided it was probably best to leave her to her thoughts for now. With any luck, one of the patrols would find Linet, and the situation would resolve itself.

They mounted his horse and said very little, both of them taking in all the activity around them. It was clear the clan was going into action, but would it be enough? He didn't know.

But for Merewen's sake and Linet's, he hoped they'd find her soon.

CHAPTER THREE

GAVIN DISMOUNTED AT THE STABLES after returning Merewen to her cottage outside the bailey. Her mother had invited him in for a bowl of porridge, and he hadn't had the heart to deny her. The blacksmith had returned while he was there, so he'd felt comfortable leaving Merewen there. For now.

She'd threatened to leave on her own if Gavin didn't agree to go with her.

He didn't doubt her.

If she did leave, he knew he only had one choice: he had to go with her. But first he'd head to the hall and convince his laird and his sire to send some guards with them. Gregor would come with him, he knew, and they'd head northeast because that was the last active location they'd heard of for the Channel of Dubh.

He wished Maggie and Will were here. As the leaders of the Band of Cousins, they knew the most about the Channel. But they'd gone back to Edinburgh to confer with their king, and they might not return for two or three days. Often times, they followed up on different information given to them by the king or one of his men. The sad fact was they never knew exactly when the two would return.

He strode inside, surprised to see the meeting was just now breaking up. Uncle Quade, Gregor, and Gavin's parents were gathered around the hearth, talking in hushed voices.

"What was decided?" he asked as soon as he noticed a break in conversation.

Uncle Quade said, "Torrian is sending out another patrol to visit each of our surrounding neighbors to see if any of their lasses have gone missing, or if they've seen or heard anything about Linet."

"When they return and have found naught, where do we go next?" Gavin asked.

His sire shrugged his shoulders. "We wait until Maggie and Will arrive. Should not be long."

Gavin would not allow them to postpone the search. They all knew how quickly the Channel could move. If they waited too long, Linet might be lost forever. "Give us ten guards. Gregor and I will head northeast in pursuit of the largest remaining branch of the Channel."

"Nay." His father moved over to the stone hearth and leaned against it, crossing his arms.

"'Tis all you have to say? Nay, Papa? Why can we not go?" Gavin stood opposite his sire behind the chairs, setting his feet apart and crossing his arms, mimicking him.

"Because you have no idea where you're going."

"Northeast." He glanced at Gregor, who nodded his head in agreement.

"Where in the Northeast? Inverness? Or are you headed all the way up to the islands?"

Gavin shrugged his shoulders. "We head to Perth and follow the path into the Highlands."

"You have no idea where to go."

"How many times have we traveled to Grant land? I'm sure Gregor and I can get there with no trouble. Our guards are familiar with the path. We'll continue on from there. Mayhap we'll meet Connor and invite him along. He'll know the paths into the north, for certes."

"'Twould be a most wondrous plan if you had any idea where to go after Grant land. To my knowledge, Connor will be little help in Inverness. Though part of your reasoning is correct, I'll commend you for that much. You've visited the Grants oft enough to know how easy it is to get lost in the Highlands, and winter is around the corner. You'll get lost in snowbanks in the mountains. You'll be no help to anyone if you're stuck."

"Papa, have you no faith in me?"

"I wouldn't send anyone into the Highlands in the beginning of winter without a solid lead." His father's hands shifted to his hips as he leaned forward to make his point. Gavin mimicked the gesture, giving his father no ground.

"Send guards with us."

"Nay, and I'll not say it again. We wait for Maggie and Will and their new guide."

"Who's the new guide?"

"Someone the king has sent to assist us with putting an end to the Channel. He knows the north better than any of us. He's from Inverness."

"And when, precisely, will this guide be here?" It struck him as overly convenient that the king should send such an expert along on the very day they needed one. He had his doubts, but he'd hold them until he met the man.

Assuming it was a man.

"They're to arrive earlier than expected, mayhap this eve. No other guards will be permitted to leave until they arrive. Understood?"

Gavin groaned his discontent with a loud growl, but then agreed to his sire's conditions. He couldn't deny it would be better for Maggie and Will to join and direct their effort to find the missing lass.

"Agreed, Gavin?" his sire persisted.

"Agreed," he finally barked out. "But fair warning, if they don't arrive this eve, I'm going without them. My fear is Merewen will leave alone, and I can't allow that. If she sets out on her own, I will follow."

"The hell you will!" his sire bellowed.

"Uncle Logan, what would you suggest he do if he learns

Merewen is leaving alone, headed north? She's as head-strong as Gavin, if I had to guess, and I've never met two closer sisters. Words will not sway her," Gregor implored.

"Logan," his mother said. "He'd be wrong not to help the lass, and you know it."

"Gavin isn't strong enough to lead anyone."

"I know you won't care for my opinion, but I've traveled with Gavin many times, and I would trust him to lead the Band of Cousins. Aye, he's a jester, but he's serious when the situation warrants it," Gregor said, shooting Gavin a sympathetic look.

"I *don't* agree with you. You took part in that fiasco, too, but even you are more level-headed than my son." Logan pursed his lips, glaring at Gregor.

Silence descended on the group around the hearth, everyone looking at the father and son with wide eyes. Gavin thought his head would explode. "What?" he finally sputtered out. "I supposed you'd trust anyone but me? Your own son?"

"Don't be daft. I didn't say I'd trust Gregor to lead the group, just that he has more sense than you. There are plenty of lads I would not trust," his sire said, moving three steps closer to him.

"But you'd trust Connor? Braden or Roddy? What about your brother's sons? Daniel and David? Would you trust Daniel? He's younger than me, but you'd trust him more, wouldn't you? Even after all the work I've done with the cousins."

His mother stepped in between them, but not before shooting his sire a withering look. "I would trust you, Gavin," she said firmly, "but you still need support. No matter what, take a few guards with you."

His father stared at his mother for a moment before, then took a sideways step so he and Gavin were eye to eye once more. "Nay, I still would not trust you as much as the others. And you know why."

Heat flushed Gavin, so intense, he feared he'd be burned. "Because of something that happened three years ago?"

"Aye, three years ago you were not strong enough, and you still are not going northeast without Maggie."

Gavin couldn't find any words. He glanced at Gregor, waiting to hear if he had anything else to offer, but he knew he could rely on his cousin. He would go along with him if Merewen proved determined enough to leave on her own. He spun on his heel and left, making sure to use his sire's signature move on the way out. He banged the door to the great hall shut loud enough to be heard into the mountains.

"That's my move, and you can't use it!" He heard his father's yelling even through the thick stone walls and oak door.

Gavin stalked back in, his face red with fury, and said, "Not loud enough for you? Then try this one!"

He left and swung the door twice as hard this time.

He hoped the damned door would fall off its hinges.

The last thing he heard was his mother's voice.

"You had that one coming, Logan."

———•———

Merewen waited patiently for any word of her sister, but when none came she grew restless. Half the day had been wasted already. Since nearly everyone was on one of the patrols, or gathered in the hall or the courtyard *talking* about the patrols, she hoped she'd be able to sneak away and do the only thing that would settle her.

Her mother and sire had gone to the great hall after the first patrol returned with no word of Linet. They were talking and pacing with the rest, but that wasn't enough for Merewen. She had to do something or she'd sob for certain. Her mission was set and she hoped Gavin would travel with her, but she'd be foolish to try to go off on her own before mealtime. The patrols and the wolfhounds would find her for certain.

No one understood her connection with Linet. They'd always been able to tell if the other was in trouble—when Merewen had tripped on a rabbit hole and twisted her ankle, Linet was the one who'd found her, and when Linet had gotten lost in the forest foraging for pine cones, Merewen had known exactly where she was. Now that special connection to Linet was telling her that her sister was far, far away.

She had to go after her.

Although she didn't know where to go this time, she trusted that if she set out, the angels who guarded her and Linet would lead her in the correct direction. Or mayhap they had guided her to Gavin, who had knowledge of the Channel.

She needed to find a way to pass the time, and she knew exactly what would serve her best. Bundled up in her mantle, she left the cottage and closed the door behind her. The gray skies had not relented, another indication that winter was indeed on its way.

She had to find Linet before the weather got any worse. But first, she needed to practice. For all she knew, she might finally be required to put her secret skill to use. She hastened along, pulling the hood up on her mantle hoping she'd not be noticed by any in the small clan village. When she reached the end of the path, she headed down the part least traveled, looking ahead to her spot.

Her favorite spot. The one she'd shared with no one but Linet, though Gavin had found her at the clan's butts once. Because of her sire's view of lasses and archery, she'd set up her own practice area, one she made just for herself. How she wished her sister had trained with her, like she'd asked, but although Linet had helped her keep her secret, she had expressed no interest in joining her.

She moved into the copse of trees, pleased to see nothing had changed.

Here it was—the key to her soul.

CHAPTER FOUR

MEREWEN LEANED DOWN TO PICK up the brush covering her crate. Lifting the top off, she let out a sigh of relief—the same sound she made whenever she opened the crate. Her things were still there. She'd have to bring her treasures home with her and hide them in the cottage until she left.

She sat on a nearby log next to the crate and lifted out the bow, which she leaned against the log. Then she removed five arrows and her quiver, something she'd made herself. The arrows she'd snuck from the Ramsay butts after dark. She had two pairs of soft leggings, too, modeled after Gwyneth Ramsay's clothing. Gwyneth had, in fact, given her one of them, along with a tunic.

Gavin's mother had been her first teacher—the one who'd given her the bow and ignited her excitement. Gwyneth Ramsay had offered to teach any lass in the clan how to become an archer, but few lasses expressed an interest, or were allowed to do so. Only Merewen and Maggie and Molly had been dedicated students. Her sire had put an end to the lessons, snapping her bow in two, insisting such a brutish sport wasn't right for his fair lassies, which was the main reason she'd kept everything secretive. Whenever she left to practice, she'd come home with a sack of apples or hazelnuts to pretend she'd been out foraging. Her sire had never caught on to her tactics.

Replacing the top on the crate over the leggings—it was

much too cold to change into them—she found her way out of the trees and over to the clearing where her target sat on the far oak tree. Her soul began to sing a familiar song of accomplishment. She was good, although nowhere near as talented as Gwyneth or her daughters. If only her sire were more like Logan Ramsay, who'd encouraged all of his daughters to learn to shoot. He wasn't intimidated by his wife's reputation as one of the best archers in all the land. Merewen sighed, something she often did when she thought of the title Gwyneth Ramsay had earned. Och, how she'd like to gain such a reputation.

A dream, surely, since she was no one of importance. She'd settled for practicing at every opportunity, for being as good as she could be for her own sense of achievement. And whenever she passed the chapel, she would say a silent prayer of thanks for Gavin Ramsay, for his generosity in replacing her broken bow. Had it not been for him, her favorite pastime would have probably ended. The bow he'd given her was exquisite, so well made that she'd thought to return it to him for one not as nice—because who was she to deserve such a gift? When would she ever put her skill to good use? But mayhap all of her practice had been for something after all—it might just help her save her sister.

Merewen moved across the clearing, limbering up the muscles of her shoulders and her arms. The cold fought against her, but her routine warmed her body. When she was ready, she took her stance, carefully placing her feet the right distance apart as Gwyneth had instructed her all those moons ago. Then she checked her body and her posture, making sure her shoulders were back and strong and that she stood at the right angle to her target.

She fired and hit her target dead center.

And again. And again. And again.

A smile spread across her face as she looked at the target, pleased to see how well she'd done. And then she startled at the sound of a long, low whistle behind her.

"God's bones," Gavin Ramsay said. "I haven't seen anyone shoot like that since my sister Molly spent all her time in the butts."

Merewen squealed, suddenly fearful that her weapon would be taken away from her. She spun on her heel to face Gavin, tucking the bow behind her back. There was no hiding her activity, but she didn't intend to relinquish her treasure to him.

Then she chastised herself for her daft thoughts. Gavin had given her the bow. Why would he take it away?

Habit. It was just habit for her to hide everything. Even now, she couldn't bring herself to hold the bow in plain sight.

"That was expert marksmanship, especially considering the clothing you have on. Have you any idea how good you've gotten, lass?"

Merewen could feel the blood pulsing through her body as Gavin moved toward her. What would be his response? She held her ground, her breathing became much faster as he stepped closer.

Gavin reached out a hand, and she flinched, tipping backward to keep him from touching her bow.

"'Tis mine. You gave it to me or have you forgotten? You said I could keep it."

Gavin lowered his voice, "Relax, Merewen. I'll not take it from you. You have earned the right to keep it. I'll make sure and find you some leggings, though you shoot well enough in a gown and a mantle."

She eased back so she could stand up straight again, dropping her arm to her side, her bow still clutched in her hand. Gavin wasn't a threat.

"My thanks, but I already have two pairs." She felt blood rise to her cheeks. "'Twas too cold to change."

"Does anyone else know you can shoot that well?" he asked. His hand came up to her face again, and he brushed the backs of his fingertips across her cheek.

She couldn't help but tremble at his touch. No man had touched her so before. Her brothers were brutes who believed women existed solely to serve men and be used by them, but Gavin had never struck her as a brute. He was different.

And she'd never forgotten the kiss they'd shared. Did he remember? The gift of the bow and the kiss that had followed had made her wish he would court her, but she knew how foolish those thoughts had been. She was the smithy's daughter, and Gavin was of noble blood. His sire was the Beast of the Highlands and his mother was the best archer in all the land.

She was no one special.

His touch was gentle and, even better, warm. She leaned into him slightly, savoring the contact, but then forced herself to pull back.

The way he was looking at her... No one had ever regarded her with such smoldering heat in their eyes. It had a most strange effect on her, causing a heat to travel inside her. That thought was preposterous because it was winter and they were outside.

But there it was again, a rush of flame through her insides.

"You'll keep my secret and not tell my sire?" she asked.

"I will if 'tis what you want, but why keep your talent a secret? There are few lasses who could compete with you. Actually, verra few men could beat you. They tend to prefer swords, even on Ramsay land." Gavin's gaze seemed to intensify even more. "I applaud your hard work. No one knows you can use a bow like that?"

"Only Linet. She would watch me sometimes."

"May I test your skills on something different?"

She nodded, feeling uncertain, but if he could teach her something new, she'd be forever grateful.

He pointed to the target. "You do verra well when you are aiming at something directly in front of you. When you're on the hunt or in the thick of a fight, your target

often changes. May I move your target from its usual location and see how you do?"

She nodded, blushing from excitement. Gavin was going
to teach her…*her*!

He moved the target off to the left and above her line
of sight. Once he stepped away, he said, "Sometimes your
target could be above you. See how you do with that."

She set her stance and took aim, but Gavin held up his
hand to stop her. Disappointed that she'd done it wrong,
she let her arm fall to the side. But he didn't wait, instead
stepping behind her. "May I show you how you should
adjust your aim for that type of target?"

She gulped, then nodded and whispered, "Aye."

He stood directly behind her, their bodies now touching
in a most intimate manner.

"Set yourself as you normally would."

She did as he instructed, grateful to have something to
do to hide her fine tremors from his closeness.

He reached over her arms, the heat of his body suffusing
her, and moved her position just a touch before he stepped
back and said, "Go ahead. Try it now."

She took a deep breath, then followed his instructions
and hit just a wee bit to the right of the target.

"You have a gift, Merewen. Did you know that? I've
yet to see someone who can adjust their shooting that
quickly."

She angled her body toward him, lifting her gaze to
meet his. Questions had tormented her ever since the day
he'd given her the bow. If they were to travel together, she
needed to ask them.

"Gavin, many thanks for your gift of the bow. Without it,
I could not have practiced this last year."

"Any Ramsay clan member who can shoot the way you
do should have a new one every year. I'll see that you do."

"Why did you kiss me then?" she blurted out.

He chuckled. "If I remember correctly, you kissed me

first."

She blushed and giggled. "Aye, 'tis true, but my kiss was not like yours."

She'd expected him to explain. Instead, he stepped toward her and cupped her face, his lips descending on hers, and stroked her, teased her, until she opened for him. The kiss was warm and sweet at the same time, his tongue reaching deep into her mouth until she tentatively touched it with hers, only to hear him growl. The kiss overtook her senses, heated, carnal, an assault on her control. Her knees nearly buckled, but she locked them.

He ended the kiss, his thumb rubbing her lower lip. "Was it like that? Because 'tis what I recall."

She gave a quick nod, her gaze now locked on his. She forced herself to speak, to give voice to her thoughts. "But you kissed me before, and I never saw you again. What did it mean? What does this kiss mean?"

He stepped back and stared at the branches in the trees overhead. "I'm sorry to have confused you, but they both mean the same thing, Merewen." His gaze dropped to hers. "I like you. Honestly, I've not been interested in many Ramsay lasses, but you? You are something special."

He didn't say anything but stared at the ground, his right foot shuffling the leaves, knocking nuts out of the way as if he were searching for an answer. His gaze lifted to hers again and he said, "I probably would have pursued you, but my cousins and I started our quest to put an end to this Channel. It got in the way."

He reached for her fingers, gently taking the bow from her and setting it down. "It doesn't mean I don't have feelings for you. I just had another commitment. My apologies if I led you to believe anything different."

She shook her head. All her feelings for him had been reawakened by one kiss. She knew not what to say.

He saved her, stating, "I'll have to bring you a pair of gloves. Your hands are too cold." He cocooned them in his own warmth, his heat traveling up her arms with a tingle that shot straight to her breasts, her nipples pressing at her bindings.

Talk of the Channel brought her back to her focus. While hope had blossomed in her heart with Gavin's confession, she reminded herself they had more important things to discuss. If her sister was in this Channel, they had to find her. "You will go with me to find my sister?"

Gavin continued to rub her hands. "Aye. I will travel with you. I've just gained a new guard."

"Gregor? Will your cousin come with us?"

"I suspect so, but I was referring to you. You will be able to assist us in most any situation. I just need to teach you how to react when fear strikes you, though you've already proven you'll be an apt pupil. I just need to work with you a bit more to be prepared."

"What do you mean?"

He let go of her hands and took a step back, staring up at the sky, which looked ready to downpour its contents on them. "I mean, you must learn how to stay focused when a boar comes straight at you, or a reiver with a sword. If you can learn that, you'll be as deadly as anyone. Come, I think we need to get out of the rain that's about to drench us."

"You will go with me? Truly? But I thought your father forbid you to leave until your sister returns. 'Tis what I heard." She followed him down the path toward his horse after retrieving her bow and several arrows. "Wait a moment, please."

She hurried back to the crate and lifted the tunic and leggings out, stuffing them under her arms. Placing the lid back on the top, she covered it with brush and branches again, knowing she'd return her things to her hiding spot someday. She returned to Gavin's side, casting him a small smile, relieved he was helping her and that he'd promised to keep her secret.

He lifted her onto his horse and mounted behind her.

"Aye, my sire says I'm not to leave until Maggie and Will return, which could be as soon as this eve. But if they do not return, I'm leaving whether he likes it or not. So my answer is aye, I will go with you. If you wish, I'll hide your things in the stables and find a saddlebag for you. I'll fill your quiver, too. You'll need both."

She spun around to face him, nearly throwing her balance off. "You'll defy your sire?"

Gavin nodded. "I'll do it for you, Merewen."

Gavin left Merewen at her cottage, promising to meet her down near the burn a quarter hour after supper began. If Maggie and Will returned by then, they would wait to leave. If not, they would set off. He found a saddle bag, stuffed a few things inside, then hid the bag and her bow and quiver inside a little-used cupboard.

He had trouble admitting to himself how much their kiss had unsettled him. He hadn't anticipated her question about the past, so he'd been as honest as possible. He did like her, and he had to admit, those feelings had just grown.

Between the taste of her lips and the feel of her arse pressed against him, Merewen Baird was an enticing lass indeed. But her skill with the bow moved him most of all. Her form, her aim, her focus were all erotic dances to him.

He'd used his bow since he was a wee laddie, but never like Merewen. Every time she fired her arrow, something fired inside of him, and he was uncertain of how to handle it.

When he left the stables, he saw his sire approaching on foot with a strange man on horseback. The man dismounted not far from him.

"Gavin, hold." His father's voice easily carried across the din of the inside bailey. "This is Rollin Fitzroy, the man King Alexander sent to assist us with putting an end to the Channel of Dubh. Fitzroy, this is my son, Gavin." Logan and his guest closed the distance between them.

"Greetings to you and welcome to Clan Ramsay," Gavin said. He glanced about, but there was no sign of Maggie and Will. If they'd arrived with this man, they'd already gone off somewhere.

"Many thanks. Your clan has quite a reputation, for both its women and its men." Fitzroy shifted his gaze back to Logan. "I've heard of your daughters, but not your son. Is he your only son?"

"Aye, but he's a fine one. My two eldest daughters have both worked hard for the Crown. Maggie still does, as you know, but Molly has health issues."

He noticed his sire didn't make any mention of Molly's seer skills, or how the headaches that accompanied her visions had pained her of late. He'd also failed to mention she was carrying her first bairn, which kept her abed at times.

Fitzroy's gaze returned to Gavin, assessing him carefully. "It must be a challenge for you to measure up."

Indeed, although who was this stranger to say so? Something about him didn't set well with Gavin, and not just that he had apparently arrived before his two escorts. He'd be interested to hear his sire's opinion of the man later. In any case, he'd not give Fitzroy what he wanted. He decided to goad him instead. "Measure up?"

"You're the only son of the great Logan and Gwyneth Ramsay. Two powerful reputations for you to measure up to." The man glanced back at his father. "How well has he met your expectations?"

Gavin would like nothing better than to show the man that he measured up with his fists, but fortunately, Gregor and Torrian walked up to them before he could.

His father shot him a veiled look before offering an introduction. "Here is our laird, Torrian, and his brother, Gregor."

Torrian greeted the man with a clasp to his shoulder.

He'd apparently heard the exchange, because he said, "Gavin measures up well. I expect he'll build his own reputation in due time. Where are Maggie and Will, and what is the latest news of the Channel?"

Gavin appreciated his cousin's kind words and how deftly he'd steered the conversation away from him, especially with two important questions, ones they all were anxious to have answered.

Rollin Fitzroy glanced at the ground, his hands on his hips. "Maggie and Will are a couple of days behind me. We were surprised at the most recent development in the Channel of Dubh. The entire operation has been moved. The leaders used to operate out of London, but now they've moved completely to the northwestern part of the Highlands. Maggie and Will stayed to find out more specific information, but they sent me on ahead. They didn't want anyone in your group to head off in the wrong direction. Due to all the information they uncovered in Edinburgh, they're changing tactics. Heading west."

"But their largest operation was supposed to be in the northeast," Gregor stated.

"*Was* the northeast. Now they're in the northwest."

Gavin glanced at Gregor, surprised by this revelation. If it were true, it would indicate a complete change in strategy. But were they truly expected to take a stranger's word for it?

"Come inside," Logan said. "I'll find a nice goblet of my best concoction to warm your insides and a light repast. Supper won't be for another two hours." His expression was inscrutable, as usual.

Rollin smiled. "I was hoping you'd offer me a nice whisky. The best part of Scotland, I say." They headed across the courtyard to the keep while Gavin, Gregor, and Torrian held back.

Gavin was the first to speak. "I don't trust the man," he said at once.

Torrian cocked his head. "I won't pass judgment yet, but I cannot disagree with you."

"He is English, so that doesn't help him," Gavin added with a snicker. "He may have lived in Inverness, but his speech is definitely English."

Torrian and Gregor both chuckled. "Aye, there is that fact," Torrian said, clapping him on the shoulder. "I'll see you both inside."

Gregor said, "I'll go with you. I want to hear everything the man says."

Gavin said, "I'll be there in a few moments."

Torrian glanced at Gavin. "Something bothering you?"

"Nay, I'll be right along. Going to brush my horse down." The two headed off toward the keep. Gavin didn't need to brush his horse down—he'd just come from the stables, and the lads would take care of the animal. He wanted to a moment alone to mull over something that troubled him.

Although his cousin and chieftain had been kind enough to tell Fitzroy that Gavin did indeed measure up, his sire had never responded to Fitzroy's question. Logan Ramsay, his beloved father, clearly did not think much of what he had accomplished. While they'd argued about it before, he knew his sire's temper better than anyone, and sometimes he said things merely for the sake of argument. But this proved it. He wasn't just arguing—he believed it.

Logan Ramsay, the Beast of the Highlands, did not think much of his only son's abilities.

Perhaps it was time to change that opinion.

CHAPTER FIVE

———◆———

GAVIN FELT COMPELLED TO DO one more thing before he headed into the keep to find out more about the Channel and Rollin Fitzroy. He made his way to the hut in the farthest corner of the inner bailey and knocked on the door of the hut as quietly as possible.

His sister Molly's husband, Tormod, answered, holding a hand up to let him know to keep his voice low.

"Is she awake, Tormod? I really need to speak with her," he whispered.

Tormod ushered him into the dark hut where the only sound was Molly's even breathing. Her thin form lay on the soft bed in the chamber off the center room of the hut. Tormod led him inside and sat on the edge of the mattress. "Your brother is here," he whispered. "Are you hale enough for a short visit?"

Molly nodded with a smile, indicating that Tormod should light one small candle on the table. She then held her hand out to Gavin—a silent invitation to sit on the stool beside the bed.

Molly was his eldest sister, adopted before Gavin was born. His parents had saved her and Maggie, her blood sister, from a horrible situation. Their birth parents had given them up to serve as maids for a family who'd beaten and berated them.

Molly had modeled herself after her adoptive mother from the first, donning leggings and a tunic and learning to be the best archer she could. She was a fierce warrior, just like her sister, Maggie, and she was also a seer, a talent that had proven useful to the clan many times. Some said his sister also had the uncanny skill of sensing evil spirits, but that had yet to be proven.

"Another bad one, Mol?" Gavin whispered, taking the stool next to her bed and grasping her hand.

"Aye."

"How does the babe fare?"

"Fine."

A curt response, which meant this headache was bad indeed. When it got like this, the simple act of speaking pained her, but she had an amazing talent of saving her words for what was necessary. He would keep their meeting brief out of respect for her.

"Did it just start?"

She nodded again.

"There's a new man who just arrived. He was meant to come with Maggie and Will, but he says they've been held back a couple of days. This man claims the Channel of Dubh has shifted its location out of England and the northeast Highlands over to the northwest. I don't trust him. I can't explain why, but I believe the worst of it is still in the northeast. I believe he's brought us bad information, whether he meant to or no. What say you?"

Molly closed her eyes for a few seconds, then opened them and gazed up at him. She pointed to his chest and nodded. "'Tis as you say. The northeast. 'Tis where you should go with the lass."

Her answer gratified him, especially since he hadn't mentioned taking Merewen along. His sister had a true gift. He was glad he'd listened to the niggling voice inside his head, the one that had whispered Fitzroy wasn't to be trusted. He knew in his gut that something bad was multiplying in the northeast, and it needed to be stopped. He smiled and kissed her forehead. "Thanks, Mol. Feel better."

"Gavin?"

"What is it?"

"Be careful. You are right, but 'tis verra dangerous, even more so than you would guess. Keep your eyes open, and do not trust all you're told. I need to speak with Maggie when she gets here. I think there will be a threat against her, or possibly Will."

"Or mayhap both?" he asked.

"I surely hope not," Molly said.

Gavin covered his sister up with a fur and moved out the door to leave. Tormod clasped his shoulder and said, "Godspeed. I think you have some challenges ahead, but you are more than capable."

He headed out the door back toward the keep. It didn't take him long to decide how to proceed—he knew his sire. Logan Ramsay had worked for the Crown for years. He would go along with the king's man, whether he liked him or not, until there was solid evidence he should do otherwise. Nay, he wouldn't share what Molly had told him because it wouldn't be sufficient motivation for him to cross King Alexander's man.

He trekked up the steps and headed inside the great hall, surprised to see how quiet it was at this time of day. Rollin Fitzroy was nowhere to be seen, and the remaining group consisted of his sire, Gregor, Torrian, and Uncle Quade, gathered in front of the fire.

Torrian got up to leave as he approached the hearth, pausing to clasp his shoulder in passing. Gavin and Torrian were often asked if they were brothers. They had similar looks, both with the lighter brown hair and green eyes. Gregor *was* Torrian's half-brother, but his dark hair and eyes favored his mother.

Privately, Gavin considered Gregor to be the best looking of the three, although he loved to crow about his own good looks to make them laugh. He didn't mind flaunting himself because Gregor was truly oblivious to things such as appearances. His cousin was focused and determined. He preferred to stand back and let others talk while he analyzed everything. He was the best strategist of all the Ramsays, or so Gavin thought, but he rarely shared his ideas with anyone other than Gavin.

He grabbed an ale from a side table on his way to join the group. No one spoke so he jumped right in with his question. "I thought Will and Maggie were coming with Fitzroy. Wouldn't Maggie have sent a missive if they were held up?"

"She did," his sire said. "Fitzroy gave me the message. They're delayed, which means you're staying here for the time being."

"Nay, it doesn't. Gregor and I may choose to go ahead to Grant land to meet up with Connor, see what the cousins have learned in the north. Mayhap Loki has some information we could use if the operation had indeed moved to the northwest. That is, if you want to take a stranger's word."

"He's a man of the king," his sire nearly growled. "Why would I doubt his word?"

Gavin shrugged his shoulders. "I don't trust the man."

"From one short encounter?"

"'Tis just a hunch I have." He pursed his lips, knowing his father wouldn't agree with him, even though the man was well known for following his own hunches.

If only his sire trusted him.

"What you think doesn't matter, Gavin. I'm giving you orders that you're to wait until Maggie and Will arrive." His father moved to refill his ale.

"And what about Linet? We give her kidnappers two days' gain on us?"

Gavin settled in a chair in front of the hearth and leaned back, stretching his long legs out in front of him. "I promised Merewen we would not give up on her sister."

Uncle Quade said, "We have not given up, Gavin. Torrian has sent a patrol out with both of her brothers along. They may turn up something. A piece of clothing, a reiver who may have seen something."

Her brothers who didn't seem to care she'd gone missing.

"Papa, I know you don't want me to go," he persisted, leaning forward now, "but I'd like to meet up with the rest of the Band of Cousins." Gavin would not give up on this quest. He still wished for his sire's support, but if Logan persisted in refusing him, he would have to move forward without it. He was convinced Linet had been kidnapped to be sold over the waters.

His father spun around. "You may take up that mission as soon as the ones in charge of the Band arrive. You'll wait for your sister."

"Nay, I won't. Two days from now may be too late. I'm leaving this eve. Gregor, I hope you'll go with me, but I cannot wait. The men in the Channel move fast."

"I said nay." His father's tone carried a silent message, one he gave out often—he was not up for a challenge in the matter.

Gavin didn't care. His father clearly didn't think much of him, so what did it matter if he had his support? He ignored him and turned to Uncle Quade. "I hope you'll allow Gregor to join me. We'll go to Grant land first, hope to gain Connor's assistance and any others in the Band. Whether we'll go east or west from there has not been decided yet, although my gut says the Channel is still in the northeast."

"I'm denying you," his father said.

"Papa—" His voice rose enough that his mother must have overheard because she came down the staircase in a rush. "I know you don't believe in me, but I don't need your approval to leave on a mission with the Band of Cousins. I'd hoped you would give it, but I'm going whether or not you wish it. I am an adult."

His father glanced at his uncle. "Quade, do you approve of them going without Maggie and Will?"

Quade sighed and said, "What I say does not matter. 'Tis up to Torrian, but I know the lass's parents will appreciate his offer. I trust my son and Gavin. Why don't you?"

Logan looked like he might explode, but instead he paced, something they all knew was not good.

Gwyneth stepped in his path, forcing him to look at her. "Logan, I agree with your brother. 'Tis time to trust our son. You need to get over that other incident. He was much younger. How many battles has he been involved with since then? You must let him go. This is not something trivial he is attempting to pursue."

Although his parents bickered all the time, fondly, Gavin had never heard his mother disagree with his father about such an important issue. Usually, his mother could soothe his sire's fury, but this time he only looked angrier, his face an unnatural red. Then the oddest thing happened—all that hot anger faded, replaced by a look Gavin liked even less: one of challenge.

Gavin's sire stared straight at him. "Don't do it. You'll regret it." His voice came out in the barest of whispers.

"Logan. You're not thinking," Gwyneth snapped.

"You don't trust me, Papa? All because of a mistake I made three years ago? Well, I made my amends. Think of me as you wish, but I'm going after Linet." He turned his attention to his cousin. "Gregor, I hope you'll come with me."

With a final nod toward his cousin, he stalked toward the door. At the base of the staircase, he caught a glimpse of something out of the corner of his eye.

Fitzroy. How long had he been standing there listening?

The man gave a brief nod and said, "Godspeed to you on your journey to the northwest. She's worth the effort." Unfortunately, the smug expression on his face belied his words. He looked quite pleased with the disagreement between father and son.

"Don't do it, Gavin. Don't go out that door!" His father's voice nearly shook the rafters.

He ignored his sire and walked out the door, but before he could step away, a thought occurred to him. One more thing he needed to do before he left. He stalked back inside, throwing the door open wide, and stood there. Once he had his sire's attention, he said, "I forgot something."

He stepped back outside, but not before slamming the door shut as hard as he could.

CHAPTER SIX

———◆———

LOGAN FORCED HIMSELF TO STAY calm, mostly because he'd noticed Fitzroy was watching them carry on from the top of the stairs. "Quade, are you out of your mind? You're leading him on."

"Nay, I'm not out of my mind," his brother said, his tone unequivocal. "You are. Our sons are grown men. They're both fine archers, and they've done admirable work with the Band of Cousins. And Gavin is a hell of a swordsman, too. Why can't you trust your own son to travel to Grant land with a few guards?"

Logan glared at his brother. Quade knew the answer to his own question, but he was going to force him to answer anyway. "You know why. Gavin doesn't have the sense of responsibility the others have. He can't be trusted to function alone."

Gwynie said, "He's not alone, Logan. And I agree with your brother. He's certainly capable of traveling to Grant land with Gregor and a handful of guards. He's traveled that trail numerous times. Respect him for trying to do the honorable deed and allow him to go."

"I cannot do that."

"Why not?" Quade asked.

"Aye. Why not?" his wife pressed.

The two of them stared at him. He glanced up at the top of the stairs, pleased to see Fitzroy had disappeared. Gregor stood behind his sire, awaiting his final decision.

The feeling of panic wouldn't leave his gut. Logan couldn't bear the thought of Gavin leading a group north on his own, although he couldn't put his thoughts into words. He struggled with what he knew the real reason was, but he couldn't bring himself to admit it to anyone.

Quade knew him well because he said, "Gregor, go follow your cousin. If he leaves, go with him. Tell Torrian and take five guards with you."

Gregor nodded to his sire and left.

As soon as he closed the door behind him, Gwynie said, "Logan? What is it? It's more than the past, isn't it?"

Quade nodded. "Aye, and I suspect you've no real reason to worry."

Logan gave a low growl before he pulled the words from his gut. "He's our only son, Quade. You have two. If something should happen to him..."

Gwynie reached out to touch him, her hand on his shoulder grounding him like nothing else could. "You would be just as upset if anything happened to one of your daughters. I know you better than to think otherwise. How can you justify that fear?"

Slud, did his wife have to know him so well?

He gritted his teeth and said, "He's our only son. Do you not know the pressure that will be put on him? Everyone will expect him to be the best archer, the best fighter, the best everything." He glanced at his wife. "I love you dearly, but consider the situation we've created for our bairns. Even Fitzroy mentioned it. People will expect him to be the best fighter because of our reputations, Gwynie. They will follow him everywhere. He'll be attacked just because of us. I don't want to do that to him until he's ready."

Gwynie moved to his side and wrapped her arms around him. "Mayhap he is ready. He needs the chance to prove himself."

"He's always been such a jester. I worry he won't focus enough to protect himself when the time comes," Logan said.

"You've done everything you can to make him a strong, honorable Highlander," Quade said. "Such a fine job that he sees a lass in need and can't stop himself from jumping to assist her. Let him go, Logan. Sometimes you have to. I didn't know Torrian would ever lead as well as he has, but I had to give him the chance."

Gwynie crossed her arms and asked, "Our son has plenty of experience, and so do his cousins. They've saved lives, Logan, many of them. Scotland needs our lads."

Logan's throat felt like it had been tied into a knot. He nodded to his brother and then hugged his wife, squeezing her close. "I pray you're both right. I have a sick feeling in my gut, one I can't ignore."

———◆———

Merewen tucked the extra leggings inside her sack and threw in a few more things she might need: a sliver of soap, hair ties, linen squares. She already had her warm leggings on beneath her wool gown, rolled up so her mother wouldn't notice them.

She sat on the bed, worried about the journey, but even more so for her sister. She had to locate her. Life in their small hut had not been easy, yet they were always happy when they were together.

By night, they whispered about lads and foolish things, about their secret wishes and dreams, and by day, they worked for the clan. The two often traveled to the keep to help care for the young ones so the women of the clan could work the wool and create garments for all. Mistress Brenna wouldn't allow the wee ones to be left out in the cold during the winter, so they came into the hall and stayed in a large chamber in one of the towers, one the Ramsays had added after the original keep had been built. It had its own hearth and heaps of extra furs.

Lily Ramsay, sister to their chieftain, often joined them

in caring for the young ones. She read to all of the bairns, but most especially to her twin lasses. When she'd noticed Merewen and Linet's interest in the skill, she'd volunteered to teach them. A year later, Gregor had broken his arm, so he had volunteered to sit with the bairns. He'd read with Linet quite frequently to help her hone her skills. Merewen had often wondered what the two had spoken about, but Linet had never mentioned anything about Gregor other than his patience as a teacher.

Books were so rare that it was difficult finding enough to read, which was why Linet had been so pleased when Lily had given her one as a gift. The sisters used to look at it together at night, Linet reading softly to Merewen.

Their father had ripped the book up and thrown it away, declaring lasses too ignorant to learn such things. Then, to Merewen's surprise, their brother, Mal, had given Linet a different book last yule—an unusually generous gesture for him.

The rest of their lives were uneventful. Like many of the clan, once they returned home from their work with the bairns, they assisted their mother with various duties— washing clothes, cleaning, needlework, and cooking. Life at Clan Ramsay was very busy, and many times exhausting.

Merewen's escape had been her archery. Linet's had been reading. They'd had to become secretive with both—while Merewen hid her archery things, Linet spent what time she could in the chapel, reading with Father Rab.

The door banged open, so Merewen hurried into the main chamber to see if there was news about her sister. Mal and Struan stood there, setting their weapons down by the door.

"Did you learn anything?" her mother pleaded, her hands wringing in her skirts.

Her sire burst in behind her brothers, slamming the door against the cold wind. "'Tis getting colder every day. Winter is nigh upon us, I fear."

Her mother waited patiently for their news, so Merewen waited also. Their sire had gone out with a different group of warriors than the lads.

Her father finally sighed and said, "Naught. Our patrol searched the forests for any clue, but we only saw signs of the other patrols that had gone through. Struan, what did your patrol find?"

"Naught." Struan shook his head and said nothing more.

"We searched everywhere," Mal added. "We chased after every reiver, hoping to see a piece of Linet's clothing. Anything at all. No one has seen anything. I fear 'tis hopeless, Mama."

"You can guess what everyone thinks, Papa," Struan said. "They think she was taken up by the Channel. The men of the north who steal lassies and bairns and sell them across the waters."

Merewen couldn't handle any more bad news, so she hurried back into her chamber and closed the door. She flung herself onto the bed and burst into tears. She had to find her sister, she just had to.

Rolling to the other side of the bed, Linet's side, she reached under one of the pillows and found just what she was searching for—Linet's favorite linen square. She'd sewn purple flowers over it, and to Merewen's delight, it still smelled just like her sister. Lavender was her favorite flower.

She tucked the linen square under her chin.

"Linet, I'm coming for you. I'll not give up," she whispered with a sniffle. In less than an hour, she'd head out to meet Gavin and they'd be on their way. Surely, they'd find her sister. They had to.

"Merewen," her mother's voice carried through the door. "Are you hale?"

"Aye, Mama. I am fine, just sad. I don't want to go to the keep for supper." She held her breath, praying her mother would accept her excuse.

"Are you sure? Papa says our laird promises a nice feast for all those who've been on patrol."

"Nay. I wish to take a wee nap. You go on without me. I'll be fine." She inhaled her sister's sweet scent again to give her courage.

Silence hung for a moment, and Merewen held her breath until her mother finally answered. "All right. We shall return soon."

She waited until the footsteps left the hut and the door softly closed before she sat up in bed. The first thing she did was stuff Linet's linen square in the pocket sewn inside her mantle.

She just needed a wee piece of her sister along with her.

She wouldn't give up until she found Linet.

CHAPTER SEVEN

G AVIN TRUDGED DOWN THROUGH THE court-yard mumbling to himself. Cursing his sire for not believing in him. Why didn't his own father trust in him? After all the battles he'd been in, he'd expected the Beast to have more faith in him. He thought he'd made amends.

It was not to be, but that wouldn't stop him from fretting over it.

A voice called to him from behind. Gregor caught up with him and said, "I'm coming with you."

"You don't care if you upset your sire?"

"Nay, my sire told me to go with you."

Gavin stopped in his tracks and turned to face his cousin. "Truly? Your father believes in me more than my own sire does."

Torrian strode toward them, a few steps behind Gregor. "I believe in you, and 'tis what matters. I'm sending half a dozen guards with you. When Maggie and Will return, I'm sure they'll choose to follow. The question is are you headed to the northeast or northwest?"

Gavin let out a sigh of relief. Aye, he believed he and Gregor could do this alone, but they would be protecting a lass, something he did not do often. They would take the six guards and be grateful.

After all, Merewen was a beauty.

"Northeast," he said firmly.

"You're not believing Fitzroy either?"

Gavin arched his brow, surprised his cousin agreed with his judgment of the king's man. "I don't believe that or anything else that man says, and Molly agrees the trouble is to the northeast. You are doubtful of the man?"

Torrian glanced about to make sure he'd not be overheard. "He may be a man of the king, but he has an edge to him I don't trust. I do hope we're both wrong."

Gregor glanced from one to the other. "Are you sure 'tis not just because the man is English?"

Torrian barked a laugh at his question. "We shall see. I suspected this would be the way of it, and I've already chosen six guards for you. The men will be ready in an hour. Expect them at the stables ready for your command, Gavin. They've been instructed to answer to you or Gregor."

Gavin couldn't have been more pleased. "Many thanks, Chief."

Torrian arched a brow at his cousin, chuckled and headed toward the hall. He called out over his shoulder. "Godspeed and get the bastards. I'll expect a missive from you every two days."

He said to Gregor, "Meet me out at the fork in the path. I'm going to meet up with Merewen, bring a horse for her."

"She'll not ride with you?" Gregor asked, clearly doing his best not to grin.

"We can use the extra horse in case one tires or is injured." Then, because Gregor expected a foolish answer from him and he was happy to comply, he waggled his brows and said, "I'll not discount the possibility that the beautiful lass will beg to ride with me once we've traveled the trail for a bit, but I'll deal with that when it happens. She rides well enough on her own."

Gregor nodded, heading back inside the keep to grab a few things if he had to guess.

"Extra cheese, Gregor," he yelled over his shoulder. He

needn't have said so. Gregor knew Gavin's appetite quite well. He'd fill an entire saddle bag with food because Gavin's belly was always empty.

Alone in the stables, Gavin grabbed Merewen's things and saddled his own horse. "Wee Paz, 'tis time to do our duty to our clan," he said, giving the great beast an apple that he happily gobbled up. He stuck two more apples in his saddle bag for later. "We have a lass to locate."

Since his horse was bred from his sire's dearest destrier, he'd given him the same name, adding the "wee" to differentiate the two. He was far from wee, having outgrown his sire by one hand length.

Moments later, Gavin was riding out of the gates, making his way to the agreed-upon meeting point.

At first, he didn't see her, and uncertainty gripped his gut. He pushed his horse from a canter to a gallop, a sudden frenzy pushing him into action. He'd do anything to prevent Merewen from disappearing the way her sister had.

But then she stepped out from behind a group of trees. Her unwavering gaze caused something to change inside him. He could almost see that wee mole above her eyelid that he wished to kiss. That and many other places. His heart sped up, pushing him closer until he could see the look in her eyes, the excitement, the curiosity, the worry, all there just as he felt it.

As if they were attuned to each other on a different level.

When he drew close, he dismounted and headed straight toward her. She hurried over to him, her breathing raspy, as was his.

"You came. I feared you would not."

"I'm a man of my word, lass. You'll see." For a brief moment, he swore he saw moisture in the corner of her eyes. Did she cry for her sister? Or had she truly not expected him to come?

That look in her eyes…

He took a few steps away from her, then turned to face

the keep, his back to her. Without saying a word, he proceeded to do four back flips until he landed directly in front of her with a flourish, turning to face her.

She giggled so hard she had to place her hand over her mouth. "How do you do such a thing? How did you learn to do it?"

He shrugged his shoulders and smiled. His wee antics had done what he'd hoped. She no longer looked as though she were about to cry.

When she was able to stop her laughter, she straightened and said, "I was afraid you wouldn't come. I thought it might be too far, or that your sire wouldn't approve, or that you wouldn't wish to leave without your sister, or that..."

He took a step closer and touched his finger to her lips. "Nay. None of those things. I'm here to help you. I have Gregor and six guards meeting us at the edge of our land. We'll head northeast." Hellfire, but that wee mole was calling to him again.

"Why northeast?" She kneaded her hands, perhaps in an attempt to stop the trembling that persisted.

"Because that's where the Channel is. I also discussed it with Molly and she agreed with me. We head to Grant land first, then northeast from there."

"You think she was truly stolen to sell?" Her eyes misted again, but this time a lone tear slid down her cheek. Her hand reached up to swipe it away with a vehemence he rather admired.

"I think 'tis possible that's why she disappeared. My sister and her husband will be coming from the south, so there's no reason to head that way. They'd hear something if stolen lasses were being moved near them. She'll be north. Could be the northwest instead of the northeast, but my gut and Molly's both say northeast, so that's where we go first."

Her voice dropped so much he could barely hear her. "Many thanks to you for believing in me and my sister."

"No need to thank me until we find her. Gregor will bring a horse for you, and I have your bow and quiver. You have leggings on underneath your dress?"

"Aye. I wore my heaviest mantle for the cold, but I also have a wool tunic, so if I must shoot, I can. I have a small sack of my own. A change of clothing and soap. Small things."

"Good. I'll tie it to the back of your saddle. Did you tell your parents what you're doing?"

Her eyes widened. "Nay, my sire would never allow me to go with you. He knows naught about my archery skills. He'd lock me in my room. Please don't insist that I tell him."

"Your sire probably would lock you in your room." He thought for a few moments, then said, "But I cannot hide this from our laird. How old are you?"

"Twenty winters. Please, I'm old enough."

"You are, but I will let Torrian know."

"Will he allow me to go?"

"I'll convince him. If you wish to come along, I'll keep you hidden while I update Torrian. Come, I'll help you mount, and then we should be on our way."

Once he arranged the sack so it would not come loose, he put his hands around her waist and lifted her into the saddle. The sweetest waft of lavender caught him, making him inhale stronger and wish he could stop and bury his face in her hair.

"What is it?" she asked timidly.

He shook his head to clear his mind. "Naught. I thought I smelled something."

"Lavender? If so, 'tis my sister's linen square. I brought it along because it reminds me of her.

"I smell the lavender, but 'tis something more."

She glanced over his shoulder. "Your cousins are both here."

Good, he thought. Torrian had come along with Gregor,

saving him the trip. "Chief, Merewen wishes to make the journey with us. I believe she can help us, and I've seen her archery skills. They are top notch. She'll be an asset."

Torrian nodded. "I suspected as much. 'Tis why I returned. Are your parents aware of your intentions, Merewen?"

"Nay, but please allow me to go. I've practiced with my bow forever, but neither of my parents are aware of my skills. Nor would they approve of them. I can help. I can sense when she's near." She gripped the folds of her mantle.

Torrian surprised them all with his next comment. "You have leggings? You'll not traverse the Highlands in a gown."

"I have them on under this gown, and I have leggings and a tunic in my sack."

"Good. Once you stop, remove the gown and save it for Inverness. You'll need to fit in there and you won't wish to ruin it. Wear the leggings and tunic while you travel." Torrian raised his gaze to encompass all of them. "I'll not tell her parents until you're well off Ramsay land. You must move quickly. I'll find something to keep Mal and Struan busy this eve. Godspeed, all of you." Having delivered his decree, Torrian turned his horse around and galloped back toward the keep.

Gregor said, "Here's the horse for Merewen. The guards will be here in five minutes. Mount up, lass. I agree with our laird. We must move quickly for many reasons."

Gavin climbed down then helped her to move to the smaller horse. It was a good thing Gregor had remembered to bring the horse for her. Gavin couldn't allow his senses to be addled by the onslaught of her scent, the sweet aroma of lavender and Merewen.

If only it were the lavender that called to him.

CHAPTER EIGHT

MEREWEN FOLLOWED GAVIN'S LEAD AND rode toward the several guards who'd just joined them. Her stomach felt unsettled. She was headed out on what could be considered to be a patrol, and everyone in Clan Ramsay knew the only females allowed on patrols were the ones related to Logan Ramsay. She was not related to him at all, so she had to accept that it was her good fortune she'd been permitted to join this journey in search of Linet. And yet…

"My parents will be furious and worried. Do you think our chief will be able to calm them?" she asked just loud enough for Gavin to hear.

"Aye. I don't know many sires who would allow their daughters on patrol," Gavin said with a sideways glance. "Even my sire only allowed my sisters on patrol if he and my mother were both with them. Then again, he considered them family adventures because he's different than most."

"This is my first time off Ramsay land," she said.

This time his head spun to face her, a shocked expression on his face. "Truly?"

"That I remember," she said, swallowing the large lump that suddenly appeared in her throat. "We came to Clan Ramsay when I was young so I don't recall."

"If you need me at any time, just call. You're about to embark on a completely new experience, lass. If you question anything—or anyone—you meet, please let me know."

Merewen decided it was best not to wonder about the meaning behind that statement, but she vowed to approach him if anything unusual happened.

He chuckled as they approached a meadow. "Yell if you must. Gregor and I will be by your side in a moment." Then he winked at her. "And make sure you are never far from your bow."

He moved his horse into a canter then, and she urged her mount to stay directly behind Wee Paz. Gavin believed in her ability to shoot, so she had to be prepared to use her skills if necessary. Perhaps that was the only reason she'd been allowed along, because it was her sister and she could shoot.

Or was there another reason?

The way Gavin looked at her was another source of anxiety…and excitement. No lad had ever watched her in such a way before.

Lads would often stare at Linet because she was so beautiful—so reserved and lovely and feminine—but Merewen rarely received such attention.

Her sister had once confessed that she hated men looking at her.

Merewen hadn't known how to respond to that comment. Why wouldn't she be flattered when handsome lads glanced her way?

Linet had just replied with a flat response: "Because I'm not. I don't like the way they look at me. It makes me… uncomfortable." She'd never said more about it than that.

Perhaps her response depended on who was doing the looking, although she'd never known her sister to moon after any particular lad. She herself had kept quiet, mostly, about her admiration of Gavin, but it felt stronger than ever now. She quite enjoyed the way he looked at her, as though he wanted more of her. She hoped the kiss that they had shared earlier would lead to more, even though the one they'd shared a year ago had led to nothing. She had no experience to guide her. How she wished there was someone to ask.

She threw her shoulders back and lifted her chin a notch. This journey was going to be into a land of men, and she would prove she could handle it. There would be no tears. Her sire and brothers hated women crying.

Once they were on open land, Gregor and Gavin pulled their horses abreast of Merewen while Gavin instructed the six guards to fan out around them, two guards in the lead. Once he'd finished his instructions, they headed out over the meadow at a nice canter, enjoying the gray day even though the sun was not out.

A couple of hours later, when the path meandered through a group of trees, they slowed their animals, which allowed them to speak without shouting.

Gregor said, "Merewen, tell us more about Linet."

Surprised by his question—Gregor had spent hours reading with Linet, after all—she sighed and considered her answer. "But you both know Linet."

Gregor replied, "Aye, we know her, but we don't know her well enough to guess her actions in certain situations. You would know quite a bit more."

If she had to guess, the spark of interest that had spread across Gregor's face was more than curiosity, but she was too far away to judge. She admitted his reasoning was sound, so she answered the best she could. "Linet has the biggest heart of anyone I know, but she is reserved and quiet and verra, verra focused. She is rarely distracted from her purpose."

"Hmmm. Sound like anyone you know, Gregor?" Gavin asked.

Gregor gave him an odd look. "Other than my mother? Nay."

Gavin just arched his brow at his friend, acting as if the other lad had just proved his point. She didn't have any idea what they were going on about, but she chose to ignore it—and Gregor's hard stare back at Gavin.

Gregor continued, "If she was kidnapped by someone in the Channel of Dubh, how do you think she would react? Would she fight, or would she follow their demands?"

Merewen shook her head. "My sister often does what's expected of her, but she also is quite clever, so I can't answer that question until you tell me more about the Channel of Dubh. I've only heard whispers. Who runs it? Why do they kidnap people and send them away?"

Gregor cast a glance at Gavin, so she turned her gaze to him. "Gavin? What will they do with her?"

Gavin nodded and made a motion to Gregor indicating he would answer the question. "They're a group of men who sell lasses across the water to the east. They make good coin from it."

"But why?"

Gavin's face turned a wee bit green. He darted a glance at his cousin before shifting his attention back to Merewen. "Lass, this is not something I'll enjoy telling you, but I feel I must if you're to be part of this excursion. They are sold for different reasons—for servitude, for wealthy women who cannot bear children, and…" His voice trailed off and he stared up at the sky.

Merewen followed his gaze but didn't see anything that should have pulled his attention away from her. "And?" she prompted.

"And for sex." He said nothing else.

Merewen allowed this to penetrate her thinking. Or tried to. That word had so rarely been spoken aloud in her presence. "What do you mean?" she asked. "Will she be forced to marry? I don't understand." Her heart had lodged in her throat at the thought of Linet being forced to marry a man she did not want. They'd have to live apart if that happened. Forever.

Or was she being extremely naïve? Would men use her

and walk away? She'd heard such talk among some of the Ramsay maids, but not about the lads in their clan.

Gregor took over for his cousin. "The truth is we don't know anything for sure, but we've managed to save many lasses from the Channel."

So she'd heard. Hope took root in her heart. If they'd saved other lasses, lasses who weren't even from Clan Ramsay, surely they'd save her sister. "However long it takes, I'm willing to follow along. 'Tis far in the Highlands, this Channel?"

Gavin shook his head. "'Tis not in just one place, Merewen, it's a forever changing group of unsavory characters who kidnap bairns, move them from place to place to keep them hidden until they arrive on the sea or even a sea loch. Then they put their captives on a boat and sell them across the water. We've caught many of the people who are involved, but the Channel keeps running."

Merewen just stared at Gavin. She'd known it was bad, really bad, but she hadn't realized the extent of it. What could this mean for Linet?

Gregor added, "Someone oversees the entire operation, and this is the person we are still looking for. We've heard a few possibilities—the leaders are in the northeast or they're in England. We'll head northeast first. For a time, they did their dark business in the northwestern Highlands and Edinburgh. Some still believe they are there, but we don't. They move about quite a bit, which is why we often depend on information gained from Maggie and Will. But this time, I expect we'll find your sister in captivity near a harbor, mayhap at Inverness."

"But Inverness…that's days away…" Merewen's head was suddenly full of fear. Days? "I thought we'd find her in a day or two and bring her home." She glanced from cousin to cousin.

"If she was only a day or two away, our chieftain's patrols would have found her already. But do not give up hope. We will find her, wherever she is," Gavin said. "And we have to hope Maggie and Will are not far behind us. They'll know how to guide us."

Merewen thought she would start sobbing.

Had she lost her sister forever?

CHAPTER NINE

GAVIN COULD TELL BY THE look in Merewen's eyes that she was about to lose control, so he tipped his head back and let out the loudest bird call he could to distract her. He had a dozen different bird calls, but this was the strangest one.

She burst into laughter, a sweet sound that he yearned to hear again. "What bird was that?"

"One I created."

Gregor said, "He has many of them, lass. Don't encourage him."

Gavin started with a "kak, kak, kak" then swiftly moved into a shrill, chattering sound that made Merewen giggle again. "What are those?"

Gregor answered, "Those are his falcon imitations. I'm sure you've heard talk of our cousin's husband who has some falcons as pets, so he's had occasion to learn them. Careful, Gavin. We're far enough away from Ramsay land to attract attention."

Gavin just glared at his cousin, then did his best imitation of another odd sound that carried through the trees.

"What is that bird?" Merewen asked.

"'Tis a puffin," Gregor replied with a grin.

"What's a puffin?" she asked, confused.

"'Tis a type of bird found on the coast."

The guard in front of them gave the Ramsay war cry as a warning they were about to be attacked. The six guards all moved toward the invading group of reivers.

"Told you, cousin," Gregor said with a clenched jaw. Merewen's heart had leapt into her throat, but it comforted her, some, that the Ramsay cousins did not seem overly concerned. They moved together fluidly, like they'd done it many times before, and she was grateful for their expertise.

Merewen stared at the chaos in front of her—men shouting, weapons drawn, even blood from the first encounter. The first man went down, but another group of strangers covered in dirt, grinning from ear-to-ear came straight for them.

But the most frightening part of all was when one of the men noticed her and yelled to his friends, "A lass. Get the lass. We'll use her and sell her."

Gavin patted the flank of Merewen's horse and guided her away from the oncoming attackers. "Go to the side and use your arrow," he said, the jesting lilt in his voice now gone. "We'll keep you safe, but you have to shoot."

She didn't need to be asked twice. Bow in hand, she turned her horse around just as one of the reivers took a swipe at Gavin. "No puffins this far away from the sea, you fool! I'll have me your pretty lassie." The man guffawed and took another swing, knocking Gavin off his horse, only to be taken out by an arrow in his side.

Merewen had shot him while she sat sideways in her saddle.

"Slud, that was great," Gregor said as he went after another attacker.

Was it ever.

Gavin switched to his bow, easily taking out two more men. But what shocked him more was the number of arrows that flew by his head, finding their target. Merewen must have taken out four of the ten reivers on her own. She was even better with a bow than he'd realized.

When the battle ended, he waved his hand to the guards

to search the area for more reivers. Then he stepped toward Merewen's horse, just then noticing she wasn't atop the beast. "Merewen?" A dull ache of dread started in his belly, but fortunately, when he headed toward her horse, she stepped out from behind it and raced straight toward him, launching herself into his arms.

He hadn't expected that reaction at all. "Lass, you were terrific. Your aim is true, and you took out many of the men." Her face was buried in his chest. When she didn't answer, he felt the tremors in her body.

She was crying.

She clung to his shoulders, her head now nestled in his neck. He had never noticed she was tall enough to reach his shoulders, but he found she fit him quite perfectly. He wrapped one arm around her waist and brought his other hand up to massage the back of her neck. "Lass, are you hurt?" Why hadn't he thought of that sooner? Had she been hit?

She pulled back, her tear-stained face shaking back and forth, her breath hitching. "I've just never, never..."

Gregor, still on horseback, approached them and said, "You've never shot anyone before, have you, Merewen? You've only practiced on targets?"

She nodded, still clinging to Gavin's arm with a tight grip, one he wasn't going to pull away from anytime soon. He quite liked having her so close. "Never been..." she hitched, "in an attack..."

Gavin said, "You did better than I would have expected. My first battle I never moved for three minutes, I swear. You took men out as ruthlessly as though you've been doing it for a long time."

Her tears erupted into a sob, and he scowled, confused by her reaction. Gregor glared at him with an expression that told him he'd said something wrong. But then Gregor had always been more adept at reading people. He'd never admit his cousin understood women better than he did, but apparently, he understood this one better.

Gregor said, "'Twas not ruthless, Merewen. If you hadn't taken them out, they could have killed you or any of us. If we'd lost many of our guards, we would have been forced to return to Ramsay land. You did this for your sister."

Merewen's tears stopped and she pulled back to stare at Gregor.

Hellfire, but he needed to get her attention away from Gregor and back to him, though it annoyed him that his gut should react in such a way.

Gavin's gaze scanned the area. "All our men have survived, though you may need to tend one wound, cousin." He waved Gregor toward the one guard who had blood dripping from his leg before shifting his attention back to the lass in his arms. "We did well, and largely because we had your help."

Gregor dismounted to see to the guard, but first he told Merewen, "Aye, you're welcome on one of my patrols any time. Well done, lass."

"The guard needs you, Gregor. You must go to him." Because his cousin knew him so well, and because the Ramsay healer's son could not leave a man in pain for any longer than necessary, Gregor turned and did as he'd been asked.

Gavin turned his attention back to Merewen and settled her head on his shoulder. He quite liked the way it fit there.

———

Merewen did her best to stop the hitching in her breath, but she failed. When she'd jumped into Gavin's arms and he'd wrapped his arms around her so protectively, she'd wished to stay there forever—somewhere safe where the evil people of the world would stay away.

But then reality had returned, and she'd remembered that the evil people had Linet.

And so she stepped back from her handsome warrior, the man who could so effortlessly make her laugh. The man with the dancing eyes and the chiseled jaw.

It struck her again that she'd killed a man…or two or three. She didn't wish to know how many. But Gregor was correct in his assessment. She hadn't done any of it out of ruthlessness. Sheer terror had motivated her.

"My thanks to you. 'Twas a shock, but I'm fine now. Do not worry about me. Were these men from the Channel?" She swiped at the wetness on her cheeks, determined to stop acting like a lass. Her vow never to cry hadn't lasted long. She wouldn't give them any reason to send her home like a sniveling bairn.

"Nay, just reivers set out to steal from anyone."

A sudden thought crossed her mind. "Could they have been the same ones who kidnapped Linet? They said they wanted me. Mayhap we should have questioned them before killing them."

"Nay, if they'd kidnapped Linet, she would still have been with them," Gavin said. "She's only been gone one day, and they would have had to keep her long enough to locate a buyer. Those men in the Channel stay well hidden."

One of the guards asked, "Where to now, Gavin?"

"Does Gregor need to stitch your leg, Owen?"

"Nay, 'tis not that bad," the guard answered. "He put some salve on it to stave off the fever. The stitching can wait until Grant land. We should be there by the morrow."

Merewen contained her surprise. She'd heard about the mighty Grant Castle ever since she could remember. It was said to be the biggest and most beautiful in all the land. All the lasses in the village told stories about it, including her and Linet. It was one of the places they'd whispered about at night, when they'd spoken of their hopes and dreams.

Grant Castle was where Linet and Merewen had hoped to find two brothers to marry.

Two Grant brothers.

CHAPTER TEN

———◆———

TO GAVIN'S SURPRISE, WHEN THEY arrived at Grant land, they were greeted by someone he hadn't expected. Connor rode up to them with Gavin's cousin, Daniel.

"Daniel? Or is it Damien? What happened to the beard, the unkempt hair?"

"Constance happened to my beard," he replied with a grin. "She didn't like my new look."

"Constance? Is she here? Are you not newly wed? What brings you to Grant land?"

"Constance wanted to visit, so we've just arrived," Daniel said. "She's in love with Grant Castle and all the tales of it. And who is the beautiful lass you have with you?"

Gavin introduced Merewen and told them about her sister's disappearance and their intention to find her as quickly as possible.

Connor arched a brow toward Merewen. "My sympathies, lass. We must act with haste. My sire received new information from a friend in the north. Daniel and I were just discussing the need to pull the Band together again. We've a lot to talk about."

Gavin said, "If we can impose, we'll stay the night so Merewen can sleep somewhere other than a cave. While we'd be grateful for your help, it's paramount we go quickly to Inverness. We'll head out at first light."

Gregor added, "Connor, Daniel. We'll explain everything in detail over an ale and a warm meal, if you'd be so kind. But I agree with Gavin. We'll need to head out at dawn. Anyone else who wishes to join us can meet us in Inverness."

Merewen whipped her head around to Gavin. "We're to stay the night? But you yourself said we need to hurry."

Gavin said, "'Tis the right plan, lass. Our cousins could have just the news we need to lead us to your sister. Connor here is much more familiar with this area of the Highlands than we are. 'Tis easy to get lost here. We will plan with the others, eat hearty because they have the best cook of all, sleep here, and leave in the morn. 'Tis nearly dusk anyway."

Merewen begrudgingly nodded her agreement, but her shoulders slumped.

Gavin held his horse back to ride alongside her. "Your teeth were chattering last eve in the cave," he said in an undertone. "Do you not look forward to a night near a hearth instead of a cold cave where creatures roam about?"

She pursed her lips, but finally nodded. "Aye, 'twas colder than I expected 'twould be, even with my leggings and the fur."

"The nights are mighty cold in the winter. I love sleeping under the stars in the summer, but not this time of year. I'll take the bed and a warm stew. We'll be better for it. We're likely still traveling quicker than Linet and her abductors, if she's in the Highlands as we suspect."

Gavin didn't know if he'd convinced her or not, but she understood there was no changing this decision. He added, "We'll do everything we can to find her, and believe me when I say Connor and Daniel are both fantastic strategists. Daniel was just in the underground in Edinburgh. He knows the Channel better than any of us. Their wisdom is priceless."

"Do they oft travel alone? Are they not both married?"

An odd question for her to ask. "Connor is not married, but Daniel's wife will be pleased to meet you. She'll tell you what she knows of the Channel. She had a brush with them herself, but Daniel saved her."

Interest sparked in her gaze at his mention of Daniel and Constance's experience with the Channel. In some ways, Merewen was quite naïve, likely due to her sire's rules and her lack of experience. Talking with Constance would likely be good for her.

When they arrived at the stables, Gavin helped Merewen down, and he stayed by her side until they entered the great hall. The Grant courtyard and inner bailey was a bustle of exuberant activity, friendly clan members doing their work, young ones giggling and following their parents.

Inside the great hall, they were greeted by several women, but Constance took a particular interest in Merewen. She led her over to a chair by the hearth and gave her a fur for her lap, pulling another chair over next to her. The second chair was presumably for herself, but she patted Merewen's shoulder and promised to return in a moment.

Gavin's attention shifted to his boisterous cousins, all settling in at a nearby trestle table. As soon as Daniel's wife had greeted the lot of them, she slipped off to grab a couple of wine goblets before returning to Merewen.

Once the lads were all seated, Gregor brought the subject up right away. "What is this you've heard? New information about the Channel?"

Connor said, "Aye. There's an active branch in Inverness. A large underground similar to the one we uncovered in Edinburgh. They hide their despicable trade with an unscrupulous front."

"Fighting again?" Gavin asked.

Connor nodded. "Aye, wagering on fighting between men…"

"And women," Daniel said with a grin. "And I'm going after both of them."

A high-pitched voice carried across the hall. "Not without me, husband."

Daniel grinned at his wife's comment. "Of course, my sweet." But as soon as he glanced away from her, he lowered his voice and said, "Constance wishes to join us, but I cannot allow it. I'll convince her otherwise by morn."

"I heard that, Daniel Drummond," Constance said, her tone as fiery as her hair, "and you'll not convince me of any such thing."

"Of course, wife."

Daniel's expression told Gavin exactly how much he was enjoying his new marriage. They seemed to be a good fit, he had to admit. Daniel needed someone to challenge him.

"If you leave Merewen behind, she'll stay here," Daniel whispered to Gavin.

"Nay, I won't." Constance's voice rang out again.

Daniel just chuckled. "Wife, have you ten ears? All right. You can travel with us so long as you agree with my terms." He added in the slightest of whispers, "Which she won't."

"Hmmph."

The serving lasses brought out trenchers of thick mutton stew, and Gavin couldn't contain his sigh. He looked up at the serving lass and said, "You just made my day. 'Tis the best aroma I've smelled in quite a while. May I have another?"

Gregor said, "Allow her to serve the rest of us before she finds more for you, Gavin." He glanced at their other cousins. "As you can see, his appetite hasn't changed."

The lass giggled and fluttered her eyelashes at him. He noticed Merewen's head swing around to stare at the lass.

Could he hope she was jealous?

———◆———

The serving lass was for certes flirting with Gavin. Merewen tried to catch his reaction, but she couldn't see his face clearly from where she sat.

Constance whispered, "You like Gavin, aye?"

Merewen blushed, embarrassed to have been caught so

easily. "Nay, why do you say such a thing?"

"He is available and he's a fine-looking man and quite talented. He's also verra funny."

Merewen had immediately felt drawn to Constance, who was warm and open and lovely—and yet she couldn't tell her how she felt about Gavin. "I'm here for my sister."

"No reason you could not find a husband."

"'Tis sad I'm here without Linet. When we were young, we used to see the Grant guards come to visit the Ramsays. We all heard the stories about this castle, and she and I used to dream that we would marry Grant brothers and we would live here forever together. Silly, is it not?" Her gaze took in the beautiful hall, the tapestries, the rushes, the weapons on the wall. All the personal touches that spoke of a woman's touch. It was even more beautiful than they'd imagined.

"Nay," Constance said, "not silly at all. My sisters and I used to dream about marrying English knights, but I prefer my Highlander. You'd have a hard time finding a free Grant brother at this point."

"Truly? Does Connor have a brother?" She didn't know why, but when she'd first set eyes on him, she'd thought he might make a good match for Linet. Their coloring was similar, although Connor's hair was so dark it looked nearly black.

"Aye, he has two, but they're both married. No two Grant brothers are single. You'd have to search for brothers amongst the guards if 'twas your true wish."

Merewen shook her head, tears brimming in her eyes. "My true wish is to find her hale. 'Tis all I ask." Thinking about her childhood plan with Linet had been a distraction, nothing more. All she cared about was finding her sister.

"I'll go with you," Constance whispered. "I'll help you find Linet."

"Are you sure your husband will allow it?" He certainly

didn't sound like he intended for her to join them.

"He cannot tell me what to do. I'll not fall for any of his trickery either. I know him too well. He'll attempt to distract me so he can leave undetected, but I'll warn him that I'll follow if he attempts such a thing. They'll take you along, will they not?"

She nodded. "I've been practicing with my bow so I can assist. Besides, 'tis *my* sister." Merewen couldn't imagine being left behind. She'd probably do just as Constance had promised and follow along until she was caught.

"You're skilled with a bow? How did you learn?"

"Gwyneth Ramsay vowed to teach any lass who wished to learn. I practiced many days once she taught me."

"Gwyneth Ramsay? She's the best in all the land. No wonder you are skilled. Teach me, please? Then Daniel would not argue with me so much."

"If you come along, I'll teach you," Merewen promised. "But I'll not stay back, even if you do. My apologies."

"Oh, I'm coming along, for certes. Daniel is mostly teasing me," Constance said. "I have a friend Rose who was kidnapped, too. We have to put a stop to this, and besides—" she shot her a significant look, "—you heard Daniel. Men aren't the only ones fighting in the Underground in Inverness."

"Aye, so he said, but what does that have to do with us?"

Constance lowered her voice. "Daniel went underground in Edinburgh. The men who run the Channel were making coin from taking bets on men fighting. Fists—no swords or jousting." She pitched her voice even lower. "If they make lasses fight in Inverness, mayhap your sister is one of them. We could find our way into one of their groups. Be spies."

Merewen couldn't imagine Linet doing such a thing. "Linet, fight? Nay, she's too tender-hearted."

"Then we have to find her before they do," Constance said. "And I'll be there with you."

Fear shot through her body, but then something else followed it, as delicate as a flower spreading its petals.

Hope.

CHAPTER ELEVEN

———•———

GAVIN DIDN'T KNOW WHAT EXACTLY had taken place between Daniel and Constance, but she sat in front of him on his horse. Merewen rode alongside Gavin, with Gregor on her other side.

Connor said, "My sire told me of an inn not far outside of Inverness. It might be a good place to start, though we'll not make it that far until the morrow."

"Any knowledge of any caves this far north, Connor?" Gavin asked, worried about the lasses in the cold night.

"Nay, but we'll find a clearing inside a thick grove of pines. They'll offer more protection from the elements," Connor said.

"I'm surprised Maggie and Will didn't make it back to Ramsay land before you left, Gavin," Daniel said. "Do you think something might have happened?"

"Nay, she and Will like to tarry and visit his favorite cave on their journeys. I wouldn't be surprised if they're already on their way. They could meet us in Inverness around the same time because I doubt they'll stop at Grant land." He didn't tell them about Molly's headache, a sure sign that something evil was about. Gavin guessed it was because of the men who'd stolen Linet, although he feared it might have something to do with Fitzroy. Surely, one of the king's men wouldn't have injured a couple traveling on the king's business. Surely, Maggie was fine.

"I hope 'tis true. We could use their insights. None of us

know Inverness," Gregor said.

"Nor do Will and Maggie," Daniel noted.

"True," Gregor added. "Though 'tis possible Will may be familiar with it. He's traveled more than the rest of us."

They hadn't gone much farther when dusk drew upon them. Gavin sent the guards off in search of a grove of pines. Earc, another Ramsay guard, returned half an hour later, three other guards following him. "There's a nice grove up ahead. Isolated and no evidence of reiver use."

Connor had brought another handful of guards along, so their retinue now numbered over eleven. With two lasses along, the lairds had insisted on more guards. They'd all been quick to agree.

Once they reached the grove, Gavin assigned each of them a task for setting up camp. "Gregor and I will take a few guards and hunt for meat. Connor, you and Daniel find a spot for a fire and get the area arranged. The other guards will care for the horses."

As they all set about their business, Constance said to Daniel, "Merewen and I are going to take care of our needs."

"No farther than the bush there." Daniel pointed to a nearby spot, and neither of the lasses put up an argument. As soon as they were out of earshot, Connor asked, "Are you claiming her, Gavin?"

"What?" Gavin spun around with a surprised expression on his face. He'd not made it more than a step or two out of the clearing.

"You should claim her if you want her. If you haven't noticed, there are plenty of others who have taken an interest in her." Connor tipped his head toward some of the guards. "If you don't, others will."

Gavin found himself thinking of Merewen in another man's arms, and a hot feeling crawled up his neck.

"You mean yourself? Or whom?"

Connor said, "I have not given it much thought, but if

you don't want her, mayhap I will pay closer attention to her." The smirk on his face made Gavin's insides start to boil. He couldn't have his cousins looking at Merewen like that. Was Connor serious or just goading him?

Gavin shot a glare at Connor, then spun on his heel and slipped off into the wilderness. He heard Gregor talking to Connor behind him.

"Good way to pish him off. He'll hunt well now."

Gavin stalked through the underbrush, considering Connor's comments. He had noticed Earc paying close attention to Merewen, but he'd assumed the man was just trying to be helpful. Was there more to it?

He'd have to pay closer attention to all the guards.

Connor was right, of course—he was interested in Merewen, but the timing couldn't be worse. Her sister was missing, and he couldn't possibly focus on a relationship with a lass when he was on one of the most important missions of his life. He wanted more than anything to prove he was indeed capable of representing Clan Ramsay with pride. He needed that victory for himself—and he also felt deep in his gut that Fitzroy was not trustworthy. The Channel was not in the northwest, but in the northeast. His sire wouldn't listen to aspersions about the king's man, so he'd have to show him the truth.

And he had to find Linet. He'd promised Merewen.

He had three important objectives to accomplish, and his interest in Merewen would only distract him. If Earc wanted her, mayhap he'd do best to step aside.

If only the thought didn't make him want to punch the man.

Gregor called out to him. "Slow down."

Gavin waited. When his friend caught up, he asked, "I suppose you want her, too?"

Gregor smirked. "Nay, I'd be more inclined toward Linet if I had my choice."

"I might have guessed that. I don't know her well." All he

recalled of Linet was that she was quiet and a studious type of person. Not outgoing at all. Certainly Gregor's type.

"I helped Linet master reading after I broke my arm in our famous endeavor. I was wandering in the keep looking for food when she tore out of the tower room through the hall. I nearly knocked her down because she ran directly at me. She was so focused on finding my mother for an ailing bairn that she didn't see me. She has a powerfully strong ability to concentrate."

He paused, his thoughts taking him back apparently. "We had interesting conversations, but I never thought of her in a romantic way because 'twas a few years ago. But she still would interest me more than her sister. Merewen suits you better, so the answer is nay. I'm not interested. And neither is Connor. He's just pushing you because he's your cousin and because Merewen appears to be interested in you."

Gregor was usually pretty good at reading people's behavior. It was one of his strengths, a skill that both of his parents also had.

"Hold." Gavin held his hand up at a sound at a soft sound in the brush, and they each nocked an arrow. Three rabbits shot out from under a bush and they fired in tandem, catching two of them.

"There's enough for us," Gregor said with a nod. "We can find a few more."

They picked up their game and continued. Gavin felt a familiar tension gather across his shoulders, and it wasn't long before Gregor said, "You were young. You won't disappoint your father. You're much more mature than you were then."

His cousin could read him best of all.

"I know. I just wish my sire would see it that way. Every time I attempt to act responsibly, he reminds me of my mistake."

Three years ago, Gregor and his half-sister, Lily, had taught Gavin how to stand up on his horse, bareback, and shoot arrows. Lily and Gregor's sire was infamous for his ability to do so, and he'd taught both of them at a young age. They'd spent hours practicing until Gavin became quite good at it. Good, and overconfident.

Then he made the fatal mistake. He suggested they recreate the famous episode of Uncle Quade saving Aunt Brenna from going over a cliff. A daft woman had tied Aunt Brenna to a sled, attached the sled to her horse, and ridden toward the cliff not far from Castle Ramsay, planning to catapult the sled over the cliff to make Aunt Brenna's death appear like an accident.

Uncle Quade had arrived in time to save his future wife. He'd climbed on the back of his horse and fired two arrows to kill the daft woman just before Aunt Brenna went over the cliff.

Gavin hadn't wanted to *actually* recreate the incident of course, but he'd thought it would be a fun bit of dramatics to stage a less violent rendition. They wouldn't have gone too close to the cliff, of course, and he'd used blunted arrows so as not to really hurt anyone. He'd asked Lily to ride the sled, but she wisely had refused and went home instead. Another young lad had gladly volunteered to play the part, simply because he would have done anything Gavin asked him to do.

"We never would have gone that close to the cliff," Gregor stated.

"You and I know that, but my sire doesn't believe it." Lily had gone home and tattled, and Gavin's parents had come flying out on horseback, putting a halt to their fun before he had a chance to fire one arrow.

The fact that he'd taken his tunic off and was bellowing bare-chested when they arrived hadn't helped matters. Nor did the fact that, upon hearing Logan Ramsay bellow Gavin's name loudly enough to be heard on Grant land, Gregor had been so upset that he had fallen off his horse, breaking his arm in the process.

He and Gregor had been chastised and lectured by everyone they knew, and they'd been kept apart for a moon. Gregor had insisted it was his idea, too, but the creativity had been blamed on Gavin—and rightly so.

"It was my idea, too."

"I know."

"You wouldn't have fallen off the horse if your father hadn't yelled loud enough to send the cows off to the next meadow all at once. And he scared the hell out of my horse so much that the animal bucked and threw me. I still say 'tis your sire's fault I broke my arm."

Gavin snorted. Someone had run into the great hall after the incident to report that the cows had been frightened by something unusual.

Something unusual. The man's bellow had frightened the cows and Gregor's horse. He could think of better names for his sire.

The Beast. He of all people surely understood how Logan Ramsay had earned that nickname.

That one sorry event had determined his fate ever since. Each time he and Gregor had ventured off Ramsay land, their sire cautioned him. "And don't be thinking up any Gavin trickery while you're away."

That had been his father's most recent warning.

No matter that he'd fought in countless battles since. No matter that he'd been an important part of the Band of Cousins' work.

Well, he would prove his sire wrong this time. There would be no jesting, no more pulling himself away from his focus.

And he couldn't allow a sweet lass to call him off his purpose.

CHAPTER TWELVE

MEREWEN STOOD IN THE MIDDLE of the clearing, trying to decide where to place her bedding. Most everyone else had already found a spot. While the bed of pine needles was quite soft, she didn't want that sap all over her, so she'd taken Gavin's proffered extra plaid to lie on while saving her fur to cover her.

Gavin must have noticed her hesitation. "If you're cold, lass, the best hearth you could ever find is right here," he said, pointing to his chest. "I promise to keep you warm. 'Tis more heat here than you'll ever need."

Connor snickered and said, "More hot air there, for certes." But then he turned serious and said, "Seriously, Merewen. If you're cold in the middle of the night, you can tuck closer to any of us. I promise we'll be honorable. The night will be cold this deep in the Highlands."

She felt her cheeks heat uncomfortably. "My thanks, but I have a warm fur."

"As you wish. The offer will be there all night," Gavin added with a smile.

Earc said, "I'll keep you warm, Merewen."

Merewen stared at the guard, not knowing how to take his offer. Was he suggesting what she thought he was? It sounded like something only a husband would do for his wife. She was so stunned she didn't answer.

"Nay," Gavin said immediately. "You're on guard duty, Earc, and you're not guarding Merewen. 'Tis my job or

Gregor's." He gave the guard a furious look that sent him
far away.

Constance came over to her then. "You might wish to
sleep between Connor and Gavin," she whispered. "They
could put their backs to you. I am so grateful for Daniel's
heat. He is like a hearth."

"I'm sure I'll be fine." She'd come along to be of assistance, not to need extra care or sheltering. Besides, her
mother had told her never to lie with a man until she was
married.

Merewen found a spot close to Daniel and Constance.
She listened to the sounds of the snoring men, hoping it
would lull her to sleep, but it didn't. The sounds of the
critters in the forest were keeping her awake.

That and her worry about her dear sister.

But she must have fallen asleep at some point, because
the next time she awakened, she heard the oddest noise,
only to realize it came from *her*. Her teeth were chattering.
Actually, her entire body shivered, and no matter how she
tried, she couldn't stop it.

She heard a deep voice she guessed to be Connor's say,
"Gavin...you or me? I'll not listen to her suffer any longer."

A moment later, Gavin appeared in front of her. He knelt
down, reached for her hands, and cocooned them inside
his impossibly warm ones. "I could warm you, lass. You're
too cold. I promise to be honorable."

The rush of heat that suffused her just from the heat of
his hands made her moan. She'd never felt so cold in all
her life.

"You'll not help your sister dead, Merewen. You have my
word of honor as a Ramsay guard."

All she could do was nod because her voice was fro-
zen and her teeth wouldn't stop chattering. Gavin moved
around behind her, lifted the fur and tucked her in close,
pulling his extra plaid up and around them. It took all

her control not to audibly sigh the way Gavin's warmth coursed through her. How did men do it? The night was so cold she couldn't move. A moment later, Connor and Gregor both backed up closer to her, giving her more heat from the front. She closed her eyes and sighed quite loudly this time, savoring the heat all around her.

Heaven. She was finally in heaven.

———————

She opened her eyes, surprised to see it was still dark. She'd stopped shivering, and she was tightly wrapped in Gavin's warm embrace, covered with her fur and his plaid. But that brought a sudden problem.

"What is it?" Gavin's breath warmed her ear.

She said, "I have to…"

"My thoughts exactly. We'll go together. You go first and I'll follow."

"But I don't wish to go alone, yet you cannot watch."

"Come." He stood up and held his hand out to her, so she took it. She had to go furiously, so she had no choice but to follow him. Either that, or she'd be gravely embarrassed for a worse reason.

He led her outside the pine grove to a copse of trees surrounded by bushes. "There. You go inside the trees behind the bushes. I'll turn my back. If you need me just holler," he whispered.

Merewen nodded at him. She didn't savor the thought of walking into that dark patch of trees by herself, but his plan made perfect sense.

"Lass," he whispered up close to her ear, his breath warming her insides. "You have to let go of me."

"Oh," she said, dropping her hand from his. She smiled, then spun on her heel and slipped into the copse of trees, the urge to relieve herself suddenly something she could no longer ignore.

When she finished, she adjusted her clothing but then

froze at a sudden rustling sound. The creature could be no more than an arm's length behind her. She whirled around and ran as fast as she could straight at Gavin, who had fortunately turned around and stood with his hands on his hips waiting for her.

"An animal behind me! I heard it!" She launched herself at him, her heart beating so fast she thought it would burst out of her chest. How she hated wild critters. "What is it? A snake? A boar?"

"Nay," he said as he enveloped her in his arms and peered over her shoulder. "'Tis one of the forest's worst beasts though."

"It is?" She jumped and wrapped her legs around his waist, afraid whatever it was would brush against her legs. "What is it?"

"'Tis a mighty red squirrel. Surprised to see one out in the eve."

Her legs dropped back to the ground and she glared at him, the smirk he wore not amusing her the least bit this time. "Are you sure 'tis only a squirrel?"

She glanced over her shoulder, but he put his finger under her chin and turned her face back toward him. "I'm sure."

She peered up at Gavin, at his strong jawline, his long fair locks, at his dancing eyes, and it happened again. Heat spread through her, from her cheeks to her neck and down her center to her core. He affected her this way, always, and the way his expression changed, turning more serious, told her that she affected him, too. But there was no time to think on it before his lips found hers.

She moaned at the sensation of his heat on her lips, parting them without hesitation, and his tongue swept inside her mouth, warming her to her toes. She wrapped her arms tighter around him, never wanting to let go, savoring the new sensations he unleashed inside her.

He ended the kiss and leaned his forehead against hers,

his panting matching her own. "I'm sorry. I shouldn't have taken advantage of your vulnerability."

"Don't be sorry. I'm pleased. I…I mean…I…"

"You what?" he whispered, his face still close to hers. "Like it as much as I do when we kiss?" He broke into a huge grin, his white teeth like a beacon in the dark.

"Aye, I liked it, and you." She didn't know how much more to say, but she finally said, "You warmed my insides." She giggled then, letting go of his neck a bit.

He chuckled and said, "Good. I like you too." He released her and held his hand out. "I'm still tired, and this doesn't change my promise to you. I'll be honorable."

"Aye, I trust you." And she did. She believed he'd keep his word about this, and about finding her sister.

Linet.

The thought of why she was here, why they were here, returned her to reality.

They were almost back to the pine grove when she stopped him, tugging on his hand. "Gavin?"

"Aye?" His gaze met hers, and her heart did a wee squeeze.

"I liked it, but I cannot be distracted. I must find my sister."

"Understood." He leaned toward her and kissed her forehead. "Neither of us will forget our purpose."

She still couldn't stop the sigh as they headed back into the grove.

As soon as she rested against him, she was asleep.

CHAPTER THIRTEEN

———◆———

GAVIN'S INSIDES CHURNED MORE THE closer
they got to their final destination. This was a new
adventure for them. While Uncle Alex and his two brothers had been to Inverness, not many Ramsays had, and
it was completely new to the Band of Cousins. This was
Gavin's chance, and he knew it. If he failed now, no Ramsay would ever trust him again.

Their group arrived at Inverness just before dusk the
second night after leaving Grant land. They found an inn
at the edge of the town, outside the ditch and the wooden
stockade built around the entire burgh.

"'Tis most impressive," Connor said, looking at the
structure from the distance. "I hope we can get past the
guards this eve. 'Tis a royal burgh. We may have to pay a
toll to enter."

Gavin and Daniel went inside the inn first with Constance and Merewen, while Gregor and Connor took
the guards a bit farther to assess what they would need
to do to get in and out of the burgh. Once they stepped
inside, Gavin and Daniel ushered the lasses over to the
big hearth at the end of the hall. The space was large and
inviting, with ample room seating—three trestle tables and
four cushioned chairs arranged around the hearth, two of
which Constance and Merewen claimed.

Gavin and Daniel then made their way to the innkeeper,
a red-cheeked man with a sizeable belly, who'd just entered

from the back of the room, probably the kitchens or the buttery.

"How large is your biggest chamber?" Gavin asked.

"My lord, there is a sitting chamber with a table and four chairs and two sleeping chambers off that. One large with several beds and one small. The small room is the only space suitable for the ladies. The sitting chamber has its own hearth and room for more pallets if necessary. Will that suit you?"

"Aye, if it will hold six."

"We've fit eight or ten before. A wee bit crowded, but 'tis sufficient for most. Garderobe at the end of the passageway for all in the upper level. Six chambers total."

"That will do." Daniel tossed the innkeeper the necessary coins. "We have a dozen guards who would prefer the stables if you have room."

"Aye, we can hold several. If there's not sufficient room, your men can go inside the burgh to the town stables."

"Here will suit us," Gavin said. "We'll make do. A meal for my men? Stew if you have it, bread and cheese for the ladies in the chamber."

"I'll speak to my cook, my lord. When I return, I'll show you to your chambers."

Gavin tipped his head to the innkeeper, and he and Daniel returned to the hearth.

Daniel came up behind Constance and snuggled her neck. "Bad news, my sweet. We must separate this eve. You and Merewen will get the small chamber, and the cousins will get the larger one. It will hold all four of us."

Constance swung around and stood up, her eyes flashing. "You're leaving us alone in a chamber, where any drunken fool can open our door and attack us?"

"Nay, 'tis a private chamber. Two chambers off a sitting chamber. If I had to, I'd sleep outside your door to guard you."

"You would?" Constance beamed, her face lighting up.

"Aye, I would." Daniel ran his fingers down her jawline.

Gavin rolled his eyes, and Merewen must have caught him because she giggled—the sound barely contained by the flat of her hand. He'd never seen Daniel so taken with someone before. Although he'd seen the couple together before, this still felt new.

"We'll station two guards in the passageway and some outside the inn," Gavin said. "Do not worry. You'll both be safe."

Connor entered the common room, followed by Gregor. "Success? Food? Chambers? Though food first. I'm famished."

"Aye to both," Gavin said. "Food to be served soon. The innkeeper has a living chamber with two sleeping chambers attached, and he's gone off to speak with his cook. The guards can sleep in the stables."

The man entered just as Gavin finished his sentence. "Your food will be out in a quarter hour. I'll have the serving lass bring the bread and cheese to the ladies when 'tis ready. Now, allow me to show you to your chambers."

Connor tipped his head toward Gavin and Daniel. "You two go upstairs and get the lasses settled. We'll let the men know we're to eat here." Connor and Gregor stepped out while the others followed the innkeeper up the staircase.

The inn was larger than he expected, but Inverness was considered the center of the Highlands. Uncle Alex had told them the town had started a large shipbuilding trade because of all the exports they dealt with—wool, hides, and furs mostly.

Were lasses and lads now part of their exported goods?

The innkeeper used a key to unlock the door, then ushered them inside the sizable chamber. A large table sat in the middle with four chairs, and a few stools were arranged opposite the small hearth opposite the door. A heavy tapestry hung over the window to keep the room warm. The innkeeper started the fire in the hearth, then showed them to the two inside chambers. One had four pallets, and the other boasted a large bed.

"Ladies," Gavin said, "your chamber for the night."

The bed was plenty big enough for two of them. They were still getting settled in the new space when a maid brought in two ewers of water. She set one next to the basin in the bedchamber and the other on the table in the main chamber. Another maid followed her in with a tray of cheese, bread, and goblets of ale.

Once they were alone, Daniel sat down, motioned for the others to join him, then said, "I'll stay here with the ladies. You go down and confer with Connor and Gregor."

The lasses sat, but Gavin stood with his hands braced on the back of one chair. He nodded. "Sounds reasonable. What would you suggest? Should we go into town this eve or wait until the morrow?"

Daniel said, "My answer hinges on two lasses." His gaze traveled from Constance to Merewen then back.

"What *about* two lasses?" Constance asked, sitting up straighter.

Daniel reached across the table to cover his wife's folded hands in his palm. "That would depend on if we could trust these two lovely lasses to stay behind. We'll leave guards outside your door, but 'tis verra important that we go assess the situation before we jump into any action. Do you not agree, Constance?"

She pursed her lips and said, "Aye. We will not follow you this eve. Will we, Merewen? I have no inclination to go to a strange place alone, especially in the dark."

"Promise, wife?" Daniel asked. "Please say the words, Constance. I know you."

"I promise we'll not follow you this eve." She lifted her chin a notch as if to challenge him.

Merewen finally spoke. "But how will you know if you find my sister?" she asked Gavin, her eyes entreating him. "Do you recall her looks?"

"Aye," he said, "and if I have any doubts, Gregor remembers her well."

"What do you intend to do if you go into town this eve?" Merewen asked.

"I intend to find myself a beautiful lass and marry her," Gavin said, winking at Merewen. "Or we could go to the river and search out the creature who lives there," he said, stretching his arms out from his body to indicate the being's size. If he were being truthful, it was impossibly large. "Wooooooo…"

"Creature? What creature?" Merewen asked, sitting up straight, her hands now on the table.

"There's an old tale about a creature from the River Ness. He's teasing you. 'Tis not something that has been proven."

"Are you teasing, Gavin? Tell me true."

"Aye, just telling a tale. I don't believe it." He stepped up behind Merewen and rubbed her shoulders. "We'll explore a bit. See if we can locate the fights. See where the alehouses are, the ships. Locate the docks and see what buildings surround them. Talk to people. There's much to do before we can make a plan."

Daniel added, "I'd like to see if we can locate Will and Maggie. 'Tis possible they arrived before us and are staying at a different inn. And Constance," he said, leaning down to kiss her cheek, "I promise we'll involve you both in our discussions. Still promise to stay?"

Constance glanced at Merewen, who nodded her agreement. "We promise."

"My thanks. I'm going to go down with Gavin for a few moments, then I'll return. I might grab a trencher of stew. Would either of you like one?"

"Nay, this platter is plenty for me," said Merewen.

Gavin stepped to the door and said, "We'll let you know what's decided before we leave."

"Mayhap we could go down with you?" Merewen asked.

Gavin shook his head. "I think 'tis best if the other men in the inn aren't aware there are two beautiful lasses in the building. Until we assess the others in the inn, please stay here. Unsavory characters who start overindulging can come up with strange ideas."

"Did you see any unsavory characters?" Merewen asked.

"Nay, not yet. We have much to learn."

Merewen sighed and said, "We'll stay."

Constance nodded.

As soon as they left, Constance whispered, "We'll stay *tonight.*"

"I heard that," Daniel said through the door.

CHAPTER FOURTEEN

————

MEREWEN STOOD AT THE WINDOW of the middle chamber, shivering while she surveyed the area. Daniel and Gavin had left with the other lads. They'd taken three guards with them into Inverness and left behind the rest of the men. Earc and Owen were to guard the door in the passageway.

Merewen resisted the urge to shout her sister's name out the window. A foolish fancy, she knew, but something told her Linet was close, and she so desperately yearned to see her.

Constance entered the middle chamber from the small one, dressed in her night rail. She sighed and flopped into a chair.

Merewen said, "You look worried. Why?"

"You noticed my husband has only one hand, I'm sure. He lost the other in an incident when he was younger. He started fighting for wagers in an alehouse in Edinburgh in an attempt to learn more about the underground. They all bet on him because of the contraption he attaches to his hand, something his clever cousin created."

"You are worried he'll fight again? Do you think they'll wager here?"

"I think he enjoyed feeling normal with the contraption. I don't care for it, but he says it makes him feel like everyone else. Perhaps I shouldn't be so against it. But he seems to take on this different personality when he wears it."

"Always or only when he's fighting?"

She considered the suggestion for a moment, then said, "I'll have to pay more attention to how he uses it. He wears it when he travels because it helps with the horse and keeps him warm. I so hope he doesn't fight in another alehouse."

"You are not planning to follow him, are you? I thought mayhap you might try this eve," Merewen said, dropping the heavy tapestry against the cold night air.

"Nay, I'd rather know more about the situation before stepping into it, but I do have another idea," she whispered as she settled onto one of the stools by the hearth. She held her finger to her lips to silence Merewen. "I don't want the guards to hear us."

"What do you propose?" Merewen took the stool next to hers, wishing to squeal just at the thought of having some activity to keep her mind busy. They had to do something. The waiting would surely kill her.

"I wish to get one of the serving lasses up here to visit with us. If there are women fighting, they might know more than some of the men. We can get our own information."

"Great idea. How will we do that?"

"I'll think of something," Constance said, chewing her thumbnail.

Merewen thought for a moment, then it struck her—Earc had eyes for her, and she could use his interest to her advantage. She opened the door and peeked out. "Earc, would you do me a favor, please?" She was pleased to see he moved to the door right away, already nodding.

"Aye, name it, my lady." The guard was quite handsome, with dark hair and eyes, but his attention only flattered her, nothing more. He didn't have Gavin's dancing green eyes. He didn't have his sense of fun, which could be immediately shifted to an intense focus should the situation require it.

Although she felt guilty for using him, she was desperate to do anything in her power to help Linet. The lads had brought her along because they thought she could help, hadn't they?

"Would you ask a serving lass to bring us some goat's milk, please?" she asked, smiling at him. "I believe 'twould help us to sleep."

Earc took a step closer to her. "Aye, I'd like to help you to sleep, my lady," he whispered, speaking too low for Owen to hear him.

The guilt she felt quickly eased.

"Earc, you need not call me 'my lady,'" she said, purposefully sidestepping his insinuation. "I'm not of noble blood."

"But you appear to be of noble blood, so I prefer it." He gave her his best smile, one that looked so much less genuine than Gavin's frank admiration.

"The milk, Earc?"

"Aye. Right away, my lady." He turned so quickly that he knocked into Owen, who growled and shoved at his chest, sending him on his way.

The other man watched him go, and after Earc turned down the staircase, Owen warned, "Do not think on a relationship with him, Merewen. 'Twill cause naught but trouble."

Merewen nodded and closed the door. She had no intention of sparking a relationship with Earc, so it was an easy promise to make.

Constance grasped her shoulders from behind and pulled her into an embrace. "I heard everything. Brilliant idea. We'll question her up here."

A few moments later, the door opened and a young lass stepped inside with a small tray. "I've brought your goat's milk."

She set it on the table and turned to leave, but Merewen stopped her. "Will you sit with us for a minute, please? My sister is missing. We believe she may have been brought to

Inverness, but we know not where to look. Have you any ideas?"

The lass, probably ten and five years old, looked stricken. She glanced over her shoulder at the door before turning back to them. "I can tell you if you promise not to say I told you," she said in a whisper.

Merewen nodded, tears misting in her eyes. Could this lass be the one who would lead her to Linet? "I promise. What's your name?"

"Abigall. I'm the innkeeper's daughter. If I help you, will you take me with you when you leave Inverness?" Her hands twisted the folds of her skirt. She was a plain-looking girl with brown eyes and light brown hair tied back in a plait.

Merewen hated the sadness in her eyes. Someone had done her wrong. Could it be her sire? Another lad?

"Aye, if we can, we'll take you with us." She sat at the table, and the other lasses joined her, Abigall sitting across from them. "How many summers are you?"

"Ten and five, but when I reach ten and six—only six moons from now—they'll take me."

Merewen's heart nearly stopped in her chest. "They, who?"

Abigall leaned toward them, her voice the lowest of whispers. "The men underground. They buy lasses for different things. They bought my sister Eby two years ago when she turned ten and six. I have not seen her since." Her eyes misted as she continued to gaze at the door. "He said she was stubborn and lazy so he sold her. Said she could work for someone else."

"But what do they do with them? Do they stay in Inverness, or are they brought somewhere else?"

"Different places, I think. Some are made to fight, some are sold across the seas into servitude, some whore."

"Truly? Lasses fighting?" Constance said, likely trying to draw more information from her.

"Aye, the men bet on them. Oh, and one other thing. They take healers, too, because some of the lasses get beaten so badly."

"What kind of men would do such a thing? Where can we find the men who run it all?" Merewen asked. "We need to know. My sister…" She couldn't bear to finish her sentence. Poor Linet. She hated the thought of her gentle sister being forced to suffer such indignities.

"Nay, 'tis a woman who manages it all. Sela. She's tall, a Norsewoman, bigger than most men, but she's mean, they say. Verra few dare to speak with her. She ignores everyone and walks wherever she wishes."

"How will we know her? Because she is tall?"

"She's tall and her hair is nearly white. You'll know her. She's beautiful and everyone fears her. She always travels with a number of guards, yet other men follow them just to watch her. 'Tis quite strange."

The door opened and the innkeeper barged inside, grabbed his daughter by the arm and lifted her out of the chair. Earlier, he'd looked jovial, but all signs of friendliness had vanished. "You do not belong here. You'll not fraternize with the patrons. Go do your work." He shoved her toward the door, and Abigall turned and ran.

Constance bolted out of her chair. "She brought us milk that we asked for!"

Merewen couldn't speak.

"Aye, I am aware of your request, but she should have returned to her duties directly," the innkeeper said. "She's my daughter and I'll instruct her on what she should do. Please do not distract her, and do not believe anything she tells you." He bowed to them. "My apologies for bothering you ladies, but I felt the need to warn you about my daughter. Everything the lass says is a lie."

Merewen didn't know what to say.

The man nodded, then stalked out the door and closed it behind him.

Merewen turned to Constance and whispered, "I believe everything she said."

Constance nodded. "I do, too."

"What will we do now?" Merewen was so upset, she fell back in the chair. But it struck her that she already knew the answer.

"We need to find a tall, white-haired woman named Sela."

CHAPTER FIFTEEN

G AVIN AND GREGOR HEADED BACK to the inn.
The cousins had split up upon entering Inverness—
Daniel and Connor had ventured to the eastern side of
town near the water while Gavin and Gregor had searched
the center of town.

Naught.

They'd learned naught.

"I hope they had better luck than we did," Gavin said.

Gregor shook his head and sighed. "We must be easily
recognizable as strangers. Someone in one of those alehouses must have known something. We entered every last
one we saw."

"We should have dressed in black."

"You think they recognized the Ramsay plaid?"

"'Tis possible. Even if they didn't mark us as Ramsays,
they must have noticed we belong to a clan not often seen
in Inverness."

Gregor glanced at the nearly full moon overhead. "You're
probably right. We'll wear black on the morrow."

"What are you looking at?" Gavin asked, glancing up at
the sky.

"I was hoping for a glimpse of the falcons. I'm disappointed we have not seen Will and Maggie or heard aught
about them."

They reached the inn and entered the common room,
surprised to see Connor and Daniel had already arrived.

They sat at one of the tables. Gavin was starving again, but he wished to see Merewen before he did anything. He motioned to Gregor, "Find me a trencher or two and an ale, if you don't mind."

His cousin nodded and greeted the others. The innkeeper's wife was bringing food out for the group.

Gavin headed up the stairs, surprised to almost run straight into Constance. "Is Merewen still in the chamber?"

"Aye, she's coming. I'll see you in the common room."

Gavin stepped back, surprised to see the door to their chamber stood open, but Daniel had sent the guards out on a wee patrol. Then Merewen stepped out, and it felt as if he'd been clubbed in the middle of his belly. The lass was a beauty, and the best part of that was she seemed oblivious to it. She had dressed in a gown this eve instead of the leggings and tunic she'd favored while traveling, probably to fit in with Constance. She struggled with the lock so he stepped up behind her and covered her hand with his. "May I be of assistance?"

She gave a start, but then turned to him with a wee smile. "Aye. Did you find anything? Is my sister in Inverness?"

He leaned over her, inhaling her sweet scent before he finished locking the door. He stepped back and found himself just staring at her, not wanting to move.

She'd let her hair down, and the silky strands fell over her shoulders to the middle of her back. Slud, but he could get lost in those strands. He wondered how she would look with nothing on, her hair covering her breasts and just the rosy nipples peeking out at him.

"Gavin?"

She pulled him out of his crude thoughts. Hell, but she affected him too much. "Sorry, lass. We didn't learn anything, and if Will and Maggie are about, we did not find them. But I've not spoken with Connor and Daniel, so mayhap they know more." He told himself he'd stop when he was an arm's length away from her, but his feet had a mind of their own, moving close enough that their toes nearly touched.

She peered up at him and asked, "Do you still believe we'll find Linet?"

His fingers reached up and brushed her cheek—barely touching her, yet she inhaled. He stood in front of her, not knowing what to do next. Turn around? Kiss her? Tell her it looked hopeless at the moment?

Hell, he'd never be able to do that.

He kissed her, his lips touching hers hesitantly, but then hungrily. He devoured her sweetness, and her arms reached up and settled around his neck. He angled his mouth because he wanted more of her, and she eagerly parted her lips for him, her tongue touching his before she retreated.

Merewen was a passionate woman, taking as much as she gave, their kisses and their breathing making a rhythm that was just theirs. He slowed his assault, lazily tasting every part of her sweet cavern until his brain finally came out of its fog to remind him of where they were—out in the hallway where anyone could see them. He stepped back and she buckled against him, feeding his ego in the most wondrous of ways, but then she pushed back and fussed with her stray hairs.

He opened his mouth to apologize for taking advantage of her vulnerability, again, but she stopped him, her finger pointing at him and her words surprising him.

"Don't you dare say you're sorry for that. I'm not, and I don't think you are either. We both liked it. But now we must head downstairs to speak with the others."

She pushed past him, but then stopped to grasp his hand because he didn't move.

"Come with me. We have news."

Now *that* caught his attention. "How can you have news? Did you leave the chamber after we asked you not to?" That club struck his gut again, but he waited for her response before he thought about throttling her.

"Nay, we did not. We spoke with a serving lass, though…"
She paused at the top of the staircase, dropping her hand.
"I was going to share what we discovered," she said in an
undertone, "but perhaps we should wait until we are back
in our chamber. The innkeeper was not pleased we spoke
with his daughter."

"Then do not say a word until we return abovestairs.
We'll see what Daniel and Connor have to say." This inn
seemed perfect for their needs so he would not risk being
sent out. He followed her down the stairs and into the hall,
pleased to see they were the only people eating at present.
It was late, and many of the guests were likely abed. Once
he finished eating, they could return to their chambers.

He ushered Merewen to a spot on one side of the trestle table, then took the spot next to her. Gregor shoved
two trenchers their way. He offered one to Merewen, who
refused, so he took both.

Connor said, "Appetite hasn't shrunk yet, Gavin? Do
you still eat six meals a day?"

"I try for ten, but my sire usually takes one or two of
them. The Beast is oft hungrier than me."

Gregor muttered, "He outeats his sire every day of the
moon. Do not believe what he says. He'll cost us much
coin. I hope you brought a few to contribute, Gavin."

Daniel reached into his sporran and tossed a few coins at
Gavin. "I'll share. You need to be in peak condition to help
us, Gavin. I can't have you searching the ditches for food
inside the wall."

Gavin pocketed the coins and glanced at Connor. "See?
Daniel understands me. Now out with it," he said, taking a
huge bite of his stew. "What did you find out? Gregor and
I had no luck."

Daniel arched an eyebrow at the two of them, but then
nodded to Connor, who was the only man not eating.

Connor said, "We went directly to the mouth of the
River Ness or *the Abhainn Nis*, and there were ships

everywhere. They're quite impressive, some beautiful. The expense must be considerable, and I've no doubt that some questionable cargo has helped pay for the detail work."

Daniel cut in, "We'll take you there on the morrow." Glancing at the lasses, he added, "Many unsavory characters in the area. Lasses shouldn't be wandering alone. I didn't see any females anywhere. Did you?" He shifted his gaze to Gavin and Gregor.

"Nay, but 'twas nightfall and dark. There should be more on the morrow. The lasses can speak with a few of the other lasses they see about, find out what they have to say about Inverness. Mayhap there will be vendors along the main pathways. The town definitely has a different feel to it," Gregor said. "I'll study it more on the morrow."

"But any questions we had about buying a ship or hiring one for transport were ignored," Connor said. "We were asked about our plaids, so we'll be dropping them and wearing all black."

Gregor said, "We've already decided the same. Any sign of Will or Maggie?"

Connor shook his head. "But we did find plenty of evidence of fighting in the underground. Ghost managed to get us into one of the dens because of connections he'd made in Edinburgh. Said he was interested in fighting."

"And?" Merewen leaned on her elbows, waiting for his answer.

"They didn't reveal much to us, but we did get definite confirmation that there are women and men in the fighting rings. Sounds like the lasses are more profitable for them. They even suggested they have a few who fight better than some men."

Constance gasped. "Truly?"

"Aye," Daniel said, as serious as Gavin had ever seen him, "and they force the women to fight. The only way out for them is to earn a certain amount of coin for the establishment."

Connor said, "We saw it for the lie that it was. Any lass earning them that much coin wouldn't be set free but forced to fight more."

Daniel said, "The entire thing unsettled with me. It sounded as if the lasses were being punished for something, but I know not what. We couldn't get any more information. We left when someone asked Connor if he wore the Grant plaid."

"Anything else?" Gavin asked, the hopeful expression on Merewen's face turning to sadness, something he hated to see. Och, he needed to bring Linet back to her, if it was the last thing he did.

"'Tis all we learned," Connor said.

Constance squirmed in her seat and said, "We have news, but we'll only tell you abovestairs." She glanced over at Merewen and the two shared a smug smile.

What the hell had they learned and how had they managed it?

"Why?" Daniel asked, removing his contraption. He winked at Constance. "I guess I've had enough of *Treun* for this day."

Merewen asked, "*Treun?*"

"It means strong. Daniel named the contraption I told you about," Constance explained.

Connor's face lit up. "I think *Treun* should start fighting again. The Demon Hand cannot be beaten." He stood and moved over to clasp Daniel's shoulders as encouragement. "We could use him in Inverness just like we did in Edinburgh."

Gavin said, "I agree. 'Tis time for *Treun* to do what he does best." He glanced at Constance to gauge her reaction. Daniel had told them of her dislike of the false appendage. "We need him, Constance."

Constance took a deep breath and let out a sigh as loud as any he'd ever heard before. "I've suspected as much, though I hate to see you go underground again, Daniel.

But you know my feelings." She pursed her lips tight.

Daniel stood and leaned over to kiss his wife. "Tell us your news, wife, so we can plan against these bastards."

"Daniel, trust me on this, please? Not here."

"Fine. Abovestairs we go. I wish to know what you learned. The rest of you can come when you're ready." He stood next to his wife and settled his hand on the small of her back, rubbing a small circle that she leaned into.

Gavin wanted nothing more than to do the same to Merewen, but would it be accepted? He didn't dare try so he grabbed an untouched trencher across the table. "I'm coming with you." Then, deciding he needed to be a bit more considerate of Merewen, he added, "Would you like to go with us?"

She stood up, nodding. "Aye, I wish to share my thoughts, too."

"More food, young beast?" Connor asked him, nodding toward the trencher in his hand.

"Aye, I'm still hungry," he said, glancing at the door as their guards came in. "We have a long night ahead of us. If we cannot go after the lasses, then I might as well fill my belly." He waved to Owen and motioned for him to wait.

Balancing the trencher, he spoke to the guard, ordering him and Earc to take up watch at the top of the stairs while two others stood at the base.

When Gavin and the rest of the group returned to the room, Daniel had already started a fire in the hearth. They settled in around the table, and Gavin sat next to Merewen. "Go ahead and share your news," he said, reaching out to squeeze her hand. "We're listening."

Constance repeated what they'd learned from the inn-keeper's daughter, slowing down for emphasis when she explained the situation with the lass's sister.

"The bastard sold his own daughter?" Gavin asked, an incredulous expression on his face. He couldn't help but glance over at Merewen, wondering how she was taking this information. It was a cold-hearted bastard who would sell his own flesh and blood. And what did that say about the group he'd sold her to? Did he know them?

And what about the Norsewoman? He hadn't expected to hear a woman was in charge, though he hoped it boded better for the lasses. He would expect a woman to be kinder to lasses than someone like Blair Lamont, who'd been in charge of the Channel in Edinburgh.

"Aye," Merewen said. "And Abigall hasn't seen her since. 'Tis exactly my fear about Linet, though my sire would never have sold her. I know that. He's not an easy man, but he adored Linet." Her hands fidgeted in her lap again.

Hellfire, they had to move quickly on this.

Connor leaned back in his chair, his arms crossed. "It's run by a tall Norsewoman with white hair? I'd like to meet this woman. Ask her why she would sell other women so callously. I've known some cruel women in my time, as have you, but even so…"

They had indeed. "Margaret nearly killed Aunt Brenna," Gavin said, reminding them of the old tale. "She put my aunt on that sled and had every intention of sending her flying off the cliff. All because Aunt Brenna had healed Lily and Torrian. She'd lost a son to red throat, and in her mind, Torrian had taken his place. The daft woman's husband could not even reason with her. Uncle Quade had to rescue Aunt Brenna."

Daniel stroked the stubble on his chin. "So she did it for her son? I doubt that would be this woman's motivation."

"I agree. Mayhap Sela is be doing this for a man she loves," Gavin offered. "Or thinks she loves."

Connor said, "Or mayhap she's just daft."

Daniel scratched his scruff again. "A daft woman couldn't control a large group of women and men. The Norsewoman cannot be daft—it must be something else."

Constance said, "I agree. She must have complete control of herself to control others in such a way." She reached over to pull her husband's hand from his beard. Leveling a fierce look at him, she said, "Do not even think of growing it out again."

Daniel grinned, but he quickly turned serious. "I can go underground again, not just visit the alehouses. I know how it all works from the time I spent in Edinburgh. I'll find out who's in charge of the fighting rings, but 'twill be easier to accomplish that if I fit in. So dark clothing on the morrow, and aye, I'll need to allow my beard to grow again." He gave Constance a nod of conviction, then leaned over and kissed her cheek. "If my wife agrees, of course."

Constance's green eyes widened, and they all waited for her to make a retort, but instead she looked at Merewen. "All right. But only for Linet and Merewen."

Merewen stood and hugged Constance. "Many thanks. I think he could find her. We must try."

"We'll start early on the morrow. If we're lucky, we'll meet up with Maggie and Will."

Constance cast a quick look at Merewen. Gavin's gaze went from one to the other. Were they planning something? He'd have to prepare his guards for trouble.

Connor's gaze narrowed. "If we're lucky, we'll find a tall, white-haired Norsewoman. I cannot wait to see what motivates her."

CHAPTER SIXTEEN

MEREWEN DRESSED QUICKLY IN THE morn, donning her leggings and tunic. She tied her hair back and plaited it tightly to her head. She'd decided to hide her bow under her mantle, which was generous and warm with a large pocket sewn inside.

Connor's voice carried through the door of the lasses' chamber. Constance was about to leave the room when she turned to speak with Merewen instead. "I wish I had leggings and a tunic. 'Twould keep my legs much warmer than the itchy wool hose. I hate wool. Did you make those yourself?"

"This pair was given to me by Gavin's mother. I've always treasured it. They say Molly and Maggie make the best leggings and tunics. They use a special weave to soften the wool in the leggings. It's easiest to shoot in them, though my sire thinks they are scandalous. He forbids me to wear the leggings...or to shoot. 'Tis why they're still in good shape. I can never wear them openly."

"I must learn how to shoot."

Merewen reached for her hand. "I promise to help you when I can."

A knock sounded at the door. Constance yanked it open, and Gavin nearly fell to the floor. He recovered quickly, standing straight and jesting, "Your beauty nearly knocked me to my knees, Constance. Daniel's a lucky man."

Constance narrowed her gaze. "You have a quick mind,

Gavin Ramsay. You must teach Daniel how to make compliments in haste. I take it the meal is ready?"

"Aye, indeed."

She winked at him and stepped into the larger chamber. The three other cousins already sat around the table, feasting on three loaves of dark crusty bread, a small container of berry preserves, cheese, and porridge.

"I see you're all wearing your black clothes. It does give you a hint of mystery," she said, waggling her eyebrows at her husband. Daniel hopped up to greet her, giving her his chair. He pulled up a stool for himself, then turned to grab another, likely for Merewen.

She couldn't get to it.

Gavin stood in the open doorway, his mouth gaping as he stared at her. She reached for the ties across the front of her tunic, afraid she'd not secured them, but they were in place. It struck her that it had been quite some time since she'd worn it in front of any lads. It had been much looser on her two years ago, back when Gwyneth had given it to her. Was that why he stared?

Well, she'd not change. She was completely covered, and the way the fabric hugged her body made it easier to shoot.

Finally, he moved out of the doorway and found his seat, still acting befuddled. Connor kicked the chair, and he immediately sprang up and offered the seat to Merewen, while he sat on the stool Daniel had brought over.

Connor said, "Have some bread and berry jam, Merewen. There's a bit of honey here, also."

Merewen took the proffered chunk of bread and sat in the chair. Connor made a motion to move his chair closer to her, but Gavin shoved his stool in between the two of them.

Gavin was acting quite odd this morn, but she would not allow thoughts of his sweet kisses to affect her focus. They would find Linet this day. She was here in Inverness. Of this, she was certain. Her sense of her dear sister had gone stronger the closer they'd come to Inverness. Linet still had a strange pull on her, and she'd not try to tamp it down. "Do we have a plan yet?" she asked.

"Aye," Daniel said. "We'll go to the docks first. We'll explore the area before we return to the center of the burgh for a mid-day meal. We're going together so as not to lose anyone today, even if we do stand out. Let them know we offer protection to one another. We're also looking for falcons or any other sign of Maggie and Will."

"Aye," Gregor said. "If we don't locate them, I'll be worried. Possibly enough to search for them. I've got a bad feeling about all of this, especially since we know Fitzroy brought us bad information."

Merewen wasn't sure what to make of that, but she'd do as they asked and keep searching for falcons. "The women who are fighting. How will we learn about them?"

"Leave that to me," Daniel said. "After high noon, we'll search the alehouses and inns."

"Shall we be on our way?" Connor said. "We cannot waste any time."

An hour later, they'd started walking toward the docks, having left their horses at the closest stables. Merewen's skin prickled with a feeling she didn't understand except to know that she'd never felt anything like it. It felt unpleasant. Dirty.

Gavin moved closer to her, wrapping his arm around her shoulder. "You look cold, lass." He gave her a squeeze and released her.

All she could do was shake her head in denial. "I'm fine, Gavin. My thanks."

But she wasn't fine at all.

Her skin crawled as they walked. Inverness was unlike anything else she'd ever seen. Filthy two-story buildings loomed on both sides of the path they followed, and the stench of human waste and urine caused her nose to wrinkle. The day was gray, and the entire town looked to match. They reached the end of the street and entered an area where shipbuilding was the main activity. Angry men yelled and scuttled about, swinging hammers and tossing wooden boards to each other. The aroma of male sweat overpowered the urine they'd smelled before. While not a pleasant smell, it was better than the alternative.

Their group had grown quiet, she guessed all were taking in the strange scenery. She'd never seen so many people bustling about. Yelling, cursing, working hard, fighting. It was a vision of darkness and despair, lads working everywhere, swinging tools and hoisting heavy loads with grunts and curses. Howls of pain and anger carried over the din of the workmanship, but something was missing.

Then it dawned on her.

There wasn't a female in view in any of the huts, cottages, or two-story homes.

Daniel led them toward the docks, where more lads carried crates onto docked ships. Here the mood was a bit lighter, with some jesting and chuckling between the men. The horizon was broken up by an array of unique ships—some small, some large—rolling with the waves. It was quite a sight.

Connor headed directly to the end of the wide dock. A large ship was anchored at either side, and he tipped his head toward the others before stepping forward to greet one of the captains. The message was clear: time to talk. Gregor joined him, and the rest of them turned toward a rough-looking man who looked to be giving instructions to a half-dozen lads loading up his boat. He had dark hair and a heavy beard that looked like it could use a washing or two.

One thing stood out to her—the size of the men she traveled with. Connor Grant towered over everyone, his shoulders so broad he looked as though he could squash some of the men around him with his bare hands. Gavin and Daniel were both a wee bit shorter than Connor, but no less powerful. All three had shoulders and upper arms that were twice the size of the dock workers. Gregor, while the shortest of the group, still looked far more powerful than anyone outside of their group.

"What cargo do you have in the crates?" Daniel asked. The lads were bringing up crate after crate, dozens of them.

"Whatever the hell we wish to have." He gave Daniel an icy glare, then waved his hand to indicate his men should continue their work and ignore the newcomers.

"Where are you headed?"

"East."

"Can I buy a berth? I'd like to travel east."

"Nay. Move on."

"Is there any ship that sells berths?"

"Nay."

Merewen cast a glance at Connor and Gregor at the other ship, but they didn't look to be getting answers either.

"How many ships have you?" Gavin asked, stepping in. "I'd like to buy one. But I'd like the best ship you have. Who can I speak with about ordering a ship built to my own specifications?"

The man strode over to stand directly in front of Gavin. "And what the hell would you know about building a ship?"

Gavin didn't back down. "I don't. 'Tis why I wish to hire someone. And I have verra specific needs." His hands went to his hips, a move Merewen knew was done to ensure his hand was close to his sword. She stepped away from him, giving him room to unsheathe it if need be.

"And what cargo will you be shipping, laddie?" The man spat after he said the last word, his spittle landing in front of Daniel's boots. He was powerfully built but short, with a scar across the side of his neck.

"Various goods. Does it matter?"

A silence fell as the men all stopped moving, waiting to hear their leader's response.

The man tugged on his heavy beard and chuckled. "Take your wealthy arse out of here before you get yourself in trouble, wee laddie. And a bit of advice. Take the lassies away from here…far, far away, or you'll regret it." With that, he spun on his heel and headed back toward the ship barking orders.

Daniel motioned for them to leave. Connor and Gregor joined them, and Gregor's shrug indicated they'd done no better with their line of questioning. They headed back down the docks together and had almost reached the end when a hush sounded. Every man in the area stopped what he was doing and stood as still as though the King of Scotland was about to speak to them.

Merewen turned her head to follow their glances, and gasped.

A woman was headed straight toward them.

Tall, beautiful, and white-haired, it had to be Sela.

And she looked furious.

CHAPTER SEVENTEEN

CONNOR TURNED AROUND AND FROZE.
The most beautiful creature he'd ever seen was headed straight toward him, and it had to be the Norsewoman known as Sela. Tall, regal, and white-haired, she sauntered down the dock, drawing every man's gaze. Shoulders back, her head tilted up at an angle, she had full lips, unadorned yet luscious.

Her hair was plaited in multiple braids wound around her head in an odd arrangement that was nonetheless as striking as any hair adornment he'd ever seen.

Her entire presentation shot straight to his loins—a reaction he'd never had at the mere sight of a lass. He changed his thoughts, fearing his reaction might be visible through the black trews he wore. If only he could have worn his plaid.

The woman, appearing as much like a goddess as anyone he'd ever seen, strode straight toward him and stopped an arm's length away.

She cast an intimidating glare at him, though it didn't affect him. Not because he fought it, but because he was so taken by that the woman's appearance he couldn't think of anything else.

She had the coldest eyes he'd ever seen. The color gave new meaning to the phrase ice blue.

Everything about her was ice blue. Her hair was so white that if the sun shone in a cloudless sky, it would reflect the blue color onto her hair, he was sure of it.

"Who are you?" Her voice was a soft, husky tone that suited her perfectly.

"Connor Grant. Who are you?" To his surprise, she almost looked him square in the eye, something that had never happened before. She was the tallest woman he'd ever met. He was taller than anyone else he knew, having bypassed his sire, the inimitable Alexander Grant, after he turned twenty summers. Now, at one and twenty, he still wasn't convinced he'd stopped growing.

"My name is Sela, and I run Inverness."

Connor just quirked a brow at her. She claimed to run the entire royal burgh of Inverness? He smirked. "My understanding is that Inverness is a royal burgh run by our King of Scotland, Alexander III."

"He's never here. I run it in his absence." Her chin lifted another notch as if to challenge him.

"You act under a direct order from King Alexander?"

"Something like that."

He waited for a smile, but not even a smirk crossed her face. Strong cheekbones and a long neck added to her beauty. Although the rest of her was pale, her skin had a slight bronze from the sun, flawless except for one mole above her lip. She wore a gown fit for a queen, the back held up by two lads when she walked to keep it from picking up the dirt from the ground. Six other guards followed her from a distance.

Her mantle was a deep purple with gold threading near the sleeves. She wore boots the same color as the mantle, and if he had to guess, he'd think there was something added to the bottoms to make her taller.

Hellfire, what he wouldn't give to see this woman nude. She filled her clothing out with ample curves, though there was much fabric to conceal any flaws. He'd bet she had the longest legs, ones that could wrap around his middle while he held her and plunged inside of her. He'd bet a large amount of coin that the woman was as powerful and passionate in bed as she was standing in front of him, unaffected by his presence.

Then it struck him with no small amount of disgust that he was having lustful thoughts about a woman who could be forcing women into servitude—fighting, whoring, and who knows what else—and that thought killed any desire he had for her.

Clearly, by the stone-cold expression on her face, *she* did not desire *him*.

He continued to play her game. "I'll have to ask my king the next time I speak with him. He's never mentioned you, and I doubt he would forget you."

He saw a slight tic in her jaw before the icy countenance returned.

"What do you want?" she asked.

Connor never flinched. "I want to fight. We heard there's plenty of coin to be earned fighting in Inverness. My friend fought in Edinburgh, but they told him he could make more here." He tipped his head at Daniel without looking away from her.

"What kind of fighting did he do?" she asked.

"My fists, no restrictions." Daniel stepped forward.

"With one hand?" she asked, although her eyes remained fixed on Connor's, unwavering.

Daniel replied, "I have an attachment I use. 'Tis part of the draw. And I promise you, in two nights, half of Inverness will show up to see me. Give me that long, and I'll prove myself."

She turned to Daniel and reached out to squeeze his biceps, then his shoulders, never saying a word as she made her bold examination. Turning back to Connor, she said, "And *you*, Connor Grant? How do you fight?"

Connor dropped the tone of his voice as if they were the only two in existence. "I fight like the warrior I am. With a sword, and I'll take on anyone who wishes to challenge me."

"Sword fighting. Hmmm." She tipped her head as she stared at him, then reached out to grasp his bicep.

He clutched her wrist, stopping her advance.

"Not without my permission."

The man whom Daniel and Gavin had just spoken to came forward and sneered, "Take your hand from her. Do you need my assistance, Sela?"

She shook her head. "Nay, Vern. I do not worry about these men." Directing her attention back to Connor, she said, "And why should I need your permission to touch your arm?"

"Because I'd never touch you without your permission. In fact, not until you begged me."

That's when the worst possible thing happened.

Sela smiled, revealing the most beautiful smile he'd ever seen. Strong white teeth and two dimples called to him, but they disappeared as quickly as they'd appeared. "I promise you that will never happen. You like to dream, Connor Grant, don't you? Fine, I can see by your size that you'll be an asset. What will you wager?"

"Wager?"

"If you win, you'll get part of my coin. If you lose, what will I get? And I have no interest in you."

"What do you want?"

"I want your lasses. They both look feisty enough to fight for me."

"Nay. Not part of this deal."

"If you decide you have enough confidence in your ability that you're willing to risk the lasses, be at the Stag's Inn at dusk. I'll arrange everything. If not, then leave." She turned to go, but then glanced back at him. "Immediately. Either leave, or fight with the lasses as your wager."

"I'll not risk them," Connor shouted.

"I'll do it," Merewen said.

Gavin clamped a hand over her mouth, but the word had

already escaped.

"I will, too," Constance said, ignoring the glare from her husband.

"Wonderful," Sela said. "I'll see you later this eve."

Daniel yelled after her. "Not the lasses. When we fight, you'll make enough in coin. You have my word on that. Blair Lamont was my boss. Take it or leave it."

"Leave it."

Connor couldn't take his eyes off the sway of her hips as she sauntered off.

Hellfire. She'd left them no choice. "I'll do it."

Daniel said, "What the hell?"

Gavin said, "Have you gone daft, Connor?"

"Nay." Then he raised his voice loud enough for all to hear. "I never lose."

CHAPTER EIGHTEEN

G AVIN WISHED TO THROTTLE TWO people, Merewen and Connor. "What the hell were you thinking,
Grant?" He was so upset he struggled not to choke on his
own spittle. "You'll not risk the women."

Daniel shot Connor a dark look, but he said, "We
shouldn't say another word here. We'll leave through the
gates of Inverness and head back to our inn. We cannot
risk someone listening to us."

"Can we not stop at Stag's Inn? If we go there for the
midday meal, we'll have the opportunity to inspect it."

Gavin shook his head adamantly. "We cannot do anything until we agree on a plan. And I don't agree with
what Connor just agreed to. We must discuss this. Alone."

Merewen refused to look at Gavin, and he had a good
idea why. But he wouldn't bend on this. True, if she fought
for Sela, she might be able to learn about her sister's
whereabouts, if, indeed, Linet had been brought here, but
Merewen had never been trained in hand-to-hand com-
bat. She'd be massacred in the first battle she had.

All were silent as they made their way back to the inn.
Although he kept an eye on the sky overhead, he saw no
sign of the falcons, or of Maggie and Will. This eve, he'd
start asking others about the pair. They would stand out,
of that he was certain. There were few females to be seen
in Inverness.

Once they were inside their chamber, all of them gathered around the table in the main chamber, Daniel said, "You cannot risk the lasses, Connor."

Merewen crossed her arms and then let loose. "This could be my only chance to find out about Linet. You may be allowed to fight with the men, but I don't believe the women will be kept there. How else can we find out?"

Gavin got out of his chair, rubbing his hands together as he paced. "I feared you were about to ask Sela if she'd seen your sister. That would be a big mistake, lass. I'm glad you did not."

Connor nodded. "Telling her we are all here to find Linet would be a huge mistake. If she learns you're looking for Linet, and she's here, she'll have her hidden in less than an hour. She's not interested in losing any fighters—she's wishing to gain you two."

Merewen was so upset she practically vibrated in her seat. "She cannot be so heartless. I refuse to believe a woman who has been put in charge of Inverness by King Alexander would risk girls' lives or take part in the Channel."

Gavin sat down and pulled her chair close to him. "Lass, she is not in charge of Inverness. The king does not know anything about her. She takes what she can when no one else is watching. That statement was a bold lie."

Gregor nodded. "Aye, and she has a group of enforcers who follow her everywhere and institute her policies. I'll inquire further, but I'm sure she forces everyone to do her bidding by having them beaten, and probably where everyone can witness the lashings."

"Or worse. My guess is she's killed a few to get where she is," Connor said.

"Truly?" Constance whispered. "You think she has no feelings at all?"

Connor said, "Those blue eyes were the coldest I've ever looked into, I assure you. She has no guilt over stealing women, selling them, or even forcing them to whore. I'd love to know what brought her to that point, as I've not met many women as ruthless as she appears, but something turned her. She wasn't born that way."

Gregor arched one eyebrow at Connor. "And is your intent to find out what that is? You were giving off a different wave of vibrations when you stood so close to her. Is she the one?"

Connor glared at him. "You jest, do you not? While I'll admit she is a beautiful woman, she has a heart made of icicles. I'm not interested in that kind of woman. Have you forgotten who my mother is? I'd never insult her by bringing a woman like Sela into our clan. She's cold, calculating, and ruthless."

Constance glanced at Merewen, then shifted her stool over to sit beside her. "We're both being naïve. I was protected by my family from such things, and I'm guessing the same is true of you. I cannot believe this situation exists, but we have both been thrust into the middle of it. We must stop trusting everyone we meet, especially Sela. I believe what Connor says."

Merewen's eyes misted, but she nodded, squeezing Constance's hand. She stood abruptly then, perhaps in an effort to try to hide her tears. "You're right, of course. We came all this way, and I wished to believe finding Linet would be as easy as asking someone and getting an answer. Clearly, 'tis not."

Gavin went to her, unable to help himself, and rubbed his hand across the small of her back, not caring who saw him. "I'm sorry to have thrust you into this so quickly, but as you can see, we've had no choice. I'm glad to hear you both recognize that you cannot trust everyone."

Daniel said, "I'm of the belief to trust *no one*."

Gregor got out of his chair and shook his hands and his shoulders, as if he'd been holding tension there. He paced along the wall, running his hands through his hair. "Connor, I'm glad you are not interested in that woman. Her job is not something she's proud of—you can see that much in her gaze."

Gavin stepped away from Merewen and fisted his hands against his sides. "This is not helping. Connor is not interested in that woman. We need to go inside the inn as a group. Daniel and Connor can go off to meet Sela, and Gregor and I will follow with Constance and Merewen. We'll have a few guards with us—two inside and a handful outside. I don't want anyone thinking they can overpower us and steal the lasses away."

"Then mayhap we should leave them behind. They'd be safer here," Daniel said.

"Nay!" The word came from both lasses at the exact same time. "I wish to see if Linet is there," Merewen added.

Connor said, "I think, for now, we take them with us. I don't want Sela thinking the lasses are alone somewhere. I think 'tis best to have them with us. They'll not steal them in front of us, and I plan to wager two or three night's worth of fighting. Daniel and I will draw a strong audience. 'Twill be good for all if the two lasses are associated with us. You agree, Daniel and Gavin?"

Gavin weighed the alternatives for a moment, then nodded. "Aye. Better to have them with us. I tend to agree with you. Daniel? What say you?"

Daniel set his hand on his hip. "I don't like this, but I'll go along with it."

"Won't you feel better if you can see her?" Connor asked.

Daniel stared at Constance, a wry grin crossing his face. "I'm always better when I can see her. Can I trust her to do what we ask? 'Tis the most important question. Lassies?" Daniel tipped his head, waiting for their response.

The lasses scowled and were slow to agree to such a restriction. Gavin placed his hand over Merewen's, "Our journey this eve is about finding information, no more. You never start your battle until you know your enemy. My sire drilled it into me."

Connor nodded adamantly. "No battles. No fights. We

will study everything—the inn, the area where the lads fight, and everyone we see. Our goal will be to get a couple of strangers to trust us enough to speak of the female fighters. We'll have to act as though we've not heard about them before. Do you understand, Merewen? Constance? We cannot reveal that we are looking for fighting women or anyone named Linet. If we do, we'll be tossed out of the inn on our backsides and sent across the bridge with no chance of returning. We must act as if we wish to become part of their group."

"We must do this slowly," Gavin said.

Merewen glanced at Constance. "I agree. This eve is about information gathering. No fighting except for Daniel and Connor."

Constance made a face. "I don't see why we cannot explore a wee bit."

Daniel said, "Because you must allow Connor and me to do so first. We'll be allowed into areas that you will never be invited into. We cannot risk losing this opportunity." He shifted his chair and leaned in close to her so their faces were almost touching. "Agreed, wife?"

She looked reluctant, but she did nod.

"My thanks. We will all search out our own information this eve, then return to the inn to discuss our next steps. Your job is to be alert to all that transpires around you. Memorize faces, listen to conversations, pay attention to which men are together. These things could be extremely valuable."

Constance sat up, her eyes wide. "Are we spies this eve?"

Daniel couldn't stop from chuckling, but then he kissed her cheek.

"Aye," Gavin said. "You and Merewen are spies this eve. Know all that goes on around you."

Merewen smirked and nodded to her friend.

"We'll be the best spies you've ever seen. I promise."

The spark in Constance's eyes matched Merewen's

exactly. Why did Gavin have a sudden uneasy feeling racing through him like a chipmunk he could never catch?

They were up to something.

CHAPTER NINETEEN

MEREWEN HELD GAVIN'S HAND TIGHTLY. They'd all insisted she had to appear to belong to someone, and Gavin had volunteered to be her protector for the night. Truthfully, it had been a relief. It would give him an excuse to touch her—and her an excuse to savor it. Constance would pretend to be Gregor's companion while Daniel and Connor fought.

Her mind bounced from one thought to another, but at the root of all the commotion was the constant thought that Linet could be here—anywhere.

They ate the late meal at the Stag's Inn, expecting to see Sela eventually, but she never arrived. When they finished, the serving girl set a large flat stone on the table. Connor picked it up and shot her a questioning look.

"Take it to the door around the back of the inn. You must go down the steps. This will get you inside." She nodded to him and Daniel. "The two of you are expected there within a quarter hour."

Daniel handed the lass a few coins for their meal, but she held her hand up flat. "The meal is free. Go now." Then she spun on her heel and left.

"'Tis time," Gavin said, standing and holding his hand out to Merewen. She glanced up at him, surprised to see he looked as nervous as she felt. He held her hand close and rubbed it in a gesture that made her insides tingle.

"Gavin? Are you worried?"

He sighed. "Aye. I am a little doubtful about this. We were with Daniel in Edinburgh, and 'twas simple enough. We'd wager, watch him fight, and collect our winnings. This feels different. This is on a much bigger level. Sela unsettles me. I don't trust her at all."

Merewen felt a twinge of discomfort. Did this mean he feared they wouldn't find her sister? "In what way does it feel different? Didn't the man in charge of the Underground in Edinburgh unsettle you?"

"Mayhap you've uncovered some of the reason I feel different. Only Daniel met with the man in charge. He did not travel out in the open. I fear this will not be quiet or easy. I hope I'm wrong."

His gaze settled on her. Oh, she did love the way he looked at her—as though she were something special and rare. Even his touch, his thumb rubbing the back of her hand as they moved through the inn, sent a hum through her body that she found both exciting and soothing at the same time. If she could just stay in this moment…but she couldn't. She needed to push forward for her sister.

"I'm worried, too," she said. "I fear we won't learn anything more than we do now." Merewen fidgeted, uncomfortable with their ruse, even more so because she'd left her bow behind at the inn. They'd decided they'd blend in better if both lasses were wearing dresses.

Gavin's arm settled around her shoulders, holding her close as they left the building and followed Connor around to the back.

The chamber beneath the building was cold, dark, and dirty, and she snuggled closer to Gavin, who wrapped his arm around her. If she could, she'd stay in in his arms all night—the place she knew she'd feel safest.

Two men greeted them, and one gave Connor and Daniel instructions to follow him. The other man addressed the four of them, plus the two guards with them. "You may place your bets in the next chamber. The fighting takes place in the large hall at the end of that passageway." With a final nod, he left to greet another group of people coming down the staircase.

Gregor led them over to the wooden counter, where they ordered ales and asked to place their bets on the new men.

"Which men? We have three new ones this eve," the man said in a flat tone, seeming disinterested in them and, indeed, the whole endeavor.

"The one with one hand and the sword fight."

"The sword fight will cost you double."

Gregor glanced at Gavin, as if to ask if he'd heard, but Gavin just nodded. They paid their coin and wove through the crowd toward the fighting hall.

Merewen's eyes took in everything they could. She and Constance were the only women in the chamber. She listened to everything she could, too, but most of the conversations centered around the men.

The four of them took seats toward the back of the chamber, off to the side. The space was impressively large, with stools on one side and benches on the other two, all at an angle above the fighting area—a large stretch of dirt floor, which would minimize the injuries, and a stone wall behind it, which would not. She noticed a few men stationed in front of the first stools and benches, likely there to keep any of the onlookers from jumping into the fray.

Too many people were present for all to be seated, so many stood in the back. The first fight started right away, but it wasn't a difficult one. It didn't look any worse than many of the fights she'd seen at the lists at home.

To their surprise, Daniel was brought in next, and the announcer focused on the fact that he only had one hand. The crowd stirred, craning their necks to see his injured arm, which the man in the center of the ring held up high for all to see.

"He's allowed to wear this special contraption to make

the fight fair," the man said, indicating Daniel's metal hand. After giving the audience a look at it, Daniel quickly put it on.

Noticing the tension in Constance's jaw, Merewen reached out and squeezed her hand. The other lass squeezed back, and mouthed 'thank you.'

Then the announcer stood back, waved his hand over his head, and the fight commenced.

As soon as Daniel took the first punch to his gut, Constance grabbed her hand again, squeezing it with a death grip. Every time her husband took a fist to his face, she squealed and gripped Merewen harder.

"Close your eyes. 'Twill be over soon," Merewen whispered to her. "Daniel's winning easily."

A minute later, Daniel's opponent fell to the ground and never moved. Constance jumped up and applauded, but Gavin leaned over and said to Merewen, "Pull her back down. I don't want Daniel worried about her attracting too much attention."

There was a brief period of time for patrons to place their next bet, and Gavin sent Owen to collect their coin. They were one of the few who'd bet on Daniel, so they made a nice profit.

Merewen leaned toward Gavin and asked, "I have not seen Sela at all. Have you?"

Gavin stood to stretch, which allowed him to survey the room without appearing to do so. "'Tis much larger than Edinburgh. Do you not agree, Gregor?"

"Aye, nearly double," Gregor said. "I have not seen Sela either, and she would draw attention from the men if she were here."

The next contestant came into the center of the arena. He wore chainmail and a helm and carried a sword with him. The crowd shouted their approval. He stepped to one side and Connor emerged in his plaid and a dark tunic. The announcer called him the Grant Stallion. The entire hall quieted after he finished saying Connor's name. Merewen leaned closer to Gavin because the tension in the air unsettled her. Why the silence?

She guessed at the cause a moment before she saw her. Sela strode down toward the center of the hall, coming to a stop between Connor and the man in chainmail. She lifted her chin and said, "The Grant warrior says he is the best swordsman in the Highlands. We shall see. This is a new risk for me, as I usually prefer not to allow swords in my establishment, because they are too bloody, but I wish to see how strong the Grant warrior is. I'll step back and let the fighting commence."

She strode away, but then Connor surprised them all by removing his tunic. He paced in a small circle, flexing his muscles as he walked, his muscles rippling across his bare back. Then he stood still, his eyes closed, moving the sword around him as though he were building a connection with the weapon.

"He is the best," Gavin whispered to her, his breath warm on her ear. "Other than his sire, his only competition in all of the Highlands would be Loki or Cailean MacAdam. He'll beat them all. I see why he was willing to fight. That puny warrior in the chainmail won't affect him."

"He will not lose? You are certain?"

Gavin leaned over and touched his lips to hers, a quick kiss to tell her not to worry. Then he glanced over Merewen's shoulder and tipped his head. "She's staying to watch."

Sela was indeed staying. Someone produced a cushioned chair and she sat, her gaze fixed on Connor as he paced. Her expression was inscrutable.

Then it began. Merewen had to admit that Connor was graceful and powerful with his sword. His arms were definitely massive. And yet, she found her mind wandering to the man seated beside her—she'd snuck to the lists to watch him fight more often than Linet knew, eager for a sight of his strong chest and arms. Little had she known she'd one day sit beside him watching his cousin fight for her freedom.

She had to force herself to pay attention to the fight. Suddenly, she had no choice because Connor didn't seem to be winning. Although he blocked blow after blow, he didn't deliver nearly as many as he received.

"Gavin, he's losing," Merewen whispered. She felt she could hear Connor in her head, telling Sela she could have the lasses if he lost.

"Nay, Connor hasn't even started," he said, pressing a wee kiss to her neck. "He's just playing with him. Be patient. It's not a fight for the owner if he knocks the lad out with his first swing."

Merewen held her breath every time the fool swung his sword toward Connor, but he never made much of a hit on him.

Constance leaned in close. "I'm worried," she whispered. "This does not look good to me. I fear he'll lose."

Merewen said, "I said the same to Gavin. He said not to worry."

And he'd been right.

Connor changed in an instant. He growled as he lifted his sword over his head, just enough room in the chamber for such a move, then came at his opponent, delivering blow after blow that was meant to drive him backward. When he finally had the man cornered, he maneuvered his opponent until he had him exactly where he wanted him, then swung around in a complete circle and knocked the other man's weapon out of his hands with the back of his sword.

The man's sword landed at Sela's feet.

She stood and strode toward Connor. Grabbing his free arm, she declared him the winner. Merewen saw her lean over and speak with Connor. She spoke in an undertone, but he spoke his answer loud enough for all to hear. "You said you did not like blood. I didn't hurt him, but he will have a headache on the morrow."

Many of the men had already filed out to collect their winnings, so Merewen was able to overhear the rest of their conversation.

"You will fight again tomorrow eve," Sela said, "and I will take the lasses with me for ten minutes."

"Nay, you'll leave them alone. We had a wager, and Daniel and I both won our fights."

"True. I promise not to hurt them, I just wish to give them a tour. If I really wanted them now, I could have my men arrange for it in a second."

"And I would have five hundred of the Highland's fiercest warriors tear your entire world down in two days. Do not be foolish. You haven't survived this long in your position by making daft decisions."

Merewen wished she could see Sela's face, but the woman was turned away from her. She caught Gavin nodding at Connor, who then nodded his agreement with the woman's proposition.

Excitement replaced the fear she'd felt. Mayhap this was just the chance they need.

"What's happening?" Constance asked.

"We're going on a tour with Sela." Turning back to Gavin, she said, "My thanks for agreeing."

He nodded, although she sensed his hesitation. It hadn't been easy for him to agree. "I'm guessing your tour will involve the fighting women. Try and remember all you see."

Moments later, Sela appeared at their side. "I'll take the ladies with me. I wish to introduce them to a different world."

"Where are you taking us?" Constance asked.

"I'm taking you to a place where women are special. A place where women rule, not men. And I promise you that this world is growing."

It was all Merewen could do to keep from squealing with delight.

Constance looked ill.

CHAPTER TWENTY

———

MEREWEN FOLLOWED SELA THROUGH A door along the wall of the passageway. She stepped inside, surprised to find herself in another, brighter passageway.

Sela led them past a few doors, then opened one and stood back, allowing them to look inside. The chamber held six beds, covered with fluffy mattresses and thick furs. A smattering of books sat on a shelf. Two women were asleep, while one sat on the bed doing needlework. She even smiled at them.

"This is where my lasses live. Don't they look happy? No men to order them around, they have no one to bother them at all."

"What about you?" Constance asked. "Must they do what you tell them?"

The only change in Sela's face was a slight narrowing of her gaze before it returned to normal. "True, they must do as I say, or there would be naught but chaos. Consider me their laird. Come along. I want you to see what you could be. You—" she surprised Merewen by pointing at her, "—you are special. I can see it in your eyes."

Merewen did not respond to the compliment, but instead looked away. Sela moved along, and they followed her. As they progressed down the passageway, she could hear men whistling and hollering—friendly but loud. When they reached the end, the passageway opened into a large chamber similar to the one the men where Daniel and Connor had found their victories.

There in the middle stood two women, each dressed in a long, fancy robe decorated with sparkly gemstones. Their hair was plaited tightly to the tops of their heads, and they both had dispassionate gazes as they looked out over the group of men seated in front of them. The man who stood between the two of them held his hand up and said, "Prepare yourselves."

Sela turned to Merewen and said, "The urge to fight is innate in some people. You are one of them. You will beat every opponent you meet, regardless of where. I can see it in your eyes. You have a burning desire to win. Watch and enjoy. Picture yourself as the victor of all the women here, because you will beat them all. You'll be admired by all the men, and you'll make huge bags of coins for your efforts."

"You think I want to fight? I don't wish to fight anyone." She worried she'd be considered trouble, but she persisted anyway, eager for any information that might lead her to Linet. "So what would you do with me? And what about my friend?" Merewen asked, clamping her mouth shut, suddenly afraid she'd gone too far.

Sela was not the least bit upset by her comments. "I have another place I'd put her. She has special skills but of a different kind." Sela smiled. Her smile never reached her eyes. Connor had accurately described her as a ruthless and cold woman.

She had ice inside, coursing through her veins.

Drawn to the battle that was about to take place in front of her, Merewen ended her questions and shifted her attention to the lasses in front of her. One had dark hair and a dark robe to match, and the other had red hair and a crimson robe. When they removed her robes, she saw they were dressed in attire her sire would have considered more revealing than her leggings and tunic. Fabric covered them from their necks to their toes, but it clung to each and every curve, hiding nothing.

The men whistled and shouted—and were soundly ignored by both women. When the fighting began, Merewen gasped. The dark-haired woman charged the red-headed one, then wrapped her arms around her waist, lifted her off the floor, and flung her onto the dirt beneath them—hard. She gasped as though the air had been knocked out of her, but the abuse didn't stop there. The one on top started to pummel her in her belly.

The men were wild over the battle, urging the two on, calling for the one on the bottom to get up. She finally did, and the fighting continued. There was no blood, but they would be very sore when they finished.

Sela leaned down to whisper in her ear. "Admit it. You'd like to fight just like them. It's innate in some people. You have what it takes."

Merewen shook her head, disagreeing with her. "Nay, I don't." While a wee part of her thought she *could* fight, she had no desire to do so. None. Sela was wrong about her. She glanced up at the tall, strange woman, noticing how beautiful she was as if seeing her for the first time.

The woman had the clearest complexion she'd ever seen, full lips, and high cheekbones. She looked as though she belonged at a queen's court. Where had she come from? Where did she find these women? She wished so dearly to ask about Linet, but the words of the cousins had left an impression.

She didn't wish to let Gavin down.

"Where do you find these women?" she asked instead.

"They come to Inverness. They hear about me and the fighting, and they come to see what they can do. Their sires send them to earn coin, or they keep it themselves. My women are verra happy."

One of the fighters began to sob, the redhead, so Sela turned and said, "You've seen enough. I'll return you to your cousins. Just know you can come to me anytime, and I'll take you in. Anytime."

Merewen trudged along behind the woman, but she took in everything and everyone she saw.

She'd seen much, but she hadn't seen the one thing she longed to see above all else.

Linet.

Gavin stuffed his hands into his pocket. They'd sat down in their private sitting room, gathered around the table on chairs and stools, to discuss all they'd learned, but none of them had gotten very far. True, Daniel and Connor had been allowed to compete, but they'd learned little because they'd been sent away after their fights.

It had unsettled Gavin to hear about the lasses' journey, particularly because Merewen seemed taken in by Sela's act. She believed the Norsewoman truly was trying to make life better for the lasses, that mayhap the lasses they'd seen had truly come there of their own volition and the stolen lasses were somewhere else.

She thought Sela might help them. Though she'd finally acknowledged that, in all likelihood, only some of the woman who worked with Sela did so voluntarily.

Constance had finally taken her hand and said, "I understand your thinking, but Sela is probably forcing them. If they don't do as she says, I'm certain there'd be some form of punishment. I'm more bothered by the fact that you didn't see Linet. I suspect Sela has a much larger group of girls hidden away."

"Why? Why would she show us some of the lasses but not the rest? Connor won his match. She didn't *need* to show us anything."

"She was baiting us, hoping we'd give in and make it easy on her. But once we are in her clutches, we'll not get away. There was another abbey hidden behind the one I joined as a novice. They sent girls there to keep them away from prying eyes. I agree with the cousins. She's hiding something. But she wants you to come to her willingly."

"Us."

"Nay, she really wants you, though I'm uncertain why. You must be verra careful."

Daniel reached over and caressed his wife's neck. "Heed her words, Merewen," he said. "Constance knows exactly of what she speaks. She's been through much."

Merewen hung her head and whispered, "I'm tired. I'd like to go to sleep." Then she turned around and went into her chamber. There was nothing ambiguous about the way she closed the door behind her. She didn't wish to continue the conversation.

Gavin had forced himself to go for a walk because he couldn't get rid of the nagging feeling that they were missing something. He headed back into Inverness and went straight for the waterfront. He stopped at an alehouse to buy a beverage then took it with him out to the docks.

The moon, though not full, lit up the area enough for him to find his way. A few lit torches bracketed to the buildings cast light on the assortment crates and boards lying about in the area adjacent to the docks. The big ship that had been loaded this morn was gone. The other huge ship remained docked, though it was quiet at the moment. A stack of crates sat not far away, awaiting the dockworkers. Mayhap the ship would leave as early as the morrow, and the shipmen were spending their last nights at home or at the alehouses drinking.

He had a bad feeling. A *sick* feeling. The last time he'd been this discomfited, something very, very bad had happened. A man had kidnapped his wee sister and his wee cousin and terrorized his clan.

He didn't have seer abilities like his sister Molly, but this bad feeling would not go away.

He strode down the dock and stood at the end, looking over the edge at the pulsating rhythm of the river in front of him. The water reflected the weather. The wind was sharp enough to cause some small waves, making the water appear quite rough in the dark of the night. The sound of the waves crashing against the rocks was mesmerizing.

But something was wrong. He could *feel* it. Intuition thrummed through him.

He swung around, half expecting to see a man ready to drive his sword through him. Naught but shadows met his gaze, which came as a relief. He'd be in trouble if someone attacked him this eve. All he had was his bow and arrow. He never carried a sword unless on horseback, just a couple of daggers in case he needed one.

He started back up the docks when something stopped him in his tracks—a rhythmic thumping. It sounded as if it were coming from one of the stacked crates. He made his way back to them, but the noise had stopped. It hadn't been loud enough for him to judge which crate, if any, it came from. He stayed put for a moment, listening for a recurrence of the sound, but the docks stayed silent, and after a while, he headed back into town.

He was anxious and high strung, and his ears were hearing things. Or so he told himself.

Gavin headed back toward the stables, paying little mind to the people he passed, until he picked up on a familiar word from a couple of drunks sitting on a bench. *Beast.* He slipped into the shadows behind the bench, hiding behind a large heap of broken boards so he could hear them.

"I'd like to have the Beast here so we could see the pain in his eyes when he watches us send his daughter out to sea. I care not where they land or who takes them. Mayhap they'll fall overboard." He elbowed his friend with a guffaw.

"Or die in the crate." The second man burst into uncontrollable laughter at this comment.

"He's a dead man by now. They planned to torture him good for all the men his clan has cost us. We'll soon be rich and free again."

Gavin froze. The Beast? All of the Highlands knew his sire by that name. Could they be talking of him all the way up in Inverness?

His sire was being tortured and Maggie and Will were destined to be sent out to sea? Had Fitzroy or someone else betrayed them?

The crate...that rhythmic noise he'd heard...

He slipped out of the shadows and started walking, making his way back to the docks. Ran.

The echo of horses' hooves carried to him, interrupting his focus. Two horses stopped not far away. Gregor and Connor.

"Gavin, what the hell are you doing out here alone and on foot?" Gregor asked.

"Help me. Will and Maggie. I think they're trapped in a crate nearby. Those men..." He pointed off toward the bench, but the men had disappeared. "Two men. They spoke of torturing the Beast and sending the Beast's daughter out to sea. They're gone, but I'm telling you they were talking about my sire and my sister."

He raced over to the area where the crates were stacked.

There were hundreds. Large, small, heavy, light, crates everywhere.

He glanced up at the sky as soon as the sound of birds caught his ears. Two falcons flew overhead. "Where? Tell me where? Land on it or something. There are too many for us to open them all."

"The birds will help when they can," Gregor said. "We cannot stand by. You start at that end, Connor can focus on the middle, and I'll start at the opposite end."

"I heard something before, like someone kicking the inside of a crate. It stopped so I continued on my way. My sister..."

The thought of Maggie trapped in one of those awful crates, struggling for air, nearly stole his own breath away. His sister's spirit could not, should not, be contained.

"Go. Start searching."

"Maggie!" Gavin yelled, hoping she'd hear him and she could respond in some way, make some noise. He moved over to the area where he'd first heard the thumping. Rats scurried away from him. He pawed through trash that had been cast aside by the men. "Maggie!"

Then he heard it again. *Thump. Thump. Thump.*

"Maggie! Keep up the noise. We'll find you!"

CHAPTER TWENTY-ONE

———◆———

"MAGGIE!" GAVIN PULLED STRENGTH FROM his gut and tossed heavy crates from one place to another. Then he heard the sound again. "Connor, Gregor, over here."

Connor was at his side in an instant, just in time to hear the noise again. "Over here, Gregor."

The sound came from a hefty crate with four others on top of it. The light beat continued, but the sound was fainter than it had been—as if the person making it was fast losing strength. Gavin wanted to vomit, scream, tear every board apart and toss it over the edge of the dock.

Connor said, "Slow down, Gavin. The two of us together can lift those crates off faster than you can swinging wildly." He climbed up onto a tower of crates next to the one they needed to move. "Here. I'll lift them down to you."

"I'll throw the top ones in the water if I have to," Gavin said.

Gregor joined them, standing next to Gavin so they could both get underneath the crates to move them. Most of them were about half the size of a person, but wide enough to fit a prisoner who'd been forced into an unnatural position. "I'd advise against it. If Maggie is in one, you have no idea what could be in the others. Will could be in one above her."

Gavin took a deep breath, changing his focus. "You're right. Of course, you're right." Then he whispered, "Maggie, we're coming. It's the fourth crate, we just need to move the three on top of it. We'll set them atop the other piles in case we need to open them."

The crate on the bottom was definitely larger than the ones they lifted and set to the side. The entire process felt like it took three years, but it was probably only a few minutes. "I doubt any person is inside the ones we just lifted. But this one weighs triple the others. We'll need something strong to open it. I have my dagger, but I don't know if it'll be enough to pry those boards apart."

Gregor said, "I found a crow over there." He pointed to a long bar with an odd end. "We can use it as a lever to get the boards apart.

Once they reached the crate at the bottom, they moved it carefully on top of another so they could more easily work on it. It was a large rectangular box and they were attempting to wrench up the largest side of it.

When the top finally detached, Gavin took a deep breath before he lifted it off as gingerly as possible

Inside lay his sister, curled up inside her husband's arms. Neither of them moved.

Gavin was sick to his stomach. Were they too late? "Maggie?" He reached into the box and touched her cheek. She was pale but didn't look waxen like the dead often did. He prayed they weren't too late. He could make out some bruising on Will's face and his hands, as though he fought his captors.

"Is she alive?" Connor asked, leaning over to touch Will's face. "I think Will is, though both look verra weak."

"Aye." Gavin felt for the beat in her neck, relaxing when he found it. "She's alive. The beat is there, though 'tis not strong."

"I'm going to find water," Connor said, "and mayhap an ale or some bread. They've probably been starved." He slipped into the night, his posture that of a man on a mission. His last words over his shoulder were, "Aunt Jennie and Aunt Brenna always make injured people drink."

"Maggie, wake up, sweetie," Gavin said, patting her cheek. "Your brother's here and he needs you to yell at him."

Gregor touched Will's forehead then his neck. "Aye, he's alive. Mayhap they were given something to make them sleep. Keep them from calling out. I'm surprised they fought long enough to make some noise inside this crate." A sharp call carried across the wind in the night.

"Will's falcons." He noticed the great birds sweeping through the air above them, circling. "Stay around, we may need you yet." He knew the falcons didn't understand him, but he had to do something. How the hell was he supposed to help his sister?

Calm down and think. What would Aunt Brenna do? He took a deep breath and focused, knowing the answer wasn't 'do nothing.'

"I'm lifting her out," Gavin said. He could no longer bear to see her in the crate, especially not when the people who'd put her there might come back at any moment. "Help me, Gregor. I'm putting my hands under her arms. You catch her head so it doesn't fall back. If she can hold it up, grab her legs. I'll put her on my horse and get her back to the inn."

"I think she's been beaten, too, Gavin. Her cheek is bruised." Gregor studied Maggie's position carefully. "My mother always starts off by checking for any broken bones. I don't see any unusual angles in her extremities. We'll lift her out, then we'll find a healer."

"No healer. Not here. I don't trust anything in this town." He placed his hands under her arms and slowly lifted her. She cried out and swung one hand limply.

"Ow. Please, nay."

Gavin smiled. When had he ever heard a sweeter sound? "Maggie, 'tis your brother. You're probably sore from being unable to move. I'm getting you out."

Her eyes flew open once he moved her entire body out.

She cried out, but not too loudly, and clung to Gavin's shoulders like she'd die if he ever let go. Gavin would kill the bastards who'd done this to her. He wouldn't rest until they were dead.

"Gavin," she whispered. "Thanks be to God. Will? Is he…"

"Don't worry about him. He's alive."

"Where are we?"

"Inverness, and we're getting you out of here," Gavin said. Needing to feel her warmth, to reassure himself she was, indeed alive, he pressed his cheek against hers.

As if on cue, Will's eyes opened and he took in the scene from his position within the crate. "Maggie?"

"She'll be all right," Gregor said. "We must get you both out of here before we're discovered."

"Where are we?" Will repeated Maggie's question, his gaze taking in their surroundings until his eyes fell on Maggie, still wrapped up in Gavin's arms. "Maggie, my love. Are you hale?" He did his best to move his extremities, but Gavin could see it was a slow, painful process.

"She'll be fine, Will. We're in Inverness, but we have to move," Gavin said. "We'll take you to our inn."

They managed to get Maggie into a sitting position on another crate while they helped Will out, his falcons now swooping down as if to check on him. If Gavin hadn't known better, he would have said they were cooing.

Connor returned with an ale for Maggie and Will, and the liquid seemed to help fortify them. Except Maggie found she couldn't stand on her own. "I can't," she said, her voice thread with a fear Gavin hated. "My legs won't allow me. They're locked or something."

"I'll not be able to walk far," Will said, although he had been able to stand. "My legs are burning in pain. Where are your horses?"

A man emerged from one of the nearby huts as Connor led the horses closer. "Och, you cannot do that!" the man shouted. "Get away from here. Naught in these crates belongs to you."

The fool made his way over and approached Connor, who swung at him, knocking him to the ground with one punch.

"We need to hurry," Connor said, nodding at some other men moving toward them from farther down the street.

Gavin lifted Maggie onto one of the horses, while Connor and Gregor together managed to lift Will onto Connor's warhorse.

Gregor said, "Go ahead. Take her home on my horse. I'll walk."

They headed back down the street, but not without attracting attention.

A couple of men charged after them, but Connor brushed his horse close enough to nudge one of them over. The other ran in the opposite direction.

Maggie leaned back against Gavin as they made their way out of town. Gavin couldn't believe how little strength his fierce sister had left. She gripped his one hand and said in a small voice, "Gavin, Da is in trouble. They were going after him next."

"Where?" he asked, heart pounding. He remembered what those drunks had said about torture, but surely his sire was too strong to capitulate to them.

"The only thing I heard them say was they hoped he would follow them. We had stopped to visit the Grants. We were only there for a night. They kidnapped us just as we left. They had plenty of guards, which confused me, but they *wanted* to be seen. They planned to use trickery to pull Papa out so they could steal him away. They wished to torture him and leave him to die in the forest somewhere between Grant land and Inverness. And Will and I were to be sold over the seas. Many thanks for having the patience to find me with my weak knocking. I tried to stay strong, but I didn't have the strength…"

"One more question, then you must save your strength. Were those men coming to Inverness?" He had to know what they'd be up against.

"Nay, not right away. They talked about going after cargo first. I fear they planned to take more lasses from their beds…"

"Hush," he said, giving her a soft squeeze. "Worry not, I'll go after him. First, we need to get you and Will to safety. We also have Daniel with us, back at the inn, and nearly a dozen guards. Gregor can come with me, and we'll leave Connor and Daniel and the guards with you."

They weren't bothered again as they made their way through the town, though if he had to guess, Gavin would wager nearly all the people they passed had over-imbibed and were struggling to find their way home. It was quiet enough that he heard little beyond the clack of Gregor's boots on the cobblestones behind him. But the rest of the men they saw seemed oblivious to their horses. It had to be late because many of the alehouses were closed.

Once they made it to the inn, they got Maggie and Will up the stairs without much trouble. Gregor fetched food and ale from the kitchens, and the famished pair ate hungrily. In between bites, the cousins questioned them.

"Who were they, Maggie? I'm going after them, but I need to know how many and what plaid they wore," Gavin said, pacing behind the group. "I'll kill the bastards."

"There were a dozen, at least," Will said, smoothing a shaking hand over his hair. "They wore no plaids and some had masks over their faces."

"Why?" Daniel asked. "Why the hell wear masks? Be proud of your work."

"They don't wish to be discovered. Mayhap 'tis someone we know or someone she would have recognized. Were there any familiar voices, Maggie?" Gregor asked.

"Nay, none. I tried to pay attention, but I was so frightened for both of us…and Papa…that I can't recall much.

Gavin, we must go after Papa. He could lay dying some-where."

Gavin gulped. "We? I'm going, but you're going nowhere. Simply out of the question. You'd be a hindrance right now, not an asset. Gregor will go along with me. If a few guards can be spared, then we'll take them. If not, Gregor and I can take the bastards out."

Connor said, "I'd love to go with you, but I agree. These two are not ready to fight, we have two lasses that we must protect…"

"And there is another shipment going out," Will said. "I know not if we would have survived until the morrow, so mayhap those other crates are empty, but they'll be board-ing a ship soon. We cannot ignore that. We'll have to split up." He stared at Maggie as he said, "We ought to stay."

The look on her face was one of agony. She was as des-perate as Gavin to save their sire, and yet she and Will had the most experience with the Channel—and she did not yet have the energy for a long, hard ride. She agreed to stay.

"Fine," Gavin said. "I'm ready to leave in a quarter hour." His gaze lifted to the door to the lasses' chamber. Merewen and Constance both emerged wrapped in extra plaids for warmth. Gavin went to Merewen at once and settled his hand on her back. "Maggie, Will, you remember Merewen Baird?"

Maggie nodded. "Aye, we heard about your sister, Mere-wen. We'll get her back. I promise we're here to help."

Gavin filled them in on the situation, then said, "We sus-pect my sire has also been abducted." He let his gaze linger on Merewen when he said it. "Gregor and I leave shortly to find him, but do not despair. Connor and Daniel and Will and Maggie will stay here to help you continue the search for Linet." Poor Merewen looked stunned. "Here, sit down, lass." He found her a chair while Daniel tugged Constance onto his lap.

"Not waiting until the morrow, Gavin?" Daniel asked.

"Nay. If they already captured my sire, he'll not last the night. I have to find him this eve. I don't understand the masks. I don't like it."

"You're not thinking of the obvious, Gavin. Worry has befuddled your mind."

He had no idea what Connor was referring to. Befuddled? His mind had never been clearer.

"Don't you see? They're not Highlanders," Connor pressed. "They don't fight with honor."

Gavin stroked the stubble now on his chin. "Slud, I never thought of that. Not this far into the Highlands. They could be English."

They split the guards up, and then Gavin glanced over at Gregor.

"English. Just like Fitzroy. We leave in a quarter hour, before my sire dies."

CHAPTER TWENTY-TWO

M EREWEN SAT ON THE STOOL, trying to take in everything she'd just heard. She'd awoken from a dream that had something to do with her sister. Her head spun from all the happenings in the last half a day. What had happened with Maggie and Will was just so unbelievable. Seeing Maggie's weakness with her own eyes made her think very hard about what was at stake for her own sister.

Maggie was tough, always had been. Linet was not. If Maggie was in such poor condition after facing these men, what would become of her sister?

"I'll go speak with the guards while you and Gregor ready yourselves for the journey," Connor said. He was looking at Gavin as he said it. Suddenly, Merewen felt the urge to cry. Gavin was riding into danger, and he might not return. She knew she should be worried for what that might mean for Linet, and she was, but she also feared for his safety.

As if reading her thoughts, Gavin looked at her and asked, "May we talk privately?"

Constance overheard and said, "Use our chamber. We're going down to the inn for an ale. If I don't have one, I'll never fall asleep. Gavin, Godspeed if I do not see you before you leave."

Merewen peered up at Gavin again, wondering what he could wish to speak to her about. She entered the small chamber in front of him and he closed the door behind him. He strode over and cupped her face at once, kissing her with a fervor she hadn't expected—as if he'd never see her again. Their tongues dueled briefly, but he ended the kiss, keeping his hands on her cheeks.

She gazed into his green eyes, wondering what he was thinking.

"Gavin, I'm so sorry about your sister. God will help you find your sire, I'm certain. This is all so difficult for you."

He nodded, his thumb brushing up and down on her cheek. "No more difficult than what you are going through with your sister. My apologies that I must leave before I can make good on my promise, but I pledge to you that Linet will be my focus upon my return. I trust that my cousins will search for her. Maggie and Will know more about the Channel than any of us, so once they have healed, they will help you. They may be our best chance at locating Linet."

He still didn't move, and Merewen couldn't stop a tear from escaping and rolling down her cheek. Gavin leaned down and kissed the tear with a big sigh. "How I wish we'd discovered each other under different circumstances. I like you, Merewen, verra much. You stir something inside me. It's something I want more of when I return. I enjoy your company." His grin stretched wider, and she thought she saw a wee bit of mischief in it. "And our kisses. We need time to get to know each other better, but this isn't the time, apparently. Please do not give up on me?"

"Nay, I feel the same way, Gavin," she said, tilting her head up to him. "I've always felt Linet is the only one who truly understands me, but now I have you, and I'm grateful for that. Even if naught comes of our friendship, I'll still be grateful for what we've shared."

"When this is over, I will court you like a queen and her ladies."

"I don't need that. I only want you."

She meant every word. It didn't matter that her dream had been different, or that he didn't have a brother for Linet to love. She'd always admired Gavin Ramsay, and now that admiration had changed. It had grown into something bigger and less easily controlled.

His lips descended on hers and he groaned when their tongues touched again. This kiss was languid and slow, and she tried to remember everything about it. How it felt to be in Gavin's arms, his tender touch, his delicious kisses.

How could she ever forget them? Gavin had shown her a world she knew little about, but she'd learned enough to know she was anxious for more.

Not now, she reminded herself. The timing was wrong.

When he ended the kiss, he held her hands in his and stared into her eyes. "Merewen, please do me a favor."

"Anything, Gavin." She stood on her tiptoes and tried to straighten the few hairs that sat in disarray on his head. Somehow the messiness only made him more handsome.

"Please try to follow Daniel's and Connor's instructions. Don't go off on your own. Everything about Sela tells me she is anxious to have you fight for her. Please don't go willingly. She's not trustworthy. Promise me?"

"Gavin, I wouldn't go off on my own. I'm too frightened, especially after seeing what happened to Maggie and Will. But I won't stay here in this room either. They have to take me with them."

"Maggie will bring you. Trust her, please. Promise?"

"I promise I'll not go out on my own. But I cannot stop searching for her. Especially knowing that ship could be departing any day now."

He kissed her forehead and said, "I have to leave. I promise to return as soon as I'm able."

As he closed the door behind him, Merewen felt her heart give a funny thump. She imagined Gavin felt much the same way.

Would they ever see each other again?

Gavin and Gregor brought two guards, choosing to leave the rest with the group at the inn. They rode in the direction that gave them the best chance of finding his sire.

Gavin was overwrought. He'd nearly lost his sister tonight, and he'd just had to leave Merewen. Worse, much worse, his sire was in serious danger. Though the man made him daft, much like he made his sire daft, he adored him. Logan Ramsay was a legend, and Gavin had looked up to him every day of his life. He didn't wish to consider the possibility he might lose him.

Will had sent his falcons with them, claiming they were very good at finding activity ahead of human ears. He'd shown Gregor how to guide them and read their chatters. He'd even given him a few treats that he knew the birds loved. While their favorite food was other birds, he'd found a type of grain they'd accept instead.

They'd ridden through the rest of the night and well into the morning before Gregor said, "Gavin, I have to stop. I have needs, and since we've found naught, we need to discuss our next direction."

They stopped near a burn to refresh themselves and the horses. They all went their separate ways but met back near the horses a few minutes later.

"I'm not sure which way we ought to head next," Gregor said. "I've seen no sign of a large group of men traveling."

Gavin sighed, running his hand through his hair, "Nor have I. Which way to go? I have no idea. I thought the falcons would lead us, but they haven't seen anything."

"So we have to make a decision."

Gavin peered around the area, standing on a rock in a clearing to try to get a better view, but they were ensconced in pines.

Something dawned on Gavin. "You know I didn't trust Fitzroy. Well, he tried to tell us the Channel was in the northwest."

"True. Where are you going with this, Gavin?" Gregor stood with his hands on his hips, giving his cousin his full attention. "It's not a time to crow about being right."

"Nay, not that," Gavin said, waving a hand, "although I *was* right. I suspect Fitzroy is in deep. If he's involved with the Channel, for whatever reason, mayhap he was trying to send us to the northwest because he intended to trap us."

Gregor's eyes widened. "We're going in the wrong direction. We have to head west. They'll have brought him there."

"Exactly. That's where we go now." Gavin relaxed now that they had sound reasoning and a plan. "We leave now."

They rode until dusk was nearly upon them. The falcons began to act differently, to chitter and dive, and there were signs a group of warriors were gathered up ahead.

Gavin heard it then, his sire's voice.

He headed straight in that direction while Gregor followed.

Gavin broke through a group of trees and nearly heaved at what he saw in front of him. His sire was hanging from a tree by his hands while a group of about ten men took their turn battering him, spinning him with each punch. His face was barely recognizable, but it was him. He was certain.

What he couldn't tell was whether he was dead or alive.

A fury shot through him like nothing he'd never experienced before. The Ramsay war cry ripped from his throat, and he fired a succession of three arrows without hesitation, taking three men out. Gregor took another man out, while the guards they'd brought rode after a couple of men who'd taken off on horseback.

He noticed his sire's sword in the dirt off to the side of the clearing, so jumped down from his horse to grab it. The rest of these bastards would know whose sword was used to kill them.

He raced into the chaos of the four remaining men, slicing two bellies with his father's sword. That left two. Gregor took one of them out with another arrow. The remaining bastard grabbed Gavin's sire and stood behind him, protecting himself from an arrow.

"That's my sire. Take your hands from him, you bastard. You're about to die from his sword."

His sire's eyes fluttered open then, giving Gavin hope he would survive this ordeal.

CHAPTER TWENTY-THREE

G AVIN HELD HIS HAND UP to Gregor and the two guards, who'd just ridden back into the clearing. "This bastard's mine. He'll die at my sire's sword. Papa, hang on. This piece of shite is weak. He shivers and sweats like a wee bairn."

"Back up," the man yelled, taking a dagger out and holding it at his sire's throat. "Back up, or I'll end his life now. Put your sword on the ground. I'm riding out of here, and you'll promise not to follow me." His hands shook with nerves, but he held Gavin's sire firmly in front of him, not giving him much room to make a move. "And your other two men are to stay way back," the man continued. "I want your warhorse. Tell your friend to throw his bow far away."

Gavin nodded to Gregor, who tossed his bow behind him, and motioned to the two guards. They did as they were bid, removing themselves from the area.

"Now your sword. Set it down carefully."

Gavin slowly lowered his weapon to the ground next to him, but as soon as it struck the ground, he reached into his boot for his dagger, swinging it out with a wild yell.

It struck the arse between the eyes, and he was dead in an instant.

"Too bad you never knew what hit you, you bastard." Gavin kicked him out of the way and said, "Gregor, help me get Papa down."

The guards helped them lower him from the tree without jostling his head, and Gavin and Gregor then settled him in the soft grass of the clearing so they could untie his bindings. Once they'd freed his arms, his sire moaned, a deep, guttural cry. "Papa? Papa! Talk to me."

Gregor said, "Check him for other wounds before we get him on the horse. Then we have to get him to my mama right away. But if he's bleeding somewhere, we must staunch that first."

The sound of an approaching horse reached Gavin's ears, so he waved at the guards to intercept the traveler.

A familiar voice carried over to them. "Is he dead? I heard there was an ambush set for your sire, so I came out to do what I could."

Fitzroy.

"Alone? You came alone?" Gavin spat hotly as the man rode up to them. "That's a story I don't believe, Fitzroy. I think you planned this entire episode. Stay the hell away from my sire."

Three Ramsay guards trailed behind him.

Gregor addressed them as they approached. "You've been with him the entire way?"

"Aye," one guard replied. "We heard your sire was in trouble so we set out to find him. Your mother will probably be a wee bit behind us."

Gavin glanced at Gregor with a low growl, still not wanting to believe the bastard, but now he had no choice. He did trust their men. "Help me get him on my horse and we'll head to Ramsay land."

"We're closer to Grant land," Gregor reminded him. "We'll do better to bring him there. Check your sire's wounds first. I'll help you."

Gavin had to agree with Gregor's reasoning. He usually knew best when it came to healing. "We'll see how he is once we ride. We may have to take him there first. It may be all he can handle."

Gavin pulled his sire's tunic up to check his belly, unable

to contain his wince when he saw the red marks and all the pounding the man had taken. "He's lucky to be alive. He won't last for long. Roll him toward you, and I'll check his back."

They saw no other indications of external bleeding, but his back was already covered in bruises. "Gregor, they must have been beating him for a while, or he wouldn't be showing all these colors already."

"True, but your sire is a tough man. I notice the one you took out had a black eye and another had a bruised face. He gave some, too, but ten to one? Those are not good odds, even for the Beast."

"Mayhap when he was younger." His chest felt tight and hot at the same time. "He looks old, doesn't he?"

Gregor arched a brow at him. "Your sire? Never. Let's get him on the horse without moving him much. Fitzroy, you can assist us now."

Fitzroy and another guard helped Gavin get his sire onto Wee Paz. Based on the amount of groaning he did when they moved him, he wouldn't be able to travel quickly.

Although still not responsive, Logan fought to sit up, and the guards helped position him in front of Gavin. There was only one problem—they couldn't get him to stay facing forward because he wouldn't let go of Gavin's tunic.

Gavin did the best he could to make his sire comfortable, cushioning his back with an extra plaid he always carried, but he winced with every jolt and bump in the road. They'd traveled about an hour when his sire started mumbling.

Gavin slowed his horse long enough to ask what he wanted. "Water." He stopped his horse, motioning for Gregor to do the same, then gave his sire a drink from the skin he carried. Though he dribbled most of it down his chin, Logan awakened enough to look straight at Gavin to say, "You saved my life."

Two days went by without a word from Gavin or Gregor. Merewen said her prayers every night for Logan Ramsay and for Linet. That second day, the group wandered down to the docks and found out the ship would be leaving in two days.

That gave her two days to find Linet first.

The night of their discovery, Merewen complained of a headache and asked Constance to help her up to their chamber while the men stayed in the main hall finishing their meal and downing ales. As soon as they were inside, Merewen closed the door behind her, leaned against it, and asked, "Will you go with me?"

"Where are you going?" Constance pulled her over to the table, then pushed her into a chair before she sat next to her. Wide-eyed, she said, "You cannot do anything until Gavin returns. You said you promised him…"

Why did Constance have to remember everything so well? It wasn't as if she'd lied to him on purpose. How could she have known they would be gone for more than two days? Sitting around and waiting for nothing to happen was akin to torture. Her sister was out there somewhere, but for all she knew, she'd be loaded onto a boat in a matter of days. "I know, but we've heard naught yet, and if I do not hear from him by the morrow, I will go in search of my sister. I cannot sit and wait."

"Let the others search for her. I know how difficult it is to wait, but allow the lads to search first. These people are dangerous, Merewen, more so than I feared."

Merewen didn't wish to go without her friend. Constance had been willing to take a chance before, she had to convince her to do it again. She reached for Constance's hands. "I know what happened to Maggie and Will was frightening…"

"Merewen, you have no idea. I was in the Channel. The

men were trying to bring me to Edinburgh so I could be sold. Would I have been locked into a crate like poor Maggie and Will? Nay, they had each other, and I would have been alone. I would have…"

"Hush, Constance. It did not happen to you, and the cousins saved Maggie and Will. We must do the same for my sister. Can you not see that?"

"But don't you see they're trying? Maggie is improving every day, and when Gavin returns, he'll continue to look for her." Constance bounced in her seat, her gaze pleading with Merewen as much as her words.

"True. But they're looking in the wrong places. They won't find her near the docks. I think she's with Sela—I'm convinced of it. Mayhap it sounds foolish to you, but Linet and I have always been especially close. I can tell when she's lost. Something inside of me awakens and does not settle until I find her. It happened in the forest, it happened when she was crying behind the chapel, it has happened so many times. 'Tis difficult to explain. Please, Constance?"

Constance released Merewen and dropped her face into her hands, covering her eyes and shaking her curls as if it could help her think. "I know not…arghhh." She took a deep breath and suddenly sat up straight, clasping her hands together to twiddle her thumbs. Then she stopped all her movement. "All right. I'll help you. But you must promise me not to take unreasonable risks. You know the danger, and I cannot bear to lose you."

"I promise to be careful." She reached over and rubbed Constance's shoulder. She was worried for her the way she worried for her sister.

"You wish to go see Sela?"

"Aye."

Constance sighed again. "I cannot disagree with you. I think Sela has a much larger operation of lasses than what we've seen, mayhap in a different inn or a different kind of building. But how can you find out where they are?"

"I'll go ask." The words that had been churning inside her burst out. "I'm going to ask Sela if I could try out fighting. Do it for one day and see if I like it." Merewen was convinced this was the only way she'd get inside to find Linet.

Constance's hands fell into her lap and the twiddling began again. "Oh, 'tis not a good idea, Merewen. You cannot trust she'll let you go."

"Why not? Daniel and Connor were allowed to leave, were they not? He's here. Connor is here."

Constance explained, "But they have to return to fight on the morrow, just as they did last eve and the eve before. Their new agreement was to fight for three nights. If they win this eve, then you and I are safe. If they lose two in a row, she'll take us. And I have no desire to fight, even if you do."

"She said she didn't want you to fight. She wished for you to do something else."

"Whore for her?" Constance bolted out of her seat this time and paced a circle around the table, her arms crossed. "Nay, I'm not interested."

Merewen chewed on her bottom lip. "I suppose you might be right." It hadn't occurred to her at the time, but mayhap that was what she'd meant. It fit with what everyone had said about the underground.

"I'm not willing to take the chance," Constance said, reaching out to take her hand again. She squeezed it, looking into Merewen's eyes as if to gauge her truthfulness. "Thank you for reminding me about that. I can't risk everything. I'm sorry, but I cannot. I love my husband. I want bairns." Her eyes misted and Merewen realized she'd pushed her new friend too far.

Constance stopped to face her. "I'll stay with Daniel, and you should wait for Gavin. Please, Merewen. Think of those crates."

She let out a deep sigh, realizing there was no sense in

arguing with Constance. In a way, perhaps this was best.

Merewen didn't wish to endanger Constance, but she was determined to act. She'd find Sela the next time they were in the basement of the inn watching Connor and Daniel fight.

And she'd volunteer to fight.

It was the only way.

CHAPTER TWENTY-FOUR

GAVIN PRAYED HIS FATHER COULD survive. "Papa, we've got to move. You can drink while we ride."

A few hours after they began their journey, his father mumbled, "I'll get them. They'll never stop Logan Ramsay. I'll…" His head lolled back against Gavin's chest.

Gavin struggled to keep his sire facing forward. He'd never had to handle him like this before. The man was a beast, and even at his advanced age of over forty years, he was still made of solid muscle.

Muscle that wished to try and fall off his horse.

"Hurry, Gregor. I don't know how much longer I can keep him steady."

"I'm fine," his sire said blearily, picking up his head and staring straight ahead. And yet with each passing mile, he swayed more in the saddle.

In the end, they didn't need to make it all the way to Grant land—a retinue met them on the road. Gavin's mother; Cailean MacAdam, his sister's husband; and three guards.

"Gavin, what happened?" his mother asked, leaping down from her mount and running over to his horse. Every line of her body spoke of alarm. "Logan! Logan, wake up! Oh my, look at your wrists. Logan, your face…"

Fitzroy said, "I warned him there could be trouble."

If Fitzroy didn't shut his mouth, Gavin would do it for him soon. The man was worthless.

"Mama, his hands were tied to a tree and they left him suspended there," Gavin said, his voice cracking. "Ten men beat him repeatedly. I have no idea how long, but he was passed out when we got to him. I feared he was dead, but he's spoken to us a couple of times. He'll be bruised everywhere. We have to get him to a healer at once."

"Gwynie? Is that you?" Logan said. "I love you." He lifted his head for a moment, then it dropped back against Gavin's chest.

"Mama, can you take him the rest of the way to Grant land?" Gavin asked. "Cailean can manage him. Maggie and Will were locked in a crate. They were almost sent across the waters. We need to get back."

"You found them in the northwest?" Fitzroy asked. Cailean rode up behind his mother, his eyes huge as he looked at Gavin's sire. "I'm so glad you were able to save them."

"Nay, not the northwest, you fool. But you knew that didn't you?" If he hadn't needed to hang on to his father, Gavin would have put a fist in the bastard's face. "But we knew better. We found them in the north*east*, the opposite of the direction. If we'd listened to you, Maggie and Will would be dead!" He glared at the bastard, thinking of the implications of this man's 'mistakes.'

"Gavin," his mother said. "We must focus on your father. You can beat Fitzroy silly later. There are lives at stake, and that's what you must do. Do you hear me? Your sire, your sister. Stay focused."

He glanced at his dear mother, just now seeing the pain in her eyes. She was right, as ever. After working for the Scottish Crown for years, she knew exactly the right advice to give him and far better than the arse behind her. He still wasn't sure if Fitzroy was affiliated with the Channel, but he didn't have time to figure it out.

"You're right, Mama. Slowing us down could be one of his objectives. Let's move Papa to Cailean's horse. Then

Gregor and I can return to Inverness."

"Aye," Gavin's mother said, looking into his eyes. "We'll bring him back. Tell me more about Maggie and Will?"

"They're both strong and will be fine in a few days. Don't worry about them, but Gregor and I need to get back to help the Band. I think we're close to finding Linet."

"Who else is with you?" his mother asked.

"Connor, Daniel, Will, and Maggie. And Constance and Merewen. We left ten guards with them. Owen and Earc are there, plus some Grant and Ramsay guards."

His mother gave a fierce nod. "Aye. Go back and help your sister. We've faith in you. Cailean, you need to lift Logan down and get him on your horse."

Cailean looked frightened of touching his father-in-law, but he dismounted from his horse and did as he was told. The man was one of the wildest and strongest warriors Clan Ramsay had. In fact, he was only afraid of one thing: Logan Ramsay. Gregor and Gavin helped him make the transfer, then Cailean jumped up behind Logan, steadying him easily with only one big hand.

Before Gavin could mount up again, his mother came over to him and reached up to cup his face so she could tug him down to kiss his cheek. "My thanks for saving your sire, Gavin. Whether he tells you so or not, we both believe in you, and you've just proven yourself."

He glanced over at Gregor, who was smiling and nodding. Accepting the praise, he said, "Cailean will get him to Grant land and he'll be fine, Mama. Do not worry." He climbed on his horse and turned Wee Paz around with a pat to his withers. "Back to Inverness we go."

The last words Gavin heard his sire say were, "MacAdam, I just might like you today."

Some of the worry dropped off Gavin's mother's face. Smirking, she said to Gavin, "He's feeling better. I think he'll be just fine. Godspeed."

Her parting words carried across the forest as they raced

off. "Show those bastards what it means to trifle with a Ramsay."

The next day, word arrived that Gavin and Gregor had found his sire and were taking him to Grant land to see a healer. They were all relieved, Merewen, too, but she knew what it meant. Gavin would not be back in time to help her.

What the hell was she to do?

She stepped outside the inn after the late meal, glancing around the area. Daniel and Connor would leave to fight soon, and unless she could think of a plan quickly, they would leave her here with Constance and the guards. She couldn't allow that. She needed to speak with Sela. If that required her to fight another lass, well, she'd do even that for Linet.

Earc approached her. "Is there something wrong, lass? Can I assist in any way?"

She shook her head, pretending she didn't see the gleam of interest in his eyes.

"We could go for a stroll this eve if you like. Once the men leave to fight, I can come back for you and escort you into the burgh. We could visit the waterfront and stroll down the dock. I hear it might be a full moon this eve."

She whirled her head around to stare at the man. Earc. She hated to deliberately use the man, but he was offering to escort her. He'd be upset if she turned him down. Besides, Gavin wasn't here to help and Constance had, quite rightly, decided the risk was too great. What choice did she have?

"That sounds lovely, Earc. I'll ready myself."

He smiled, and she took her leave, her mind already piecing together a new plan as she turned around and headed up to their chamber, doing her best to rethink her clothing. She'd wear a gown with her leggings underneath so no one would suspect what she had in mind. Once she was finished, she headed back to the common room downstairs to wish the lads luck with their venture.

Earc winked at her.

Constance promised Daniel to stay behind when the group took their leave, then she and Merewen headed back upstairs. Earc left with the group, while three guards stayed behind, posting themselves in front of the inn.

Constance grabbed her hand and dragged her up the stairs. The moment the door closed behind them, she whirled on her. "I saw that look in your eye. Tell me you are not planning on going to see Sela alone."

"I'm not planning on going alone," Merewen said.

"Good," Constance said, flopping into a chair at the table. She blew out a breath, ruffling her red curls. "I couldn't handle it if I had to worry about you, too."

"I'm going with Earc."

"What? You cannot! What if you don't return? I'll never forgive myself," Constance cried.

She took her friend's hand and said, "I must go. I understand the lads are looking to stop the entire Channel, thinking that will help Linet, and mayhap they're right. But 'tis a large undertaking. I'm only looking for one lass. If I can talk to some of Sela's lasses, I suspect I can find out where they're keeping Linet. Then I can go after her on the morrow, and I'll take the cousins with me."

Constance's nose was scrunched prettily, but she finally nodded. "That sounds like it may work, if Sela will allow you to leave. Try to get Earc to bring you home before the lads return, please? Otherwise they'll come after you." She gave her friend a squeeze.

"I'll do my best," Merewen said. "I cannot wait here any longer. I must do something."

A half hour later, Merewen went down the staircase to wait for Earc. Once he arrived, they set off for the burgh. Earc talked sweetly to her all the way, but she did her best not to encourage him.

"Earc, I'm looking for someone. 'Tis why I wished to come along. Please do not get your hopes up for anything more. I'd like you to take me to Sela." She didn't give him the chance to deny her—she simply kept walking.

"I understand," he said after a moment, darting a look at her. "But a man can hope."

They walked to the waterfront where they'd met Sela the first time, but she was nowhere to be seen.

"Mayhap we must return to Stag's Inn, Earc. Can you find your way there?"

"Aye," he said, fortunately not casting her any more unwelcome looks. She'd told him the truth of their relationship and he'd accepted it. As soon as they rounded the corner where most of the alehouses were situated, she spotted Sela. She raced over to the woman and stood directly in her path, stopping her forward progress, though her retinue of guards quickly stepped in to protect her.

Sela made a motion with her hand for the men to stand back. She didn't smile, but her demeanor was that of a cat with a bowl of goat's milk as she stepped closer and said, "I knew you'd come see me. Ready for your first fight?"

Earc caught up with her, but he clearly didn't understand what they spoke of. He cocked his head, listening.

"And *he* cannot come." Sela's tone was scornful as she tipped her head toward Earc.

"I'll only fight if I can leave when I'm done."

"'Tis not how it's usually done with lasses."

"'Tis how I wish it to be done." She crossed her arms, hoping to convince the tall woman that she would not budge on her demands. Sela had done her best to convince her and Constance that she tended to the women in her care, that she did what was best for them and treated them better than any husband would. Merewen hoped to use that to her advantage. "You do so with men. Why not lasses? Or do you give men preferential treatment?"

Sela stared at her for a few moments, not speaking, and her silent, cold assessment made Merewen grateful for Earc's solid presence behind her. He did know what she was about, but he knew his ultimate job was to protect her because she was a member of Clan Ramsay.

"I'd like to try it. If I make good coin, I'll return another night."

A few moments of silence passed before Sela answered. "Fine," she said. "You'll be in the next fight. When you're finished, I'll have one of my men return you to this spot." She glanced at Earc. "Understood?"

He waited for Merewen's nod, then said, "I'll wait for the lady."

"Follow me," she said to Merewen, but instead of heading toward Stag Inn, she led her around the back of another building. There were no signs to indicate which inn they were entering, or even whether it was an inn.

She followed Sela down the stairs and through the back door. The basement of this building looked to be double the size of the other one and there were twice as many men milling about. They passed two rooms for fighting, both of which appeared to be for lasses, one larger than the other.

At the end of her quick tour, Sela opened the door and called to a matronly woman, "Get her dressed in something appropriate. She'll be in the next fight, and she leaves after one battle."

The woman quirked her brow, but followed Sela's instructions, leading Merewen into a chamber already occupied by several lasses, some nursing wounds while others paced to get ready for their turn.

"Here," she said, handing her two garments. "Try this on. The next fight is in five minutes. If you don't make that one, you'll have to wait until the next one, which will be in fifteen minutes."

The older woman left, so Merewen scanned the chamber

more openly. She didn't see anyone who looked like her sister, but a girl with red hair and kind eyes came over to greet her. "My name's Runa. Would you like some help?"

"Aye, if you please." She fumbled removing her gown and leggings, then attempted to pull the tight garments on. "I could use some help. I don't think these will fit me."

Runa smiled. "Aye, they will. They're meant to be verra tight. I'll help you put them on. Then you must bend your legs and walk around to loosen the fabric or you'll never be able to fight."

Runa seemed nice, and Merewen wished more than anything to ask her about her sister, but she didn't dare trust her yet. If she made the wrong decision and this lass told Sela...

"I only have a few minutes," she said. "I appreciate your assistance."

"I didn't know there were any new lasses tonight."

"It just came up. How many lasses are there?" While she didn't wish to rouse any suspicion by discussing her sister explicitly, she thought there were some general questions she could ask without sounding suspicious. Fortunately, no one else paid them any mind.

"Too many," she sighed. "How did you get caught?" she whispered.

She glanced over her shoulder and noticed the matronly woman had returned and was watching her.

"Don't worry about Bera," Runa said, waving a hand dismissively. "She's forced to work here like the rest of us. She'll not tattle on you."

"Mayhap we can talk after my fight. That is, if I survive. I hope my opponent isn't too tough."

"You can beat her. Whoever it is. You look tough enough. Make your face a wee bit meaner and you'll do fine."

Merewen didn't know how to react to that comment, so she didn't. Instead, she did what Runa had advised—stretching her outfit enough to allow movement.

Bera waved to her. "Now. Hurry." She ushered her out the door and into a passageway, then shoved her through another small door. When Merewen glanced back over her shoulder, the last thing she saw was Runa's smiling face. Glancing quickly at her surroundings, she found herself in the middle of an area with a dirt floor, surrounded by layers of yelling men standing in a circle. Their mantra at the moment was, "Kill her, kill her, kill her…"

She turned around just in time to see a lass a head taller than her weighing twice what she did barreling straight toward her.

She was about to die, for certain.

CHAPTER TWENTY-FIVE

MEREWEN DID THE ONLY THING she could think to do. She waited until the very last moment then stepped aside. The brutish lass flew past her, though she tried to stop her forward movement. Merewen spun around quickly and gave the lass a kick, sending her flailing to the ground. She jumped on her back and grabbed her arms, pinning them behind her. The brute couldn't move.

But then the brute did the unexpected and bucked against the soft dirt floor, sending Merewen flying. She landed with a big "oof" and the other lass was on her in a moment, attempting to pin her to the ground. Because she was big, she was slow, and Merewen, still on her back, managed to get her legs pulled in tight to her chest and kicked the lass full force in her belly, sending her flying backward. Her head struck the stone wall, knocking her out.

Merewen was declared the winner and shouts filled the big chamber. The announcer held her hand up, shaking it so all could see. This was the first time she'd looked at the audience of all men closely. A sea of dirty faces surrounded her, fists swinging in the air, goblets of ale sloshing and spilling as they shouted and whistled at her. With each spittle-laced bellow, they collectively moved in closer, though a few men stood at the edge, forcing them back. The spectators wore wild, daft expressions, as if intent on hurting someone...was it her?

A moment later, the crowd was chanting something,

although it took her a moment to register the word.

"Kicker, kicker, kicker…"

She'd gained a name. As soon as the big woman was removed, another lass came in through the door from which Merewen had emerged, running straight at her. Merewen had no idea what was happening. She glanced at the man in bafflement. "Another one? But I thought I was only fighting once."

He smiled at her and said, "Nay, you've got another one to beat."

She spun her head around and took a fist straight to her eye from a solid but thin brunette with a nasty grin.

Merewen was driven back into fight mode by the thought of Linet being forced to fight this lass. She had to save her—she just had to. She swung her fists the same way she'd seen the men fight, protecting her face with one hand while she attacked with the other, and got in a kick where she could.

At one point, the lass's eyes glazed over in an odd way, so Merewen bent at the waist and delivered a side kick, catching her in the chin and sending her to the floor. She didn't move, so Merewen was again declared the winner.

When the crowd started chanting that word—"kicker"— the man shook her hand over her head again. That was when she noticed the blood running down her cheek and her neck from the blow she'd taken to her eye.

The judge said, "Get your eye treated." He pointed to the door, and she ran to it, not wanting to get forced into another fight. To her delight, two other lasses came in, and the chanting changed instantly.

There she was in the middle of an empty passageway. With the swing of a door, she was forgotten. She took a deep breath and headed back to the chamber on the other side of the passageway, the one where she'd met Runa.

Once she had changed, with help from Runa, Sela returned, again with no expression, and motioned for

Merewen to follow her. Then she turned slightly and added, "Runa, come with us."

The two followed her back into the passageway, down a ways, and into a small chamber at the end. This one had a small table, a pallet on the floor, a small chest, and three stools. Sela pointed to the stools, and Merewen felt she had no choice but to sit. Runa did the same, but Sela remained standing. "Runa, take care of her eye," she said. "Linen strips are in the chest."

Runa did as she was told, pouring water from an urn into a bowl, then tearing linen strips to work with.

All the while, Sela stared at Merewen. "Well done," she said, speaking with no emotion. "I'll hold up my end of the bargain, and I'll send a guard with you in a quarter hour. Think on it, but as I said, 'tis in your blood—just as I suspected. Come back on the morrow if you wish to continue, though if you return, you'll be staying.

"Your men have one more night of fighting, possibly tonight, although I suspect neither of them will lose. You will not be sacrificed as part of a wager, so the choice is yours. Do you wish to spend your life chasing bairns and cleaning up their waste, or live a life of luxury where the men will adore you and scream your name? Here's your coin for the night. You did well."

She handed her the small but heavy pouch, then left without another word or a smile.

Runa dipped the cloth in the water and continued to tend her wound, which wasn't too bad.

The red-headed girl clucked her tongue. "You'll have a darkly colored eye by the morn. 'Twill be quite sore, but you paid the lass back. Sela will want you back. You won twice and the men loved you—partly because of your skills and partly because of the way you look in your outfit. I'd advise you to be careful. She has a way of getting whatever she wants."

"How many other lasses fight for her? Would she really

want me with so many others?" Merewen was hoping the question was vague enough not to alert Runa to her purpose.

"I'm unsure. This building is divided into two sections. One side is for the new lasses and the other for those that have been here for a while. I hear the other side is much nicer. On each side, there are two sleeping areas, one for those who win her the most coin, and a larger area for the rest of us."

"She treats you differently? 'Tis not fair."

"The ones who do well think 'tis perfectly fair. They get the best food, they are sometimes allowed outings with guards, and they get books. I heard that on the other side, there's a lass who teaches the others how to read when she's not healing. She does both."

Merewen felt a strange thrumming her chest. Linet could read. Could it be possible that this was her job? She had to ask more questions. "How did she get such a position?" she asked cautiously. "'Tis much better than fighting."

"She was made to fight in the beginning, but she cried too much. Sela said she was the only one who could read, so 'tis how she earned it. That and a few other things. She actually just started teaching a couple to read because she's new. They had to find her books to use, but word passed quickly because we all wish to learn how to read."

"And the other lasses? If they do not fight, what are they made to do?"

"Some are made to whore, but no one knows how she decides who whores and who fights. But the one who teaches reading, she's quiet and rarely talks. She never questions Sela."

Now that her insides had calmed, she sensed something—the feeling in her chest she experienced whenever she was near Linet.

Linet was here. She could *feel* it.

Perhaps not in this chamber or even this side of the

building, but she was here. She'd never been more certain of anything. But she also noticed something quite odd. At times, she'd been able to sense Linet's fear when they were separated, but this time she could not. It was as if there were no strong feelings in her dear sister's heart at the moment.

Linet always did as she was told, with one exception—she hadn't given up reading at their sire's command. And while Linet wasn't a healer, she'd assisted their mother with treating all their family illnesses and wounds. She'd also helped Lady Brenna, the clan healer, several times because she enjoyed it. Could this person be Linet?

Merewen wished to ask more questions, but she was afraid to arouse the other lass's suspicion. She didn't trust Runa completely yet.

"Do not ever question Sela," Runa whispered as footsteps approached the chamber.

Sela stepped in a moment later, a guard behind her.

"You go now."

With Runa's advice fresh in her mind, she thanked Sela for the opportunity and followed the guard out without another word.

But she'd be back, and despite what Sela had told her, she wouldn't be staying.

She felt sure the reader had to be Linet.

———◆———

Gavin and Gregor couldn't get back to Inverness fast enough. They'd done all they could for Gavin's sire, now it was time to assist the Band of Cousins. To assist Merewen. There was much to do, and little time, if they were to stop the Channel and discover the secrets of Sela's underground network.

When they arrived at the inn, he realized how much the journey had exhausted him. "You as tired as I am, Gregor?"

"Aye. We didn't get much sleep in the last two days.

Naught but a couple of hours. 'Tis late enough they should all be inside. After we get an update, I'm headed to bed. I need sleep, if only a few hours."

Gavin could run on just a few hours of sleep, much like his sire, but Gregor needed more rest. He knew what his cousin had given up for him and his sire.

He was pleased to see that Connor and Daniel were in the common room of the inn with Will, Maggie, and Owen, and there was no one else about, not even the innkeeper. Earc and the rest of the guards were outside patrolling.

"Greetings, all. Have you any news?" Gavin sat on the bench, rubbing his one shoulder as he sat down.

"You found your sire, we heard, and sent him back to Grant land. Was it a tougher fight than you expected?" Daniel asked.

Gregor sat opposite Gavin on the bench. "For him, aye. I used my bow, but Gavin jumped right in as he oft does…"

Connor gave him a smug grin, and nodded, "You made the bastards pay for touching your sire, did you not?"

"Aye, we did, and he'll survive, but tell me what's happened in our absence."

"Not much, except there is a big ship heading out on the morrow," Connor said. "Relax for a moment. You've earned it. Grab an ale and talk with us." He settled them with ales, then said, "All I learned while you were away is that there's a different building where the majority of the women are being held. There are two levels of fighting for the lasses: one level for those just starting, and a different level for the experienced fighters. We haven't uncovered where this building is exactly."

"Merewen and Constance are abovestairs?" Gavin asked, unable to stop himself. He longed to see Merewen's fresh face, her long brown hair, and breathe in her scent. "Both hale?"

"Aye," Daniel said. "Both were in their chamber, ready for bed. I told Constance it would be a while before I turned in. You two look exhausted."

"Papa?" Maggie asked, reaching for his hand and giving it a squeeze. "Please tell us all. I've been so worried about him."

Gavin said, "'Twas not good, but he's safe. Ten men had hung him from a tree by the hands and beaten him pretty badly. Looked as though it had gone on for a while."

"Ten?" Will asked.

"Aye," Gavin nodded. "They paid for their mistake. We met Mama and Cailean on our way to Grant land, and she took him back there to be healed."

"How badly is he hurt?" Maggie asked, swiping a tear from her eye.

"Not as badly as we thought. Before we left, he woke up and told MacAdam he just might like him."

"He did?" Maggie's face lit up with a bright grin, and Gavin found himself grinning back.

"Aye. It took Cailean, Gregor, and me a bit to get him down from my horse and onto Cailean's. He was dead weight. The man is still a beast, all muscle. He woke up once Cailean climbed up behind him and stopped him from falling off his horse."

He took a deep breath, finally realizing how much had happened over the last three days.

Too much.

But they'd done what they'd needed to do, and now they could focus on Linet.

"Hellfire, it took all my strength to keep the Beast on my horse." Gavin rubbed his shoulder again, then added, "I'm famished. Anything left to eat?

"There's stew in the pot over the hearth and bowls next to it."

"As soon as I finish, I'll go check on the lasses."

Gregor said, "Have you forgotten who we met not far from your sire?"

All talk stopped as Gavin abruptly stood from the bench,

his hand falling from his shoulder. "How could I forget? That bastard."

Maggie, wide-eyed, stared up at him. "Who? Who could have been involved in such a horrific scene? Who hated our sire enough to beat him senseless before killing him?"

"Fitzroy. I did my best to make him out to be the liar he is, but he had an answer for everything. I wished to beat the fool with my bare hands, but my mother reminded me of my focus."

Gregor added, "And you realized yourself that his entire purpose could be to slow us down and get us away from Inverness, so you wisely ignored him. He can return to Ramsay land or Grant land. He'll find no backing at either place."

Gavin's jaw clenched. "But I will kill that bastard if I find out he had anything to do with that attack on my sire. You can count on that."

CHAPTER TWENTY-SIX

—◆—

MEREWEN DIDN'T HAVE ANY TROUBLE finding Earc. Upon their return to the inn, Earc said, "If you wish to go back, I'll take you."

"Why?" She couldn't help but wonder why he was interested in this venture. Did he expect something from her, or was he merely helping her because he was a Ramsay guard?

"Because I can help you get into Sela's den of lasses, if you're interested."

"How would you know about that?" Merewen had to hide her surprise at Earc's pronouncement.

Earc stared far off into the distance "I know more than you would ever guess, about many things. If you decide you'd like to go, I'll be out here for half the night."

They parted ways, but his comment had stayed with her. What if he could help her get inside without being available to Sela? She didn't wish to risk raising the woman's ire.

Merewen was definitely not interested in joining Sela's fighting ring. It was way too painful. She rubbed her temple near her swollen eye as a reminder of what the last one had cost her.

She snuck in through the back entrance of the inn, a path that Earc had showed her. As soon as she entered the room, Constance pulled her into the small chamber and led her to the bed. Both of them sat and Constance gripped her hand. "Tell me everything," she said, her eyes sparkling. "The lads arrived before you did, but I pretended you were asleep in the room. They're in the hall downstairs."

Merewen told her what she'd learned without mentioning Linet's name. She told about the fighters, the whores, and the lasses who were treated better than the others. She told her all about her fights.

"But you didn't see your sister and you didn't ask about her specifically?"

"Nay, I was afraid to. I feared Sela would keep me there if I was too bold. I didn't see anyone who looked like her, but the lasses in the building sleep in four different chambers. Imagine how many there are all together." Merewen pulled her hand away and started to pace. "I don't know what else to do, but I must go back."

"If you didn't see her, why do you wish to go back? Mayhap she's not even in Inverness. We could be completely wrong."

"Nay. She's here. I can feel it. And I think I have proof."

"What are you talking about?" Constance asked with wide eyes.

She sat down next to her friend again, whispering. "Runa said there's one lass who teaches the others to read. Said she was new. Sela tried to make her fight, but all she did was cry."

"Why do you think that lass is your sister? You think she would cry?"

"Aye, I don't think she would wish to fight, and she also loves to read. Gregor and Lily taught her. The other thing Runa said was that this special lass always does what Sela tells her. That's my sister. No matter what, she almost always does as she's told. Papa and my brothers rule her about, and she always does as they say, even if they make her clean up something nasty. That's Linet."

"I wonder if Sela keeps her hidden." She paused, her forehead scrunching up as she considered something, then said, "And where do the girls do their whoring? You said there are four chambers for the lasses. It doesn't sound like there's room for a brothel. There would have to be a place with many private chambers for the women to do their whoring."

"How do you know this? 'Struth?"

Constance blushed but said, "I'm of noble blood. I used to listen to the stable lads and the guards talk when they didn't know I was around. Each lass has her own chamber to use. 'Tis part of how it works. They all spend time in the hall first, the men choose who they want, then they go off to private chambers."

Merewen thought for a moment. "Aye, you're right. The women who whore must be in another building. I don't know which one the reader would be kept in." She paused, then sat up with a start. "Och. I forgot. This lass also helps with healing. Linet always assisted with those things at home."

Constance said, "Then she would have to be near the women who fight, though sometimes the women in a brothel get beaten by the men." She scowled and stared at Merewen, tipping her head toward the candle. "What's wrong with your eye? 'Tis turning colors and swelling." Her hand jumped to her mouth. "Were you punched there?"

"Aye," Merewen replied sheepishly.

"Did you retaliate in kind?" Constance asked, a wee grin on her face.

"Aye, I kicked her arse."

The two giggled, and Constance wrapped her arms around her neck and gave her a squeeze. Their laughter ended quickly. "Then how will you return? You said Sela wishes to keep you, so how can you risk going back?"

"I must take that risk, but I'll talk with the cousins first. See if they learned anything that will help me. Then I'll have Earc take me back on the morrow, unless Gavin returns. In fact, I'm going to go talk to the cousins in the hall, then I'll check with Earc. See if he'll take me back."

Merewen pulled her hair out of her plait so she could cover her eye, then crept out of the door and made her way downstairs.

She changed her mind and decided to seek out Earc first. If he knew something, she wished to know it too—and to understand how he knew. She snuck past the hall, not even looking in that direction because she didn't wish to be seen. Outside, she saw Earc off to the right, talking with a group of men. She made her way over to him and said, "Earc, could I speak to you privately, please?"

He pointed to a spot away from the others, hidden from the front of the building, so she followed him and leaned back against a tree, hoping it would hide her even more.

Something struck the side of her head, and she crumpled to the ground.

A new group of men came into the hall. They'd all been imbibing and were stumbling, but they found a trestle table and made their way to the hearth for stew.

Gavin's appetite was as strong as ever, so he got up to fetch another helping before it was all eaten. He'd intended to ignore them like he usually would, but he got caught up in their conversation.

"My favorite was the kicker lass. What a body, and she knew how to use it. She was a beauty with all that silky brown hair. I'd like to tup her."

"I liked the other one, the one who could punch."

"Where were you two?" Gavin finally asked. "Lasses punching?"

"Aye," one said. "'Tis great sport to watch the lasses fight. They're always different ones. The one we saw tonight, she was new."

He'd like nothing more than to punch the fool himself,

but instead he forced a smile and said, "I'd like to see that! Where do you watch them?"

Connor, who'd either overheard the conversation or noticed Gavin's interest in the men, had come up behind them. "Aye, I'd like to wager on lasses, too."

"'Tis the huge building not far from the docks. Past all the fishermen's cottages."

"The name of the place?" Connor asked.

"No name. There are no signs. You have to just know to go inside. But anyone can go as long as you have plenty of coin. And you wouldn't want to miss the brown-haired lass with the nice tits and the brown eyes."

"With gold flecks in them," the other lad added. "When she was knocked down, she landed right in front of me. And she had a mole right above her eye."

Gavin felt as if he'd been punched in the gut. Connor kept asking questions but Gavin couldn't take it anymore. He needed to see her. Needed to know she was safe. He patted Connor's shoulder and said, "Have to go abovestairs for a moment."

It made him ill to think Merewen had gone to fight after all. How had she found her way in?

He didn't need to think much on that—Sela. She'd located Sela and asked to fight for her.

He headed upstairs, and Daniel joined him without comment. No doubt Ghost had overheard the conversation. When he entered the main chamber, he immediately made his way to the door for the small chamber.

He knocked lightly, but there was no response. He opened the door quietly, surprised to see only one person in a bed. The other was empty.

Merewen was gone. A roil of nausea crept through his insides, even though his mind tried to reason through all the places she could be—the garderobe, the other chamber, down speaking to a serving lass or one of the guards.

He didn't need this worry after what he'd just been

through. Why couldn't she have stayed put?

Constance sat up, wiping the sleep from her eyes.

"Where's Merewen?" he whispered, that sick feeling getting worse.

"Och, you're back. She went down to speak with the cousins. It was a while ago, but I fell asleep, so I know not how long ago."

Gavin spun around. "Did you see Merewen at all?"

Daniel shook his head, his expression tight and serious. "Not since we returned from the burgh. She was abed when we got back."

Gavin turned back to Constance. "Are you sure she said she was going to speak with us? Did she say anything else?"

Constance opened her mouth, then clamped it shut.

Daniel slipped past him. "Constance, tell us what you know," he said. "She's not belowstairs. Now where else could she be?"

"Earc. She said she was going to see Earc."

Gavin raced out the door, not allowing himself to think about the significance of Merewen speaking with Earc. He just had to find him.

Find *her.*

He reached the guards out front and asked, "Where's Earc?"

Owen sighed. "We don't know. He's missing."

Gavin let out a war cry.

Where the hell was she?

CHAPTER TWENTY-SEVEN

———◆———

GAVIN'S CRY MUST HAVE MADE its way to all his cousins, because they surrounded him in a few moments.

"What is it?" Gregor asked. The others gathered in closer to hear his response.

"Merewen was stolen. I'm going into Inverness now. Owen, you will keep half the guards here, and two of you are to be in the passageway outside Constance's door."

"Shite," Daniel said. "We've got to move fast. Back to Inverness."

Connor said, "The drunks just told me about the house where the lasses fight. It's not far from the docks and it's totally unmarked. The biggest building there." He nodded to Gavin. "We'll find her."

Daniel said, "Constance just confessed that Merewen snuck out this eve and met with Sela while we were gone. Earc took her, and she planned to go back on the morrow. She thinks Linet is the healer for all the lasses who fight and whore. Reads to them, too."

"I'm leaving now," Gavin said. "I hope someone will come with me, but if not, I'll go alone."

"Nay," Connor said, clapping him on the back. "You'll not go alone. I'll go with you." He cocked his head at Daniel, who nodded.

"Aye, I'll go if Maggie and Will stay with Constance. I'd rather not leave her alone, tonight, guards or not."

Maggie nodded. "Godspeed."

———◆———

Merewen awakened to a roaring headache. She was in a small room with no windows, on a pallet with a plaid thrown over her. She pushed herself up and glanced at her surroundings.

The last thing she recalled was trying to arrange for a trip back to Sela's with Earc.

A voice called out to her in the dark. "You're awake. Please don't call out."

She recognized Runa's voice.

"Runa, what happened? Why am I here?"

Merewen waited for her eyes to adjust to the darkness, then noticed Runa pushing herself to a sitting position on the opposite wall.

"Please do not scream," the lass said quietly. "Please listen to me first. I'm already in enough trouble."

"But why?" Panic raced through her body, nearly over-taking her ability to think.

"Because you asked too many questions, and I answered. So Sela sent someone after you. You're one of us now. We've all been taken, same as you were, and she won't let you go. The only ones she allows to leave are ones who don't act the way she wishes. Those lasses are sold across the water. Trust me, you don't want that. Many of them die on the ship."

"What happens now?" she whispered.

"You'll fight on the morrow again. Until then, rest, and ask no more questions."

Merewen was stunned and didn't know how to react. She knew one thing for certain. If she was a prisoner here, at least she'd have the opportunity to find her sister.

She would force Sela to tell her what had become of Linet.

She banged on the door until a large, hairy brute came

over and said, "Stop now or you'll be punished."

"I wish to speak with Sela."

"She's busy. Hush and sit. You'll see her when she's ready to see you." He turned around and walked away.

Merewen took her boot and banged on the door again. "Now. I want to see her now. You have no right to keep me here. I have plenty of friends who will come looking for me."

She heard Sela's voice. "I'll speak with the new one. She needs to learn the rules. If she continues to carry on after that, then you can take her to the punishment room."

Merewen put her boot back on and waited for the door to be opened.

There she stood in the opening, the icy Norse queen. "Follow me and speak to no one," the woman said, her voice completely without inflection. Sela led her down the passageway, guards along the walls, and up the staircase to a larger chamber with a table and three chairs, a large hearth, and a pallet along one wall.

Sela pointed to a chair so Merewen sat. She decided to wait until Sela spoke first. There was a period of silence before the woman finally addressed her. "You are mine now. You will live here, do as I say, and fight for me. If you do well, I can make life better for you. Everything must be earned here. The cornerstone of that is obedience."

She folded her hands and waited.

Merewen asked, "Do I get a chance to speak before I'm condemned to a life of servitude to you? Allow me to remind you I've done naught wrong."

Sela waved her hand, indicating she could speak. "My thanks. First, I'll tell you that I'm from Clan Ramsay. You've met the warriors who travel with me, and if I do not return, they will be all over Inverness searching for me." She paused to see if this had an effect on Sela, but it did not so she continued, "I'm here, we're all here, because my sister was stolen from my home. She was taken from

Clan Ramsay. Her name is Linet, and I believe she's here. Allow me to see her please."

Merewen swore she caught a slight tic in the ice queen's jaw, but it disappeared as quickly as it had appeared.

Sela shook her head at once. "There is no Linet here."

"Fine. So you changed her name to keep her from being discovered. I know she's here. I will find her, and my clan mates will find me. Just let both of us go, and your life will be much easier."

Sela never twitched or moved. After a long pause, she said, "First of all, you are young, so I'll forgive your naiveté. You live in a world that does not respect women. Men are in control, and their preference is to tie each woman into a life of servitude. They do it through marriage. Your husband is chosen for you, you are forced to have relations whenever he wishes, you wash his clothes, feed him, and take care of his children. He can beat you, kick you, do whatever he wishes, and no one will say a word to him. Why? Because he owns you."

"'Tis not that way in Clan Ramsay."

"Aye, 'tis that way in all of England and Scotland. You're just too young to understand it. I take women away from that sad existence and give them a chance to enjoy life. True, they have a job to do for me, but when they're finished with that job each day, they may relax and do as they wish. Trust me, they live a better life than all of the wives in your clan."

Merewen shook her head vehemently, even though everything Sela had said reminded her of her own mother's life. There was no love between her mother and her father, her sire was a brute who barked his orders to all of them, but her mother did love all of her children. Of that much, she was certain.

So her home life was less than ideal, but she knew better than to think every marriage was the same. Gavin's parents supported each other in everything they did, and Brenna and Quade Ramsay were as fond of each other now as they'd been at the beginning of their marriage. There were so many others she knew to be happy together.

Gavin. If she wed Gavin, it would be different.

"So you take lasses from their clans, their families, and think they'll like your lifestyle better? What if they don't? Are they allowed to leave if they'd like?"

Sela just stared at her.

"Aye, I thought not. Where is my sister? I wish to speak with her."

"There is no Linet here."

"She's the one who teaches others to read. She has brown hair and…"

"The person who teaches reading has red hair. She's not your sister. I did not steal her from Clan Ramsay."

"Then she's your healer. She has brown hair and brown eyes, and she's most submissive."

"Why can't you be more like her then?" That wee smirk was the only smile she'd ever seen on Sela's face. "She's not here. And if she were, she wouldn't wish to leave. All my lasses love it here. We are a family, but a kind one."

"Forcing them to fight and whore is kind?"

"I must earn coin to feed them all. They don't mind making a small sacrifice for their family. Do you have any other questions? If not, I'll send you back to your chamber. I would suggest you try to get some rest because I promise you that you'll be fighting this eve. You've lost most of the night. 'Tis nearly daybreak."

"I'll go back, but I'll promise you that I *will* find my sister. You cannot stop me."

CHAPTER TWENTY-EIGHT

IT WAS NEARLY DAWN WHEN the men returned to the inn. Maggie and Will sat inside the chamber awaiting their arrival.

"She's gone," Gavin said, every word cutting into him. "Completely disappeared. I don't understand it."

"Did you find Earc?" Maggie asked.

"Aye," Connor said. "He had a bump on his head and a discolored eye. Said he was knocked out, and when he woke up, she was gone. He didn't stir until after we'd left for the burgh. He confessed to taking her into town but claims he doesn't know where Sela took her. He was instructed to wait in a different location."

"We found the building the men at the inn told us about, but 'twas locked up. There's no sign of her anywhere."

Gavin felt like he would jump out of his own skin. He wanted to scream, to shout, to fight all of Inverness. Anything to get her back.

"I think you'll have to wait until the morrow to find her, or at least until dawn," Maggie said softly, looking at Gavin. "You won't want to wait, but after speaking with Constance, I think I know where you'll find her."

They all looked at Constance, who'd come out to join them.

Daniel wrapped her up in his arms. "You need to tell us everything," he said. "Where can we find her on the morrow?"

Constance was nearly brought to tears, but she answered him. "She'll be fighting. She fought last eve and did verra well. The lass she met warned her that Sela would want her back. She said…" She stuttered to a stop and glanced at Gavin.

"Everything, sweeting," Daniel said. "If you want us to find her, we must know all."

Constance swiped at her tears and said, "She said the men loved her and she won, so Sela would want her back. The men named her 'the kicker' because she knocked two lasses out with her feet. Oh, Daniel. What have we done? She's just trying to find her sister. She tried so hard to wait for you, Gavin, but she just couldn't sit still. She kept getting those feelings she gets from her sister. Linet is here. Merewen believes it with all her heart."The tears came out in a flood then. "How could Sela treat her like this?"

Gavin said, "You've no reason to feel guilty, Constance. Merewen would do anything to find her sister. She would only have taken such a risk if she thought she was close. I'd wager she was going to speak with Earc to see if he'd bring her back tomorrow eve."

Constance gulped on her tears and nodded her head, leaning against Daniel. "Aye, she did think she was close. Said there's a lass who teaches the others how to read and is also the healer. She thinks it's Linet."

"I think we have to sneak inside," Connor said. "We can follow men to the second building now that we know where it is."

"Before we make plans, I have a question for all of us," Gregor said. "Earc is playing the innocent, but is he? We've been quick to judge Fitzroy, but mayhap he's innocent or in league with another bastard. Someone is a traitor to the Ramsays in my view. Is Earc the one who led men to Linet, to the one who set men after Uncle Logan, and the one who is now trying to make more coin by selling Merewen? Is my thinking so wrong? Fitzroy wasn't around to steal Linet. Is someone in league with him?

Silence settled over them all as they considered his words. Gregor was absolutely correct. While he wished to blame it all on Fitzroy, how could he have been involved with Linet's disappearance? He hadn't arrived until after she was gone.

Could there be more than one person involved?

The thought of Earc's possible betrayal made Gavin grit his teeth. He'd disliked the man for flirting with Merewen, and if this were true…

"How long has he been in Clan Ramsay?" Connor asked. "And how long as a guard?"

"I think only a year," Gregor said. He glanced from Maggie to Gavin. "If I'm correct, then we have all the more the reason to suspect him."

Will said, "'Tis true. We suspect the Channel has been sending men to learn of our plans so they can stay ahead of our group. What think you, Ramsays? Aye or nay?"

"'Tis possible," Gavin said. "Not probable because I don't think he's quick enough."

"How much more do you know about him?" Connor asked. "Why did he join Clan Ramsay?"

Gregor shook his head, "I'm not aware of his reasons. Gavin?"

"No idea," he said, shaking his head. "I'll promise you this. If 'tis Earc's fault, I'll kill him, choke him with a smile on my face."

"So we need to be aware of him at all times," Maggie said. "He's more likely to lead us to Merewen if we don't let him know we suspect him."

"Connor, are you and Daniel going back in to fight?" Will asked.

"I'm done," Connor said. "I'm not going back because if I do, I'll kill someone for certes. They have no sword skills. As I promised, she didn't win the lasses."

"So do you think that upset her? Could she have sent

someone for Merewen?" Constance whispered, her thumb twiddling about.

Gavin took in what Constance had suggested, and the suggestion unsettled him terribly—because she may have just hit upon the truth. He couldn't stand by any longer. "Daniel, are you returning?"

Daniel glanced at him. "I don't have to, but I can. Whatever approach we decide to make, I think we should wait until after dusk."

Gavin knew they would let him decide because this was about Merewen. His Merewen. He couldn't lose her.

God's blood, he'd just found her again.

All faces turned to Gavin, waiting for his answer. His thinking was becoming sluggish because he'd been without sleep for too long, so he was no good to Merewen in his present condition. He stood up and swiped the sweat off his forehead, then said, "Aye. I think I have little choice. 'Tis nearly dawn, and neither Gregor nor I have had a full night's sleep since we left. I can sleep most of the day away. Gregor may not awaken for two days." He glanced sheepishly at Maggie, who was now standing next to him. "Why did you stand up?"

"I stood up so I could catch you when you fall over. You're exhausted. You both need to sleep or you'll be tripping over each other and me."

Gavin turned his head to smile at her. "I promise to follow your instructions, sister." He nodded his head at her, then closed his eyes just for a second.

When he opened them, he turned to her, surprised she was so close, and said, "Hellfire, why are you pushing me?"

"Because you fell asleep standing up and leaned against me. I didn't want you knocking me over," she said with a chuckle. "Go find a bed. Gregor needs to get started on his sleep if he's to be any help at all." Maggie grinned, for it was a well-known fact that Gregor valued his rest. "We'll see what we can find out in the meantime," Maggie said.

"But I think Daniel is correct. We'd do well to wait."

———— • ————

Merewen returned to her small prison and said little to Runa—not because she disliked the lass, but because she didn't wish to get her into any more trouble.

She did her best to sleep on her small bed, but she was tortured by too many thoughts.

What if she couldn't find Linet?

Was she stuck here forever?

Would Gavin and the others try to save her?

She couldn't stop thinking about what Runa had said about lasses being sold across the waters. She had to make sure Linet wasn't in those crates. Could she count on the cousins to take care of that? Were they still checking crates?

She'd have to make sure she wasn't put in one of those crates either. While it would be difficult not to argue, she could hold her tongue for a few days. This was her best chance to find her sister, so she couldn't be reckless.

She must have fallen asleep because the next thing she knew, someone was knocking on the door. It opened, and the old woman threw an outfit in. "Put this on. You'll be on in a quarter hour. Do not tarry. When she's dressed, Runa, bring her abovestairs."

Merewen didn't need another invitation. She jumped off the pallet and dressed.

She was finally getting out of this dreaded chamber.

———— • ————

Gavin was on his fifth bowl of lamb stew when Connor sat down next to him. "If you keep eating like that, Sela's people will have an easy time chasing you."

Gavin chuckled as Maggie and Constance came down the stairs. "Gregor and I didn't eat for two days. Naught but three oatcakes, and you know how filling those are." He filled his goblet with ale and said, "Besides, I've decided on a plan for this eve."

"Please do tell, brother," Maggie said. "We'll give you our opinion. I don't think you're capable of thinking clearly when it comes to Merewen."

"What in hell are you saying?" Gavin blasted at her.

"I'm saying you have too many emotions involved to think rationally." She put her hand on Gavin's arm. "I am pleased to see you interested in a lass, do not take my meaning the wrong way. But allow us to help you think this through."

Gavin heaved a sigh and slumped back in his chair. "Aye, you are the best at strategizing. You and Connor are better than me."

Gregor joined them at the table, having refilled his own bowl. "As am I. You're too headstrong and stubborn. You explode just like a..." He glanced at his cousins with a grin.

Daniel finished for him, chuckling. "...just like a beast."

"Aye, I cannot argue with you. I do act like my sire at times." Gavin knew this to be true. His mother had accused him of it often. She claimed it was the source of most of their arguments.

Gregor just arched a brow at him.

"Go ahead," Maggie said. "Your new thoughts."

"I think Daniel should fight tonight, and he and Connor should go to Stag Inn to see what they can learn. Gregor and I will go to the lasses' building and see what we can uncover. Merewen is quite stubborn when it comes to her sister, so she may well have gotten herself in trouble already. She could be stuffed in a crate much like you were, Maggie."

That thought caused them all to pause.

"And if you find her?" Maggie asked.

"I'll ask her how I can help."

"And if she refuses? She may not want to leave if she thinks she's closer to finding her sister."

Gavin hadn't considered this possibility. He gave it some thought and finally said, "Daniel, I have an idea."

"What? If it's about fighting, I have everything under control."

"Do you recall the times when we were younger and the three of us—" he pointed to Gregor, "—used to pretend fight? We'd wrestle and take false swings at one another, yelling and bellowing all the while?"

Daniel said, "Aye. I thought my mother was going to pass out when you pretended to punch me and I yelled and fell down."

"Until you jumped up and told her it was all in fun," Gregor said.

"If I cannot find Merewen this eve, then I wish to get deeper into their operation. So I'll return and volunteer to fight Daniel."

"I don't follow," said Will, who'd been silently taking in all that was said. "How will this help you?"

Connor nodded, already understanding Gavin's meaning. "'Tis brilliant. If they do it long enough, the men will realize they're faking the punches. They'll think it's staged…"

Gregor added, "…and demand their money back."

Connor nodded. "Sheer chaos will reign, and all the guards will be sent to control them."

Gavin winked at Maggie. "And I suspect we will be able to get to the lasses. You may not have noticed, but the two buildings are close. I'm sure they are connected underground."

CHAPTER TWENTY-NINE

GAVIN AND GREGOR ARRIVED AT the lasses' building before the fights started, sneaking in a side entrance. They roamed the interior, hoping to gain insight into the layout. They did indeed find a set of stairs that led to a floor underneath the building. The fighting took place in the cellar, so this additional space was below it, or off to the side but at a half level. By their guess, it appeared to be a tunnel, but there were two guards posted at the mouth to keep people from wandering inside.

Who knew what was held there?

They knew the moment the fighting began, because the hooting and hollering from the men filled the building. They were only interested in the side where the new women were kept, so their first task was to find which side was which.

They didn't have to wait long—the yells of the men calling for one of the fighters to kick the other caught their ears, and Gavin snorted and pointed, elbowing Gregor. Hell, but the woman he cared about was a true fighter. How had Sela surmised as much from merely looking at her?

Gavin followed the taunts, then stepped into the darkness of the arena, and despite the dim lighting, he saw her at once—Merewen on the ground getting pummeled by her opponent. He forced himself to sit on a nearby bench, pushing down his instinct to go after her attacker. The lass who had her nearly pinned was larger and clearly older, not that it appeared to affect their battle any.

Merewen did some squirming and her supporters began to chant: "kick her, kick her, kick her." To his surprise, she did. She squirmed until both knees were bent against her chest, allowing her to push against her opponent with both feet, sending her flying into the air. Merewen followed her to where she fell and sent a powerful punch to her temple, knocking her out.

"Hellfire, she's good," Gregor whispered.

"Thank the Lord for that. I couldn't watch that for long without getting involved." He watched to see if she was to fight again, but she was shuttled through a door and two other females came inside. He bolted off the bench and ran into the passageway, hoping to see where she had gone.

Not a clue anywhere.

They paid for an ale and asked the men gathered around the wagering area. "Do you ever get the chance to speak to the lasses who fight? Do they come out and chat?"

"Nay," one man chuckled. "And you'll never see them in Inverness either. They're kept well hidden. Probably to preserve their strength. Plus they don't want them to run off with some man."

Gavin took a deep breath. Turning to Gregor, he whispered, "Off to Stag Inn. It appears I'll have to fight Daniel. But we'll have to find the tunnels that connect the building before the fight."

They left forthwith, Gavin marking the distance between the buildings as they walked. Just as he'd thought, they weren't far apart at all. They found Connor soon after they arrived, and Gavin asked, "Has he fought yet?"

"He's next. But I've been wandering around, and I believe I found what we're looking for. There appears to be a tunnel from here."

"Where?"

Connor pointed down a passageway. "That door on the

right. I was standing there when it opened, and someone appeared to be emerging from a staircase leading down below, though just a few steps."

"Good. I couldn't get to Merewen. She fought a match, but they removed her immediately. We found the other end of the tunnel. 'Tis guarded by two beasts, but I think they'll come over here if there's trouble. So let's find a seat in Daniel's arena. I'll volunteer to fight him, and then we'll play our game."

"I hope it works," Connor said, clasping his shoulder.

A quarter hour later, the man in the center of the arena asked, "Any challengers for the man with the demon hand?"

Gavin stood up and yelled, "I'll beat his arse."

He was waved forward, so he stripped off his tunic and approached the announcer. He held Gavin's hand up and said, "Here's the new challenger. What's your name, lad? I need a catchy name."

Connor yelled out, "He looks like a beast."

"Beast, it is. Place your wagers, Demon's Hand or the Beast."

A few moments later, the fight started. Daniel went straight for Gavin, lifted him into the air and tossed him over to the side. Gavin released pained bellows, while Daniel faced the crowd to urge on their calls and cheers. Gavin jumped to his feet and tackled Daniel, grabbing one of his legs and tugging it until Daniel fell onto his back. Standing up, he beat his chest while he yelled, then dove onto Daniel and started punching him.

Daniel kicked Gavin back and punched his face several times while the crowd screeched with joy. Until someone noticed something odd. "There's no marks on either one of them!" a man screeched. "They're not really hitting each other."

One caught on, then the next and the next, until the entire group began demanding their wagers back. "Cheat,

cheat! I want my coins back."

Gavin jumped up and said to Daniel, "Cover me so I can get through the door."

It took longer than they'd planned, and Gavin took a few punches from the unhappy bystanders, but he finally made it to the door. Guards raced out of it, heading in their direction, because the guests were crowding in on the man who took the wagers.

Gregor stood waiting by the door. He nodded and said, "Well done. I think Daniel may need Connor and me to get him out of here safely. Can you handle this tunnel alone?"

"Aye. Go assist Daniel."

Gavin hurried down the dark staircase and followed the tunnel. Though it was dark and gloomy, with only a few torches along the way, he didn't waste any time. To his surprise, he arrived in a large chamber with several small chambers off of it.

It was most unique because the small chambers all had locks on the outside.

It reminded him of the tales of dungeons his older cousins had told him about, except the doors were made from wood rather than stone. A small window was roughly cut out of the top of each door. A stool sat at the end of the passageway, next to the stairs that headed up, but the brutish guards had left. He peered in each of the windows, but they were all empty.

Except the last one.

One lass inside lay flat on her back, a cloth, partially soaked with blood, across her forehead.

A brown-haired lass.

"Merewen?" he whispered.

She sat up and tossed the cloth to the side. "Gavin. What are you doing here?"

"I've come to set you free. As soon as I find the key. Are you hale? Can you walk?" He glanced at her, then scanned the walls, searching for a key.

Merewen approached the door. "Gavin, I'm fine, but I'm not coming with you. I cannot."

He stopped and whirled back around to face her. "Look, I don't have much time, Merewen. I'll get you out, and we'll argue about this somewhere else."

"Nay. I'm not leaving. My sister is here and I'm not going anywhere until I find her."

"Are you sure she's here?"

"Aye, I can feel it. I'm so close. Please, Gavin. I don't know where they're keeping her, and I need a chance to save her. Come back in a sennight, then I'll leave with you if I haven't located her yet."

"Merewen...nay. 'Tis not safe for you. And I'm not leaving you here for a sennight. 'Twould be daft of me."

Tears rolled down her cheeks. "'Tis not safe for Linet either. She'll not defend herself. I must do it for her. Please go."

Gavin put his face up to the small window. "On one condition."

"What?"

"Kiss me. One kiss through the window."

Merewen didn't hesitate. She stepped over to the window and boldly pressed her lips to his, but it wasn't enough. He deepened the kiss and savored the taste of her, wanting so badly to pick her up and take her away from this place.

When he ended the kiss, neither of them moved. Finally, he whispered, "I'm worried for you."

"I am, too. But I'm this close. Please, Gavin. I must try. I have a plan."

"I'll do as you ask, but I'll be back. Be careful."

Noises came from the end of the passageway, telling him the guards were returning, so he said, "Please be careful."

"I promise."

And he left her, but he was sick over it.

Something was not right.

CHAPTER THIRTY

MEREWEN SLEPT LIKE THE DEAD, not waking up until the sun was up. To her surprise, her face had swollen more than she expected. Which was hopefully the perfect cover story she needed to get what she wanted. She called out to the guard at the end of the passageway.

"I need to see the healer. Look at my face," she cried. While she couldn't see it herself, she could feel it, and when her fingers touched it, it hurt terribly. "Something's wrong!"

The guard came over to the window, stared at her, and said, "I shall return."

He must have believed her because he did go up the stairs. She used the water on the small side table to freshen up and rinse her mouth, spitting out a bit of blood when she did. This didn't please her either. She'd fought twice last eve, and every part of her body ached.

She heard the man's footsteps as he came back down the stairs. He opened her door. "Follow me."

"Where are you taking me?" How she prayed it was to see the healer. She had to find out the truth. Her heart ached because she missed her sister so much.

He led her to another chamber, opened the door, and shoved her inside, closing the door behind her. It was larger than her sleeping chamber on the lower level, but there were more pallets on the floor, four to be exact. And the back wall had a pallet up against the stone.

Rather than consider the meaning of it all, she turned around and waited for the door to open again, hoping, no, praying it would be Linet.

She waited several minutes, though it seemed an eternity passed before the door finally opened.

The person who came in wasn't her sister. It wasn't a lass, but a huge brute with a mean expression on his face. Sela came in behind him. "The man who came to visit you last night. Who is he?"

"No one visited me."

The brute slapped her hard across the face, sending throbbing pain through her wounds..

"Tell me the truth. Was he from Clan Ramsay?" Sela showed no emotion. She just stood with her hands on her hips, as if Merewen were a misbehaving child. "Are your friends who are fighting for me from Clan Grant or Clan Ramsay?"

Merewen thought about lying again, but she'd already told her about Clan Ramsay, so what did it matter? Then she had a thought. "I'll tell you the truth if you'll let me see my sister."

Sela nodded to the brute, then stepped out of the chamber, closing the door. The next thing Merewen knew, a fist came straight to her belly. He hit her so hard, she thought she would vomit, but she managed to hold it inside.

"You'll learn, you wee fool. Don't argue, don't disagree, never question, and do as you're told."

She then proceeded to get the battering of her life.

When the brute finished, he kicked her in the belly and left her curled up on the floor. All she could think was she would die here alone, looking like a wee bairn.

She passed out.

The next time she woke up, her sister was at her side humming softly, the scent of lavender reaching her.

"I've made it to heaven, have I not, Linet?"

The Band of Cousins met outside the next morn and made plans for the day. Daniel and Connor went off to collect Daniel's winnings, but they'd vowed to see what else they could uncover, while Maggie and Will stayed back with Constance.

Gregor and Gavin decided to have a chat with Earc, whom they found in front of the inn, doing his duty as guard—or so it seemed. Only four men had stayed back, the others had gone into Inverness on Maggie's orders.

"Earc, come talk with us for a few moments?" Gavin said.

Earc joined them. "What is it, my lord?" He stepped away from the front of the building, the place where he and another man had been assigned to watch for stragglers who didn't belong at the inn. There wasn't much activity during the day. Most of the activity took place in the early morn or near dusk, men traveling either to earn coin or spend it.

Gavin hated being addressed as a lord. Officially, Gregor was the lord, as were Connor and Daniel because both of them were direct descendants of their respective lairds. Gavin was a nephew, but he had learned to ignore the mistakes. Gregor oft reminded him it was a matter of respect.

"Why did you come to Clan Ramsay a year ago?" he asked Earc.

"I'd been part of Clan Buchan until our chief was killed. I spent some time in Edinburgh on my own, but I wanted to live with a clan again. Clan Ramsay's reputation is the best."

"Better than Clan Grant?"

Earc grinned sheepishly. "For warriors, Clan Grant is the largest and the best, but they are far in the Highlands. Clan Ramsay is on the border between the Lowlands and the Highlands. 'Tis my preference."

"Cannot argue with that reasoning." He paused, taking in Earc's stance, his expression. He wished to unnerve the man, but was he succeeding? No, Earc appeared completely calm, his chin lifted with that air of confidence. "How did you know where to take Merewen?" Gavin had to see if he could use some trickery on the man, catch him in a wrong answer. He still couldn't decide on Earc. Fitzroy was a traitor, for certes, but Earc? He just wasn't sure. Gregor came up behind him and studied the man silently, watching his every reaction.

"I took Merewen to Sela. 'Twas what she asked me to do. I knew not where to find her, but you must admit she's quite unique. Sela told me if I stayed where I was she would return Merewen to me."

"You shouldn't have allowed Merewen to go off on her own," Gavin said with a low growl. "In fact, you should not have escorted her into Inverness."

Earc nearly smirked, but he covered it the best he could, his hands now on his hips. "If you knew Merewen well, you would know that she's a wee bit stubborn. Would it not be my job to follow her if she went on her own?"

Gregor stepped in and said, "'Tis a conjecture, Earc. You shouldn't have brought her inside the burgh without more guards. You know that. I'll report it to my brother upon our return."

"But Sela brought her back as promised." Earc's face had turned bright red—with fury, not embarrassment, though he kept it out of his words.

"Aye, true. Where is she now? What can you tell me about her disappearance?" Gavin would find out all he could before the man's mouth clamped shut.

"I don't know much. I had asked her to step aside to chat. There were only two other men in the area. They were guards but wore no plaids."

"How do you know they were guards and not just residents of Inverness, or fishermen?"

"Because of the weapons they carried. Swords and daggers."

A sound caught both of them and they turned in unison to see where it had originated. To Gavin's surprise, his sire was headed their way with Fitzroy and a handful of Ramsay guards. Earc would have to wait. Innocent or guilty, they'd decide later.

Thrilled to see his sire riding on his own, Gavin hurried over to Logan's horse and grabbed the reins. Gregor followed on his heels.

"Papa, you are hale?" He certainly didn't look hale, but he was upright and riding alone. That alone was a good sign.

"Aye, I'm fine, thanks to Fitzroy here. If it hadn't been for him, I wouldn't have made it back to Grant land. I would have been killed by those fools who kidnapped me."

Gavin couldn't help but stare at his father and then Fitzroy, who quickly said, "I'm heading into Inverness to see a friend. I'll return by nightfall."

"Many thanks again," his father called out to him. The Beast had a darkly colored eye, plus numerous bruises and cuts on his face. While he did his best to mask his pain, Gavin could see in the clench of his jaw that he had a long journey to healing yet.

Gregor asked, "You think Fitzroy saved you, Uncle Logan?"

"Aye, he was the one who killed all the reivers by himself. He had a couple of guards, but had he not followed me, I'd be dead by now."

"Papa, you have no memory of the attack?" Gavin couldn't believe the falsehoods coming from his sire, falsehoods that he clearly believed.

"Only when they strung me up. One blow to the head knocked me out. 'Twas probably a blessing. I was in pain at the Grants. Caralyn helped me tremendously. But I'm on the mend, and I was worried about you all here. Had to promise your mother I wouldn't fight. Maggie is hale?"

"Aye, Maggie is fine and inside." Gavin couldn't believe the bastard Fitzroy had taken credit for what he and Gregor had done. Surly pig-nut, as Loki would say. Devious and cunning at the same time. But Gavin's mother knew the truth. Why hadn't she told him? "Where's Mama?"

"Once she knew I would recover, she returned to Ramsay land for Brigid's sake."

"But you know MacAdam was the one you rode with, not Fitzroy, aye?"

"I don't recall any of it, but Fitzroy said I rode with him. If he says so, I believe him."

Gregor whispered to him, "Tell him the truth or I will."

His father climbed down off his horse, slower than usual, but he was fit.

Gavin ground out between his clenched jaw, "What good would it do? I should have known better than to think he'd respect me. 'Tis no use bothering to convince him. I'll not waste my breath. 'Twill only start an argument."

"What are you two mumbling about? Doesn't matter. I'm here for another reason. We received word that there is a load of lasses coming here for a shipment this eve. Many are already in crates. We need to stop it from happening."

Gavin pointed to their lodging. "Will and Maggie are inside. Shall we join them in the inn? You look like you could use an ale and a hot bowl of stew, Papa. They have a great cook."

"I am hungry. I was beaten up pretty badly, though you probably haven't heard the half of it. I'm lucky to be alive and walking, son. Fitzroy has proven his worth." He clasped his son's shoulder, then went into the inn. "I've seen his true colors. I hope you can now believe him."

Gavin believed him all right.

He believed he was a traitorous bastard.

CHAPTER THIRTY-ONE

MEREWEN'S SISTER SAT ON A stool while she lay flat on a fluffy mattress. How beautiful and serene Linet looked. "You're not in heaven, Winnie, but in Inverness." Linet carefully cleaned her wounds with a bowl of water and fresh linen strips, then applied a cooling salve to them.

Merewen teared up at her sister's favorite name for her. She tried to sit up to hug her, but the smallest movements nearly made her scream in pain.

She'd forgotten about the brutal beating she'd taken, proof she was indeed still in Inverness and not heaven. How could she get Linet out when she could barely move?

"I'm the healer for all these women. 'Tis the only reason I've been allowed to see you. They call me Leena here. The Linet you knew is gone. We must talk quickly, and then I must go. There are many others who need me."

"*I* need you."

Her sister paused and Merewen could see the tears mist her eyes. "Winnie, why did you come? You should have let me be. Just forget me."

Merewen grasped her sister's hands and said, "Linet, I love you. Remember our plan? We wished to marry brothers so we'd be together forever. What happened? How did you end up here?"

Her sister took a linen square and wiped her tears. "I don't really know. I had to use the garderobe in the middle of the night and I was abducted by two men. I heard a puppy crying and I went after it. I don't recall anything after that. Those men…they were… Sela took me away from those horrid creatures. 'Tis not been long, I know that, but I've made a life for myself here. One that suits me better than living at home with Mama and Papa."

"Sela bought you. Men steal women and sell them to these people in a Channel. Sell them for lots of coin, especially lasses. I'm here to bring you home again."

"Nay, I'll stay with Sela. I know naught about any Channel, but I'm needed here." She returned to her work, fussing over her sister.

"Linet, we have so many guards here from Clan Ramsay and Clan Grant, nearly twenty. We'll get you out and take you home," Merewen whispered, gripping her upper arms. "We'll find a way. I promise."

Linet stopped her ministrations and set her salve down. "I won't go with you, Winnie. I like it better here."

"What? How could you? Sela is a bitch. She had me beaten for no reason."

Linet dropped her gaze from Merewen's, refusing to look at her. "Sela did not have you beaten. If the men did it, 'twas their decision, not hers. Sela is not that bad. Most of us are verra happy with our situation. We've been taken out of our homes, true. But for the first time in my life I feel valued. Not just valued but needed. People *need* me, Merewen."

She had so many arguments against Linet's reasoning that they bubbled out of her. "But you're a prisoner. Don't you want a family, many bairns at your feet?"

"Nay, I don't. You know how 'twas at our home. You and I did everyone's bidding and received naught in return. At home, I had to read in secret. Here, I take care of women who've been hurt. I read stories to them whenever I can, and they are all so appreciative. Sela finds me books. What did Papa and our brothers ever do to let you know they appreciated anything we did? I used to wash their clothes on the rocks at the burn until my knuckles were bloodied. They never once thanked me for it. And I had to hide my reading. I'm tired of that life."

"But don't you remember our knights? Or the brothers at Castle Grant? I've been there, Linet. You would love it. You could fall in love and marry and have bairns…"

"How naïve you are. Being forced to spread your legs every time a man demands it is not my idea of a wonderful life."

Merewen gasped at her sister's crudeness, but Linet had not finished. "I'm treated well," she continued. "I have my own chamber, my own books, and I help people. 'Tis not so bad that I cannot walk outside alone. I can travel with a group and a couple of guards once a month."

"And are you beaten like I was because I didn't wish to answer Sela's question?"

Linet sighed. "Winnie, you have always been headstrong. If you would just do as you're told and try to get along, they'll find a place for you, too. Stay. I'll miss you if you don't, but I'm not coming with you. I'll stay with Sela for as long as she needs me. I'm sorry you were beaten, but a husband would do the same to you."

Merewen didn't know what to say. Was she wrong to imagine a life of happiness? Did most husbands truly beat their wives and force them to couple against their will?

"Winnie, I'm happy to see you, and I appreciate all you're trying to do for me, but…" An awful expression crossed her face as she stared at the hands clasped in her lap.

"What were you trying to tell me the night before you disappeared? You wished to say something. I'm so sorry I didn't listen. I'm here for you now."

Linet lifted her head and gazed at her sister with heart-breaking sadness. "It does not matter any longer. You had cramps. I should not have bothered you."

"Aye, you should have," she implored. "Please tell me. I

feel awful that I ignored you."

Her sister gave her a hug and said, "Do not feel awful. I've made my choice. It was naught important. You are the best sister I could have ever asked for."

"Linet," she cried, tears tracking down the sides of her cheeks. "I don't want a life without you in it."

"Then you must make a choice. Stay with me or return to Clan Ramsay. You cannot have both because I'll not go back. I'm grateful I was brought here."

Merewen forced herself to a sitting position, ignoring the pain, in order to grasp her sister's arms. "Nay, Linet. You're my sister. You belong with me at Clan Ramsay. We can set up our own home, work with Mistress Brenna. Help Lily with the twins and read to all the wee bairns. Please, Linet," she cried, tears now covering her cheeks. "I need you home with me. I've come all this way because I miss you. They've done something to your mind. You should trust your sister, not some strange tall woman with odd plaits."

Linet pulled back and shook her head. "My name is Leena. Sela is a friend to me—she's my protector. Aye, I'll miss you, but I'll not go back."

Merewen had a difficult decision to make, one she might regret for the rest of her life.

The entire group, except the guards, met inside the chamber abovestairs at the inn to avoid being overheard. Maggie said, "We know the crates are somewhere in town, so we shall search all of Inverness for them this eve. We have to find them before the ship leaves at dawn. We have one night. Any questions?"

"I'll be going after Merewen," Gavin said. "If she hasn't found her sister yet, I'll bring her out. I can't leave her in there knowing the crates could be going. I'll keep my ears open about any treasure in the burgh."

"Do you want assistance, Gavin?" Maggie asked.

"Nay," he said. "You'll need as many people as possible searching for crates."

"Has anyone seen the innkeeper's daughter Abigall?" Constance asked. "If not, please be looking for her in Inverness. I think she's missing. She claims her sister was sold, so I suspect the same may have happened to her."

A round of "ayes" filled the air.

Maggie glanced up at the rest of them. "Any other questions?"

Gavin pursed his lips because he knew what kind of response he would get. "I have one. Where is Fitzroy? He still hasn't returned."

"He has friends in Inverness," Logan said. "I'm sure we'll see him when we are near the docks."

"I'm sure we will," Gavin muttered, "and he won't be doing what you expect."

"What the hell was that, Gavin?" his sire shouted. "I couldn't hear your mumblings."

"I said, I'm sure we'll see him, but he won't be doing what you expect. Are you ready to accept the fact that he might be working against us?" Gavin had heard enough of his sire's defense of the rotten bastard, Fitzroy.

Logan shook his head as if in disbelief.

"You have no proof of that. Disregard my son's sour comments. His jealousy is showing." His sire stalked out ahead of the rest of them. "I'll await you at the wall, Maggie," he called over his shoulder.

"Why the hell don't you tell him the truth?" Connor asked, giving Gavin's shoulder a wee shove.

"Because he'll not believe it coming from me. 'Tis fine for now. I must focus on Merewen, not Papa or Fitzroy. He'll find out the truth someday. I only hope the man doesn't have to stab him in the back for it to happen."

Gavin mounted his horse and headed into Inverness. After stabling his horse, he made his way to the cellar of

Stag Inn, and even placed a wager so as to look legitimate. He'd thought he needed to stage some act to distract the guards so he could get to the tunnel, but there were hardly any guards at all.

He took the opportunity and slipped down the passageway to the other building. When he came to the opening on the other end, he peered out, shocked to see the stool empty. He feared she'd been moved upstairs, but then he heard her.

Sobbing.

His heart nearly broke from the sound of her wrenching sobs. He made his way to the last door. "Merewen?" Through the opening in the door, he could see she lay face down on the pallet.

Her tears stopped and she jumped up off the bed, just before she yelled, "Ow!" She bent over at the waist driven by some pain.

Then he saw why. Fury swept through him in an instant. One look at her, especially her face, and he vowed to kill the man who had inflicted the painful blows to her beautiful skin. These were not marks from a battle with a woman, these were intentional blows placed by a strong man.

The bastard had hit her everywhere.

"Gavin. Take me away from here. Please. I'm so glad you came for me." She reached for his hand through the window.

"Who?" He needed the bastard's name. "Who did that to you? I'll kill him." He clutched her fingers in his, trying not to squeeze them too hard, but his fury was a powerful force just now.

"Gavin, I know not who he was. One of Sela's men. But it does not matter. I found Linet."

"You did? Great! Tell me where she is and we'll get her out, too." The words were out before the inconsistency struck him—why was she crying so inconsolably if she'd found her sister? Was Linet alive? Had she been beaten too?

"She said she'll not leave. She says she likes it better here than her life before. She's the healer for all the girls and teaches them how to read. She loves her work and says she's appreciated more here than she was by our parents." She wiped away the tears running down her cheeks.

"What?" While Gavin had guessed a dozen different ways this could have ended, this wasn't one of them. Never once had he considered that Linet might choose to stay. Poor Merewen. "They've used trickery on her. I'll just drag her away. Tell me where I can find her."

His hand rested on the edge of the opening, and she reached up to rub his hand. "Nay, Gavin. I must let her go. She made her choice, and I've made mine. I'm going with you, but I don't know where they keep the key for this chamber. Look for it. Please just get me away from here."

Gavin hurried over to the area near the stool, looking for a nail upon the wall or anywhere a key could be hidden, but he found nothing. Light footsteps at the top of the stairs came rushing down. He barely made it back into the tunnel before the person appeared.

It was Linet. Her appearance hadn't changed, but a new air of self-confidence surrounded her, something he'd never notice before. What had happened to her?

"Winnie, I'm letting you out and you must take your leave." She dropped her voice to the barest of whispers. "While I like my purpose here, there are some things I don't yet understand. I want you to leave. I just heard something terrible. Something about you and a crate. After all you've told me, I must stay and learn the truth. Please go. You're terribly hurt and you need to heal. They'll keep you fighting if you stay. Or worse."

Gavin came out of his spot in the shadows of the tunnel and said, "Then unlock the door. I'll take her to safety."

Linet started, but then whispered, "Gavin Ramsay? Logan's son?"

"Aye. Unlock the door before 'tis too late. Have you the key?"

She pulled her hand out of the folds of her skirt and slid the key into the lock.

"The crates. Where are they, Linet?" Gavin asked. "These people you work with shut lasses and lads into crates. If what you say is true, then Sela planned to sell your sister, have her put into a crate to load onto a ship sailing east. Who knows where she would have ended up."

Linet shook her head, clearly upset. "If 'tis true, then 'tis because Sela's being forced. She doesn't talk of it often, but there is someone who forces her to do things. Possibly two people. One in Edinburgh and one in England. One is of noble blood. They oversee the whole operation and I know she is afraid of them."

"And the Channel probably. Where?"

She unlocked the door and Merewen stepped out, falling into Gavin's arms, though he didn't dare squeeze her too much.

"What is the Channel?" Linet whispered. "I've never heard of this."

"Then you won't wish to know. The crates. Where are they being kept?"

"North of the docks in the small forested area. There is a section of trees that hides everything for them. Some are kept there, and some are brought in. I was told they shipped wool and whisky. I thought that's why they were so quiet about it—liquid gold. Oh, Winnie. I'm so frightened for you." She leaned over and hugged her sister. "I love you, dear sister. Gavin, please take good care of her."

"Are you sure you'll not join us, Linet. Please?" Merewen clasped her sister's hands.

She shook her head and released Merewen, folding her hands in front of her. "Do not worry about me. The lasses here need me and Sela protects me. Please just go before you're caught. The guards won't be gone for long. Here, there's another passageway over here. It exits behind the buildings."

"My thanks to you, Linet," Gavin said. While he hated to leave her here, he had to believe that when they finally broke up the Channel completely, Linet would find her way home.

Merewen gave her sister one more hug, then Linet pushed her away. "Go."

Gavin grabbed her hand and led her through the passageway until they came to a door at the end. He opened it slowly, peeking out to see if they could safely exit. When he thought it safe, they left and he led her over to the town stables to find his horse.

The town was eerily strange. Usually full of the roar of drunkards, this eve the burgh was much quieter, men hustling to destinations unknown, some milling around as if searching for something. He searched for his cousins, doing his best not to draw the attention of anyone else. There was nary a sign of them, and he didn't dare enter Stag Inn with Merewen, so they headed toward the area Linet had described. He dismounted, helping Merewen down before they scanned the area. He moved his horse into the trees.

Not far from the trees, he spotted Connor. Relief surged through him. They caught up with him and Gavin asked, "Where is everyone else?"

"Searching for the crates because we heard they would be north of the docks."

"'Tis what we were told, too. Hidden in a forested area. In fact, this looks exactly like the area described by Linet." He pointed to it and glanced at Merewen, who nodded her agreement.

"Linet? You found her?" Connor asked, his eyes wide with surprise, a reaction he rarely saw in this cousin.

"Aye, but she wished to stay. Personal reasons." He squeezed Merewen's hand. "We'll explain later."

Connor turned to face Merewen, a dark expression on

his face. "Lass, did you get all that bruising from fighting?"

She shook her head, and Gavin said, "We have much to tell you, but it will have to wait." He could tell just by looking at her that she was about to fall apart. The pain of losing her sister, again, clearly hurt worse than any bruise.

Connor said, "Take care of her. She looks to be in considerable pain. I'll find the others and bring them here to search the woods. I'll come find you if we need you."

As soon as Connor left, Gavin bent down to speak with Merewen. "Mere? You're hurting, are you not? Can you make it over there?" He pointed to a secluded area in the trees—somewhere they wouldn't be seen by passersby.

She shook her head, so he did what any Highlander would do.

He scooped her into his arms and carried her away from the chaos of town.

CHAPTER THIRTY-TWO

———————

AS SOON AS GAVIN LIFTED her into his arms, the tears started. Merewen wrapped her hands around his neck and buried her face in his shoulder, ignoring the pain in her body as she hugged him tight.

It was all she wanted at this point. She wished to bury herself in Gavin Ramsay.

He had a scent that was all his own, and every time she was close to him, she wished to sigh and stop just to absorb it, allow it to wash over her. Being wrapped inside his arms was the best place in the world. Here, she felt protected, she felt revered and special.

When he set her down onto a mossy spot behind some trees, he knelt to ask her a question, but she cupped his face and kissed him. He let her set the pace, and when she tentatively touched her tongue to his, he moaned. He tasted like ale, and she savored everything she could of him—his scent, his taste, the warm touch of his lips against hers, the sounds he made in the back of his throat whenever they kissed. She loved to squeeze the hard muscles in his arms, reminding herself of his strength, his power.

She pulled back and said, "I love you, Gavin. I wish I didn't have all these bruises so we could kiss properly, but 'tis most painful."

He ran his tongue across her lower lip, even where it was cracked open. "I'll do anything you want, but you must guide me so I'll not hurt you, love."

"I don't think you could ever hurt me, Gavin Ramsay."
He was so different from the men her sister had described.
So much kinder. So much gentler. She considered herself quite fortunate to have found him. He was, without a
doubt, the man for her.

He sat down and settled her on his lap. "I love you, too,
Merewen. It made me ill to think of you being trapped
in that place or stuffed into a crate." He ran his fingers
through the fine hairs at the edge of her hairline. "Does
this hurt?"

"Nay."

"I'm sorry about your sister."

"I'm grateful to have found her and spoken to her
myself. They've used some trickery on her, but mayhap
'tis not so surprising she doesn't wish to go home. I know
she was unhappy. We used to talk about finding knights
to marry so we could escape home. My brothers were so
unpredictable. Sometimes they'd treat her wonderfully, and
other times all they did was taunt her. Mal especially could
be terribly mean and inconsiderate. And our sire was only
kind when we acted as he thought a lass should. No shooting. No reading. He kept us from the things we enjoyed
most."

"You wished to marry a knight?" He said it with his
usual smirk, leaning over to nuzzle her neck. "But Highlanders are so much better."

"We were young lasses, Gavin. 'Tis what young lasses
dream about. In fact, we'd hoped to marry brothers."

"Then you probably wouldn't be happy marrying a warrior like me, would you? I have no brother for Linet."

She peeked up at him through her lashes, wondering if
he was teasing her again. "Are you asking me, Gavin Ramsay? Because 'tis not something you should tease about."

"Aye," he said, his tone serious and his eyes even more
so, "I am asking you if you would be my wife. Merewen
Baird, will you marry me?"

She broke into a wide grin, cracked mouth ignored. "Aye, that would make me so happy." Her tears erupted again.

"I made you cry? Och, I take it all back. I can't be known as the husband who made his wife cry when he proposed, can I? It must be because I'm so hideous. All the warts on my nose bother you, don't they? They shan't rub off on you, I don't think. Will they?" His hand reached up to touch his nose, and he then looked at his fingers as if searching for a wart or two.

"Gavin Ramsay. Stop your jesting. There are no warts and you know it." She giggled and squeezed his shoulder. "These are happy tears, grateful and joyous tears."

"Good, then when this is finished, I say we find a kirk and marry here in Inverness."

She tipped her head, thinking about his suggestion. "But your family will not be here. Your cousins are, some of them, but your parents? Your sisters?"

"I'm so upset with my sire at the moment that I don't think I want him there."

"Why? 'Tis so sad to hear you say that. Tell me." But she wouldn't get the chance to hear his explanation. The docks were erupting in activity.

A growing din called to them, so Gavin put his finger to her lips. "I'll tell you about my sire later. We should investigate. I have my bow so we can help if necessary." He helped her up from their spot, then slipped behind the trees to check on the activity near the docks. He noticed Gregor, Daniel, and Connor not far away. A short distance from them stood his father, who was with Maggie and Will. Fitzroy was nowhere to be seen, fortunately. With any luck, he'd fallen off the docks and been carried off by some strange sea creature.

"Come, we'll join my cousins. Because of your injury,

you should stay hidden. Do you agree with me about this, my lady stubborn, or should I say my lady kicker?"

She giggled but covered her mouth with her hand. "I agree. I'm in too much pain to do aught but watch."

They approached the cousins. Gregor saw them first and said, "Glad you're here. Connor filled me in on what happened with Merewen. I think the night is about to change." He tipped his head toward the center of Inverness.

Down the middle of the burgh came a long, wheeled cart, multiple pack horses pulling it toward the docks. The beasts were headed straight for the ships.

His sire came over to join them. "Holy hell. What is that creation?"

Connor was taller than the others, so he had the best view. Will and Maggie came up behind them. "What do you see, Connor?" Maggie asked.

"Crates. The cart is covered with crates of all sizes. They didn't stow them here after all."

"We have to make a plan," Will said. "How many bows have we? Gavin, Gregor, you have yours?"

"We're ready," Gregor said. "And there are plenty of trees we can climb to shoot down at them. Where are the guards? We could use their help. We have nearly twenty with the men Uncle Logan brought."

Gavin's sire nodded. "They'll be here soon."

"They're milling about, but most are over there waiting for our instructions." Maggie nodded to a few men making their way over to their group. The cart was such a distraction that no one paid the guards any mind.

Merewen gasped and grabbed Gavin, burying her face into his neck. Fear seemed to explode from every one of her pores.

"What is it?" Gavin asked, holding her tightly. He could feel the fear radiating from her body. Hell, but when had he ever felt this protective of someone? He scanned the area searching for anything that could have frightened her so, but saw nothing.

"'Tis him."

He could feel the tremors that surged through her body. "Who?" he asked. "Who and where?"

"The man who beat me. 'Tis him leading the pack-horses. He's the one."

His blood began a slow boil, building to a point he fought to contain his reaction. He'd kill the bastard, whoever he was. He struggled to maintain his control, not wanting Merewen to feel his rage. She'd been through enough. He also didn't want the bastard to notice his reaction either, even from this distance.

Logan Ramsay turned to her and asked, "He put those bruises on your face? You look like someone beat you for hours. Are you sure 'tis the right man?"

"Aye, I'll never forget his face, his build. He smiled all the while he beat me."

Gavin glanced over her shoulder to see who she pointed to.

Fitzroy.

"We know him. I'll beat that man to a bloody pulp myself." He glared at his sire. "Your new friend is a dead man."

Merewen's body visibly shook with fear, something he had to put an end to.

She held a death grip on him. "Nay, Gavin. Please don't leave me. If you're not with me, he could come after me. He could use trickery or send someone to get me. Please, don't allow him to come at me again." Tears slid down her cheeks. "He'll kill me."

The look on her face crushed him. "Hush," Gavin whispered as he cupped her face. "I'll not let him touch you. You're safe. Do not worry." He brushed her tears away with his thumb.

"I cannot believe it," Logan whispered, the bluster taken out of him. "He tricked us all."

"And was probably the one who ordered us put in the crate," Will said. "I think I recall someone saying they were doing this to free up the Channel. He outsmarted us, came right into our keep and found out everything we had planned."

"Not all of us were surprised," Maggie said. "Gavin knew he was false. And by the way, now that you know the man's measure, Papa, 'tis time you know all. Fitzroy did not save you. Gavin and Gregor are the ones who killed your attackers and cut you down from that tree. I cannot believe you thought Fitzroy could handle that many men. As soon as Gavin heard there was a plan to attack you, he took off in a fury.

"Fitzroy did not take you home either. Gavin took you part of the way and Cailean took you the rest of the way to Grant land, although I hear Fitzroy traveled with the group on his own horse. He couldn't have handled you. You were dead weight, according to Gregor. The only lads strong enough to have maneuvered you are Gavin, Gregor, or Cailean. If you doubt my word, ask Mama. She's the one who took you from Gavin."

His father swung his face to stare at Gavin. "'Struth, Gavin?" His voice came out in the smallest whisper he'd ever heard from the man.

"'Struth, Papa."

"Then why the hell didn't you tell me?"

The shock in his sire's face struck him as true. Could his sire actually hold regrets?

"Because you wouldn't have believed me. You were too taken by Fitzroy. If you recall, I'm the son who can't do anything right."

His father turned to Gregor, who only tipped his head and said, "All true, Uncle."

Logan Ramsay looked as if he'd swallowed a goat, but he had no time to process the revelation. Their attention was pulled to the cacophony unfolding in front of them.

The procession continued toward the docks, lines of men following it, presumably to load the cargo onto the ship. The ship looked like a barely restrained beast in the dark of night. It was the largest ship Gavin had ever seen, by far.

Gavin felt eyes on him and turned to see his sire staring at him. The shock on his face was still evident. "Gavin, I'm so sorry. I should have believed you."

Daniel quirked a brow at his uncle as if to say, "Aye, you should have."

"I saw that, Drummond. And I…" The man suddenly looked totally defeated. "I was wrong and you were all correct. My apologies to you."

It was the first time Gavin had ever heard his sire say those particular words. He would have choked on his shock had he not been so focused on Fitzroy.

Logan's gaze drifted back to the man on the packhorse. "Rotten bastard. I'll kill him."

"Nay, you won't, Papa. He's mine."

Logan Ramsay looked at his son and nodded. "Fitzroy needs to pay for many things, but what he did to Merewen is the worst.

"Make it painful, Gavin."

CHAPTER THIRTY-THREE

—◆—

MAGGIE GAVE INSTRUCTIONS ON WHERE she wished everyone to be. The archers would initiate the battle, then the guards would go after the men guarding the crates.

"Fitzroy is mine," Gavin reminded them.

"Aye, Gavin may have Fitzroy. He won't be your toughest opponent." Maggie smirked. "The man is a coward. Our plan is to wait until they are almost to the ship. As soon as the men start moving the crates onto the ship, we shall attack. Once we've dealt with them, we'll see what we find in the crates. Understand, some of them could have wool or other goods. I think if you move them slightly, you'll get a feel for what kind of cargo they are carrying."

"I'm not sure if you've noticed," Daniel said, "but there are more men milling about than we can take on. At least we know there can't be anyone back at the inn to bother Constance."

"We left Owen and four guards to protect her. She'll be fine," Maggie said. "Until she learns to use a weapon, we have no choice."

Daniel sighed. "I have work to do, do I not?" He quirked his brow at Maggie.

"Those are men hired just for this load," Will said. "I suspect they have no idea what they're loading. You can tell the difference because they are hanging back as if awaiting instruction. They probably come once a month to make extra coin and have no idea what they're doing. The men of the Channel are Fitzroy, probably the ten behind him, and the ones coming off the ship. We want Fitzroy and the men from the Channel."

They were just a little too far from the docks to start anything yet.

Will said, "The first arrow will go into the air as a warning to the newly hired men. They'll run. Those hired by the Channel will stay and fight. They're the ones we want. The more we take out, the fewer there will be for the Channel."

"I'll stay back and use my arrows," Gavin said. "You can stay with me, Merewen," he added, squeezing her. "But I'm aiming to take Fitzroy down. When he drops, I'm going for him, so I need all of you to watch out for Merewen. Agreed?"

His sire stepped forward and said, "I haven't fully recovered. When you go after Fitzroy, I'll stay back with Merewen. If anything happens, I can use my war cry now as well as ever."

Gavin, shocked, said, "My thanks, Papa." They moved off to their assigned locations, and Gavin took Merewen by the hand and led her to a couple of trees that he would shoot from. The spot would give him a perfect vantage point to Fitzroy. All he had to do was wait.

"Patience, son," his sire said, coming up beside him. "I see your mind churning. You want to go after him first, but 'twould be a big mistake. Take it from someone who learned the hard way. Allow the big man to stay until the end. Finish him once his men have been dealt with. Then he won't be able to send them after you while he runs the other way."

Gavin gave his father a quizzical look.

"Aye, many of the most wicked refuse to fight. Too afraid. Fitzroy strikes me as one of them now that I see his true colors."

They waited. They waited until Gavin wished to rush
the bastard with his bare hands and tear him apart limb by
limb. But he didn't. About a quarter of an hour later, the
enormous cart was nearly at the docks, at least as close as
they could get it. Fitzroy had started to unhook some of
the pack horses, moving them out of the way, which would
also be to the Band's benefit. The two men they'd all seen
at Stag Inn took over, shouting instructions to those who'd
been paid to assist with the heavy work.

The time had come.

Two arrows shot into the air, chaos erupted. Daniel
and Connor moved forward, swords drawn, and charged
toward two men. Just as they'd predicted, many men ran
for their lives, never to return. Others drew weapons or
found places to hide so they could stand their ground.

The rest of the cousins stayed back to shoot arrows at the
men coming off the ship.

Gavin wanted the bastard so badly that as soon as Fitzroy
headed away from the docks, he started to move, but his
sire said, "Wait, Gavin. He's got someone willing to die for
him. Wait until he's moved out of the way."

The Ramsay guards moved in on horseback from behind
the group, striking many of the Channel men down and
killing others.

Men fell right and left as Connor and Daniel moved
in their familiar dance. The first two to fall were Fitzroy's
protectors.

"Now. In the leg, Gavin."

Gavin grinned, because he'd been thinking the same
exact thing. Shoot him in the leg so he'd go down. Then
Gavin would have him.

He aimed but missed because the bastard turned at the
last minute.

Fitzroy stood, staring directly at Gavin. He scanned the
area, likely looking for his men, but most lay dead. Just as
he was about to turn, Gavin fired again and caught him in

his upper thigh this time. He wrenched in pain but then tried to run away, dragging his injured leg behind him.

Gavin dropped his bow, turned around to give Merewen a quick kiss, then catapulted straight into the action, dagger in hand should anyone try to stop him. He dove at Fitzroy's waist, taking him to the ground.

"What the hell! I'm on your side, Ramsay. You're a fool."

"Am I? You're the fool, Fitzroy. I suspected you from the beginning. And now you'll pay for the beating you gave my lass."

He almost made it to a standing position. "She was a sweet thing," Fitzroy said, dropping the act. His head fell back as he laughed.

"You're a dead man," Gavin whispered, punching him in the face, his head snapping to the side. He pummeled the bastard everywhere he'd dared to touch Merewen. When he finally stopped moving and laughing, Gavin stood up, wiping the blood from his hands onto the arse's clothing. If he didn't stand back, he would kill the man with just a flick of his wrist. Something had stopped him, but he didn't quite understand what.

Merewen's voice called to him and he glanced over his shoulder, seeing her running toward him. "Don't be like him, Gavin. Stop, please."

Gavin opened his arms and she flew into them, and he knew all would be better. He was so wrapped up in holding his love that he never noticed the bastard rise up and grab a dagger from the ground.

No need, because another arrow sluiced through the sky and hit Fitzroy between the eyes. Gavin didn't need to know where that arrow had come from. He glanced over his shoulder in time to see Gregor standing there with a grin on his face, shrugging his shoulders. "He deserved it."

A silence settled as a sound finally interrupted them.

The ship was sailing. Apparently, the men had decided it was a better move to abandon their cargo than to risk losing men. In the quiet, Maggie walked forward, making sure it was safe, wiping the tears from her face before she strode over to one of the crates the same size as the one she'd almost died in.

She motioned to Will, who pried it open, then reached in and helped a sleeping lass out of her prison.

The Band of Cousins all stepped forward, joining Maggie in the task she'd started.

Gavin and Merewen exchanged a look and then moved forward, hand in hand, to see how they could help.

Crate after crate was the same thing:

Runa

Abigall

Abigall's sister, Eby

One of the other fighters.

Lass after lass after lass.

They'd made it in time. And that was what really mattered.

CHAPTER THIRTY-FOUR

TWO DAYS HAD PASSED AND the group had decided it was time to head back to Grant land.

Merewen had searched for Linet—she'd even gone back to Stag Inn with Daniel and Connor—but they'd been told Sela and all who were part of her group had gone. From what they'd seen, it seemed to be true. While she was disappointed, bitterly so, she knew Linet wouldn't have changed her mind even if they'd found her.

She sat out in front of their inn, staring up at the rare blue sky they'd been gifted with that morn. Runa, Abigall, and her sister, Eby, had all agreed to go to Rose and Roddy's castle with Constance and Daniel. They'd said their goodbyes last eve. The lasses were grateful to be leaving. The innkeeper was adamant that he'd done nothing wrong, which was technically true. A father could indeed sell his children if he chose. Maggie had insisted there was nothing they could do within the law. Yet the look she'd given the man had made it clear what she would *like* to do. Regardless, they were all happy his two lasses were safely away from him.

Gavin came around the corner, surprising her. He held his hand out to her and said, "Do you trust me? Come along with me?"

She smiled. "Of course, I trust you." She took his hand, and they strolled down the road a ways until they came to a fork in the path—one path headed into Inverness and the other led into the forest.

He led her down the latter path. They hadn't gone far when she saw it. There in the middle of the towering pines sat one of the prettiest kirks she'd ever seen, decorated with firs, pine cones, and winter berries. She fell in love with it.

"Marry me now, lass?" he said, staring into her eyes. "I'd like to go home as husband and wife."

She glanced at the church and then nodded. "Aye, I'd like that, too. I'd like naught more than to be your wife, Gavin."

He opened the door and gestured for her to walk ahead of him. She did so, pausing in the doorway for her eyes to adjust to the dark, though there were a few lit candles. The priest stood at the far end of the church near the altar, his hands folded in front of him. The kirk was small but quite beautiful. Elegant linens decorated the altar, adorned with carefully-stitched needlework. Rows of benches sat in perfect lines, while greenery decorated the windows and the top of the altar.

"You found your lass, I see. Are you agreeable to this match? Do you wish to marry Gavin?" he asked. He had brown hair and a beard that he kept rather trim. His kind eyes sparkled and danced.

"Aye, but do we have anyone to stand with us, Gavin? Did you ask anyone to come with you?"

"I didn't. I wished to see if you were agreeable. I was afraid you'd turn me down." He took her hand in his and looked to the priest. "Father, how many do we need? I'll find someone."

"Well, I'd say you might like two to stand with you."

Merewen peered up at Gavin and held his gaze. "Who shall we ask?"

A voice called out to them from the door that had just opened. "I'm hoping you'll allow me to stay, Gavin. I've never been prouder of you than I have been during this entire event. I'm privileged to call you my son, and I'd like to see you wed to this wonderful lass. I welcome her as my daughter-in-law."

Merewen glanced up at Gavin to gauge his reaction. She knew how much he'd struggled with his sire of late, and how much he had always looked up to him. "Gavin," she whispered, "I know you're upset with him, but I want you to remember the father who taught you how to ride a horse, who carried you on his shoulders to pick apples and shoot your bow from the tallest vantage point. The man who would pull you and Gregor on sleds and ride with you down the highest hills in the winter. I remember all of that. Can you not? He adores you, but in your heart, I think you know that."

He nodded, squeezed her hands, and kissed her forehead. "Papa, I'd love to have you stay."

Logan smirked. "Good, because I didn't come alone, and 'twould be embarrassing if you turned me away in front of your sister and cousins. Once I knew where you were headed, I went back to get them." He stepped inside the door, and a string of people followed him in: Maggie. Will. Connor. Gregor.

"We wouldn't miss it, dear brother," Maggie said with a grin. "Are we welcome?"

"Of course."

Maggie came in and handed Merewen a basket of pine cones and berries with ribbons. "Seems to be my job these days. Winter isn't the best time for bouquets, but I made this for you."

Merewen was too excited to pay much attention to the words of the priest when he began the ceremony, but the lilt of the Gaelic warmed her heart as she glanced up at her husband to be. The priest took Gavin's Ramsay plaid and wrapped it around their wrists, binding them together forever, and it was all she could do to fight the misting in her eyes. But she was happy, so happy.

When she nearly gave in to the tears, Gavin wrinkled his

nose and waggled his brows, then gave her that sideways smirk of his that always made her heart sing. The urge to cry left her, and she wished to shout to the world that she was in love, and she would love this silly, wonderful, braw man of hers forever.

At the end of the ceremony, Gavin let out a huge yip of happiness, kissed her passionately in front of everyone, then did backflips down the length of the aisle until he reached the door.

He let out a whoop, then glanced back at the priest. "Sorry, Father. Just had to let that out."

They returned to the inn for an ale and a toast, and when they were preparing to pack up and leave, the innkeeper's wife came up to Merewen with a package.

"Your name is Merewen?" The sadness in her eyes told her exactly how she felt about losing her daughters.

"Aye."

"A lass stopped last eve. Left this for you. My apologies that I forgot to give it to you earlier."

Merewen took the package wrapped in fabric and tied with twine. She opened it, surprised to find a new night rail embroidered with lavender flowers. She knew her sister had made it because the scent of lavender filled the air. A note fluttered out of the middle of the gown.

Merewen,

Please forgive me for leaving you. I will always love you dearly, but there are things you don't understand. I have my reasons for staying with Sela.

My guess is you and Gavin Ramsay will marry, and my prediction is you will be verra happy. Please accept this as a token of my apologies that I could not attend your wedding. It was carefully done just for you. I love you with all my heart, always and forever.

Linet

She inhaled her sister's sweet scent, savoring the peace

it gave her, then folded the garment up and set it on the table. She tried to say something to Gavin, but no words came out.

Fortunately, Logan stepped forward and said, "If you'll pack your things, I have a wee surprise for you. From your mother and me, Gavin. I suspected what was coming ever since someone saw you two kissing in the woods, so I made arrangements for a private place for you to spend your first night together as husband and wife. I sent a messenger ahead. 'Tis a lovely inn almost to Clan Grant, so we'll be riding most of the day, but I think we can get there before this eve."

Gavin gave his father an incredulous look. "You had us followed in the forest on Ramsay land, Papa?"

"Nay, but I cannot help it if your laird catches you in the act. Torrian had quite a smile on his face when he told me. His first comment was that he wagered you'd marry within two moons." His father's smile was as broad as he'd ever seen it, demonstrating just how proud he was that he'd kept his efforts secret.

"Torrian?"

"Aye, and your mother agreed. She suggested the special inn."

Merewen grabbed his hand and said, "I think it sounds wonderful."

"What makes it so special, Papa?" Maggie asked.

"The inn is nice, but there's a separate hut in the back meant for one couple. I've reserved it for the newly wedded couple. The rest of us will stay in the main building."

"Truly?" Merewen whispered. "I'm so excited. I'll go pack."

Grabbing her sister's gift, she took her husband by the hand and led him up the stairs. She'd think on her sister on the morrow.

This would be *their* night.

CHAPTER THIRTY-FIVE

———

MEREWEN STEPPED INSIDE THE SMALL cottage, passing beneath the bow of greenery that hung above the door. She sighed and squeezed Gavin's hand. "Oh, Gavin, 'tis beautiful."

While the cottage was small, there was a big hearth at the back with a roaring fire. There was a tub in front of it that made her giggle with surprise. "A bath. A real bath." She glanced at Gavin, who looked completely indifferent to her declaration.

A table with four chairs sat in the middle of the chamber, and there were two plush chairs to the side of the hearth, misplaced by the tub if she were to guess. A long table against the side wall to the right held utensils and pots for cooking on the hearth.

A doorway on the left led to their private chamber, filled with a large bed and a hearth against the back wall. The bed was the largest she'd ever seen, covered with plump cushions and thick furs.

"Oh, Gavin." Her gaze took it all in one more time. A platter had been left for them on the table, she noticed. Wine and two goblets, bread and cheese. It was decorated with candles and fragrant dried flowers.

Gavin said, "It is wonderful, but I'm hungry. Shall we eat?"

She shook her head slowly from side to side. "Nay, I wish for a bath first." Releasing his hand, she wandered into the bedchamber to place her satchel on the chest. She pulled out her sister's carefully sewn night rail and carried it back into the main chamber, holding it up for him to see. "I cannot wait to wear this for you."

Gavin snorted. "I cannot wait to take if off you, but if you wish to wear it, please do. I promise not to rip it."

While she knew the first time would be painful, she wasn't worried about Gavin hurting her. She'd listened to all the tales, but something Lily Ramsay had said had stayed with her.

"There is no better way to be close to the person you love."

She'd thought of that comment again and again on the way to the inn, convincing herself that tonight would be wonderful.

She glanced up at her husband, who had a different expression on his face. He strode over to stand in front of her and ran his finger down her jawline. His eyes were serious, for once, and full of emotion. "You are a mighty strong woman, Merewen Ramsay. All the bruises you carry, and you never complained once on horseback. You deserve that bath and should enjoy it while 'tis still warm. Take your time, and if you wish to wait for our bedding, I will. I don't want it to be overly painful for you."

She stood on her tiptoes and kissed him. "Husband, I am anxious for our first night together. But I would like the bath first. I think the heat could help with my bruises. I wish to cherish this night."

"Go ahead with your bath, and I'll go to the main build-ing and grab an ale for myself. I will knock before I come in. I know you'll be shy, but you shouldn't be." He smirked. "I know every part of you will be beautiful."

She sighed as he strode over to the door and left, throw-ing her a wink over his shoulder. As soon as he closed the door behind him, she stripped bare, tested the hot water with her toe, and climbed in, not wanting to give him enough time to return before she submerged herself. She decided to face the doorway rather than have her back to it because she wished to be certain Gavin was the only one to step inside.

The water was heavenly, a scent of wildflowers wafting up around her. The innkeepers had thought of everything. She washed her hair after she scrubbed every inch of her body, needing to cleanse herself of the filth of Inverness and the underground. When she finished, she leaned back and closed her eyes, savoring the warmth still engulfing her body.

Later, a soft knock on the door awakened her. "Gavin?"

He peeked around the door and closed it, using the bolt to lock it behind him. "You're mine for the night, lass."

"Have they settled well?"

"Aye, they had their fun teasing me, but they're eating and downing ales faster than my sire. Even Maggie is giggling. 'Tis good to see them enjoying themselves."

"Your hair is wet."

"Aye, I found a waterfall not far away. 'Twas cold, but I survived."

The closer he came, the more she wished she'd thought about what she was to do when he entered. He couldn't see much of her bare body from his vantage point, but if he came to stand over her, he'd see all.

And what was she to do about it? If she rose from the bath, the problem would be the same.

Merewen reminded herself that he was her husband now and he would get to see her with naught on often enough. Cottages were small, so it was not likely she'd have her own private bathing chamber like the queens and kings had.

But he surprised her by walking around the perimeter of the chamber to blow out the candles. Although she didn't know exactly why he did it, she liked it.

"Gavin? Is everything all right?" she asked, trying to stop

her hands from covering her breasts.

He finished his chore, then sat in a chair at the table—not far away but at enough of a distance that he wasn't staring directly down into the water. "My love, I'd like to tell you I did that entirely for your tender sensibilities because I would suspect you to be shy, but 'struth is I mostly did it for myself."

She gave him a questioning look but said nothing, waiting for him to finish.

He leaned forward, resting his elbow on his knees. "I'm hoping the darkness will hide the bruising on your body. I know the man's dead, but if I see those bruises, I will still react to what you've been forced to bear, and I don't want that to be your memory of the first time I see your beautiful body."

Merewen nodded glumly, not knowing what to say to that. "Gavin, I don't wish to hide from you. I love you. I want you to love me. I wish to share our love this night with no reservations. You do whatever you must do to ensure that happens."

He stared at the floor, his elbows still on his knees. A low growl erupted from deep inside of him, but he ended it quickly and lifted his gaze to hers. "There's a stool by the hearth. May I pull it closer?"

She nodded, blushing. He removed his boots and tossed them toward the door. She couldn't take her eyes off him. He was so handsome. He grabbed the stool and set it near her head. "I just have to kiss you. You're so beautiful and I'm so excited that you're mine. Do you mind, or do you wish to get out of the tub first?"

Her hand moved up and reached for him, tugging him down. "I want you, too."

Their lips met in a soft touch, but it quickly turned to a hungry mating—the kind of kiss that was intended as a prelude to something more. He devoured her, his tongue stroking hers until she thought she'd come undone. She sat up to get closer to him, and his hand fell to her wet breast, cupping her and touching her with a reverence that humbled her.

She ended the kiss and looked at him. "Gavin, you won't hurt me. Please don't worry. I want you to touch me."

His response was to growl and reach into the water, sending it over the sides with waves of sloshes, and lift her out. He tipped her toward the linen cloth the innkeeper's wife had left on the stool and said, "Take it with us if you wish to attempt to dry yourself. We're going to the bed, where I can see your beauty and feel it."

She grinned, kicking her feet back and forth in glee as she grabbed the towel on the way into the bedchamber.

He growled, "You better dry yourself quickly because you'll not get much of a chance. You're way too beautiful to be just stared at. If I watch you dry yourself…" Then he paused, looking at her. "Mayhap I *should* watch you…"

He set her feet down and she wrapped the linen cloth around herself. At first she thought to tease him, but if she taunted him too long, she suspected he'd toss her onto the bed before she was dry, and they'd be sleeping in the wetness all night.

She tipped her head to him. "Are you to remove your clothes, too, or am I the only one involved in this venture?"

He laughed, dropping his plaid onto the floor so quickly she hurried to finish drying ahead of him. First she dried her backside, wiggling it his way intentionally until she thought he'd fall over in his haste to tear his tunic off. Then she dried each breast slowly, amazed at how he'd stopped, mesmerized by her slow movements, especially when she rubbed each nipple until it peaked.

"God's bones, but you're torturing me, lass." He stepped closer and cupped her breasts, his thumbs encircling each nipple. "I think 'tis my job."

She moaned and he dropped his head to taste her, his tongue traveling a path beneath the mound before making his way back to the center and suckling her until she cried out.

Hell, but she'd never been so aroused in all her life.

———◆———

If the lass touched herself one more time, he might as well just reach down and finish himself with his hand because it would fly out so fast and hard it would hit the side of the wall. If that wasn't something to scare the hell out of a virgin, what else would?

Gavin had to take control or he'd embarrass himself like a laddie.

He caressed both breasts until Merewen moaned, then he lifted her and set her in the middle of the pile of furs. "I'll try my best not to hurt you," he said, removing the rest of his clothes in haste, "but if I do, tell me and I'll stop. I fear your bruises may be too much for my weight." He lowered himself down next to her, caressing his hand down her sides and over toward her center.

She reached up and cupped his face with one hand. "There are so many furs beneath me, you'll not hurt me. Make love to me, husband."

He did as she asked, kissing her tenderly at first, then ravishing her mouth the way he'd always wanted to, delving deeper until she moaned with a passion that shot straight to his loins. His hardness pressed against her belly and she started, so he ended the kiss and took her hand, leading her over to his erection. "Touch me. I'll like it when you touch me there."

"It does not hurt? They say a woman can hurt a man there."

He showed her. "This is where you can hurt a man. My bollocks as they say," he said with a chuckle. "And they aren't nice to look at either, but this is for touching." He taught her how to hold him and how he liked her to move her hand on him.

Hell, he was being tortured, but it was such sweet torment, he'd be happy to succumb to it. His head fell back to her breasts, taking her nipple in his mouth, suckling her and grazing his teeth across the pert bud until her head fell back and she arched toward him with a deep moan. His hand found its way to her center, parting her curls to see if she was ready for him. His finger slid inside her and she gasped at the invasion. "Lass, am I hurting you?"

She shook her head and waited, watching his face while she continued to touch him. Slick with need, she parted her thighs to give him better access. The more she opened, the more she moaned, her hand now gripping his arm. "Gavin, what's next? Please?"

"You're a quick learner, but I think you best end my torture or I'll never be able to finish." He pulled her hand away and settled himself between her legs. "This will hurt but only for a few moments, I promise."

He breached her entrance, coaxing her with sweet words as he pressed up against her maidenhead. Although he hated to hurt her, there was no avoiding it so he gave a quick thrust and broke through. She bucked against him a wee bit. "Mere, I'm sorry. I won't move until you tell me to. The pain will ease, I promise."

She nodded and gripped his shoulders. "I think 'tis better already." She began to move against him, testing their rhythm until he could no longer stop. Leaning on his side so he could touch her woman's spot, he caressed her until she cried out and then thrust into her until he was fully seated.

He picked up his pace and drove into her with a roar, doing his best to hit her in the right place, but she demanded more. He knew he wouldn't last long, so he touched her again and she exploded, her orgasm causing her to clench against him. She milked him until he finished with a low growl, calling her name out in the dark of the night.

He couldn't speak or move, so humbled by the experience, by how much she'd given him after the pain he'd caused her. He nuzzled her neck just to make sure she knew how much she'd pleased him. "Mere, that was wonderful. Did you enjoy it?" he whispered against her neck, pulling back to gaze into her eyes.

"Nay," she shook her head emphatically, doing her best to calm her breathing. "I loved it, every bit of it, just the way I love you, Gavin Ramsay."

EPILOGUE

—————◆—————

THEY ARRIVED AT CASTLE GRANT at the end of
the next day. To their surprise, they were greeted by
cheers and a huge group of well-wishers in the courtyard,
led by Connor's family. Gavin's sire had sent word ahead
that they'd be ready for a nice feast for the newly wedded
couple.

And feast they did. Gavin ate everything in sight, ignoring the teasing from all his cousins about keeping his
energy up for his new duties as a husband. He just replied
with a snort, "Jealous people. Your jealousy is showing. I
know I have one of the most beautiful wives, but you all
have lovely wives, too." This he said to his married cousins,
while he chided the single ones. "Och, I forgot. You are
not lucky enough to have found the lass of your dreams,
are you?"

The hall was full of minstrels and dancing, and Merewen
danced until he thought her feet would fall off her.

At one point, he'd teased her. "Wife, where do you get
your energy? Och, that's right. You are the one who keeps
me up half the night with your amorous attentions. I may
have to sit for a bit, just so I can keep up with you this eve."

Merewen laughed and ignored his jests, tugging him
behind her to dance the next one.

When they did retire for the evening, they both fell into
bed exhausted, too tired to do more than hold each other.

It wasn't until the next night that Gregor called to Gavin

and asked him to meet him outside near the stables.

"Merewen, too?" Gavin asked. He had his suspicions about what his cousin might want.

Gregor nodded then left.

Once he found his wee wife, Gavin took her by the hand and said, "Follow me."

"Where are we going?"

"Gregor wishes to see us. I'm not sure why. He asked us to come to the stables."

By the time they made it outside, Gregor was nearly mounted and Connor was saddling his horse. Ten guards were gathered around them.

"Returning to Ramsay land so soon? We've only been here for a couple of days."

Gregor, most serious, said, "Nay. We may stop, but 'tis not my intent to stay for long."

"And your intent?"

Gregor turned his attention to Merewen. "Merewen, I wanted you to know. I'm going after Linet."

Merewen's face lit up, and she squeezed her husband's hand. "After my sister? Truly?"

"Aye. We have no idea where they are, but we'll find them with Maggie and Will's help."

Maggie and Will appeared from behind them. "We may have stopped the shipment, but we didn't end the problem. We still don't know who's in charge of the Channel. We plan to follow Gavin and Connor in two days, but I wish to make certain Papa is hale before we leave him."

"I do," Merewen shouted. "I know who's in charge."

All the faces swung in her direction, mouths agape.

"Well, not exactly, but Linet told me there are two people who force Sela to do things. One is in Edinburgh and one is in London."

"Did she tell you anything more, Merewen?" Will asked.

"Just that one was of noble blood. I think 'tis all she knows. Do you think 'tis where they went?"

"Aye," Maggie said. "My guess was Edinburgh, but we've long heard of London as being the center of the Channel. Once I'm certain Papa is home and doing well, we'll start in Scotland. I'm glad you remembered. 'Tis most helpful to know we're headed in the right direction."

Merewen glanced at her husband. "Should we not go along?"

Gavin squeezed her hand. "I'll do whatever you wish to do. I'd love to help, but we're newly married. 'Tis your choice."

Merewen looked to Gavin, then said. "Aye, I think we should go home first, share our good news with your mother and my family. But then I wish to help them," she said.

Gavin agreed. "That sounds like a good plan. We'll come with you, but we'll stop at Ramsay land before following you to Edinburgh."

Maggie nodded, "Good, we could use your skills. We'll be behind you by a few days, so we may be ready to leave for Edinburgh at the same time."

"Will you wait for us?" Merewen asked, looking at Gregor. "My bag is nearly packed."

"Aye, we'll plan on leaving in a quarter of an hour. Will that suit you?"

"Aye, my thanks." Merewen said, almost heading toward the keep but then she stopped to turn back to the group. "Forgive me, but first I must ask a question."

Connor said, "Ask your question."

"Why, Gregor? Why are you searching out my sister? And Connor, why are you going?"

Gregor sighed and thought carefully before he answered. "I know your sister well enough to know that she doesn't fully understand the group she's wrapped up in. I want to be there for her when she learns the truth. Besides, where is Earc? He never returned with the other guards. I suspect he was with the Channel all along. He could have fallen at

Inverness, but I never saw him or found his body."

Merewen looked at Gavin. "We have to catch up with them within a sennight. I think we can help."

"Connor?" Gavin asked. "What are your thoughts?"

Connor said, "I'm going after Sela."

"Why? What is Sela to you?" Merewen asked.

"Sela is naught to me, but I have some questions for her." He swung up onto his horse and turned the large snorting destrier around. "And I intend to get my answers."

DEAR READER,
Thank you for reading Gavin and Merewen's story. As you know, many times I leave small strings that will carry into the next novel. These aren't meant as cliffhangers, but as a reflection of life's messiness. Things are not usually tied up in a nice bow. Gregor, Gavin, and Connor's stories will all be closely related, so I apologize if there is more than one string left out there. Sela, Linet, and Merewen might just be in all three stories, too.

Will the sisters both marry? Will it be cousins? You'll have to come back to find out.

If you enjoy my stories, please, please leave a review. I read them all and it's the best way for me to know what you are thinking.

Happy reading!

Keira Montclair

www.keiramontclair.com
www.facebook.com/KeiraMontclair
www.pinterest.com/KeiraMontclair

NOVELS BY

KEIRA MONTCLAIR

———

THE BAND OF COUSINS
HIGHLAND VENGEANCE
HIGHLAND ABDUCTION
HIGHLAND RETRIBUTION
HIGHLAND LIES
HIGHLAND FORTITUDE
HIGHLAND RESILIENCE

THE CLAN GRANT SERIES
#1- RESCUED BY A HIGHLANDER-
Alex and Maddie
#2- HEALING A HIGHLANDER'S HEART-
Brenna and Quade
#3- LOVE LETTERS FROM LARGS-
Brodie and Celestina
#4-JOURNEY TO THE HIGHLANDS-
Robbie and Caralyn
#5-HIGHLAND SPARKS-
Logan and Gwyneth
#6-MY DESPERATE HIGHLANDER-
Micheil and Diana
#7-THE BRIGHTEST STAR IN
THE HIGHLANDS-
Jennie and Aedan

#8- HIGHLAND HARMONY-
Avelina and Drew

THE HIGHLAND CLAN
LOKI-Book One
TORRIAN-Book Two
LILY-Book Three
JAKE-Book Four
ASHLYN-Book Five
MOLLY-Book Six
JAMIE AND GRACIE- Book Seven
SORCHA-Book Eight
KYLA-Book Nine
BETHIA-Book Ten
LOKI'S CHRISTMAS STORY-Book Eleven

THE SOULMATE CHRONICLES
#1-TRUSTING A HIGHLANDER

THE SUMMERHILL SERIES-
CONTEMPORARY ROMANCE
#1-ONE SUMMERHILL DAY
#2-A FRESH START FOR TWO
#3-THREE REASONS TO LOVE

STAND-ALONE NOVEL
FALLING FOR THE CHIEFTAIN-Book Three in
Enchanted Falls Trilogy

ABOUT THE AUTHOR

KEIRA MONTCLAIR is the pen name of an author who lives in Florida with her husband. She loves to write fast-paced, emotional romance, especially with children as secondary characters in her stories.

She has worked as a registered nurse in pediatrics and recovery room nursing. Teaching is another of her loves, and she has taught both high school mathematics and practical nursing.

Now she loves to spend her time writing, but there isn't enough time to write everything she wants! Her Highlander Clan Grant series, comprising of eight standalone novels, is a reader favorite. Her third series, The Highland Clan, set twenty years after the Clan Grant series, focuses on the Grant/Ramsay descendants. She also has a contemporary series set in The Finger Lakes of Western New York and a paranormal historical series, The Soulmate Chronicles.

Her latest series, The Band of Cousins, stems from The Highland Clan but is a stand-alone series.

Contact her through her website, *www.keiramontclair.com*

Made in the USA
Coppell, TX
09 October 2021

63711631R00152